who have made their homes in the U.S. May there be more fine police procedurals featuring the complex and likable Romilia Chacón!"
—*Drood Review of Mystery*

"A high-intensity plot that will leave readers begging for more!"—*Library Journal*

"Marcos Villatoro is a skilled writer and a gifted story-teller. *Minos* captured me from the very start with its keenly observed characters, perfect pitch of language, and its suggestion that a brooding and intelligent mystery was about to unfold. It certainly did. The tale is rich in history and myth, rich in setting, rich in character. This book reminded me of *The Da Vinci Code*. It is a pleasure from start to finish."—T. Jefferson Parker, Edgar Award winner

"Villatoro's lyrical writing style provides the perfect vehicle for describing his fascinatingly flawed Salvadoran protagonist. . . . This is a compelling, character-driven novel in which Villatoro generates tremendous sympathy for his complex and very human heroine."—*Booklist*

"A fast-paced and entertaining read . . . reminiscent of *The Da Vinci Code*, with plenty of fascinating literary references, except here the object of pursuit is devilish, not divine."
—*Memphis Commercial Appeal*

"A well-told tale, replete with richly drawn characters. Highly recommended."—*Kate's Mystery Newsletter*

"Scintillating, densely plotted . . . Villatoro creates a compelling, dramatic balance. The ending resolves beautifully, but that is really secondary considering how well the story works as a whole."—*Publishers Weekly* (starred review)

"The hottest murder investigation the FBI has seen in years . . . Brainy and literate . . . Nicely written, it's a quick read with a racing story. . . ." —*Rocky Mountain News*

HOME KILLINGS

A ROMILIA CHACÓN NOVEL

MARCOS M. VILLATORO

A DELL BOOK

HOME KILLINGS
A Dell Book

PUBLISHING HISTORY
Arte Público Press edition published 2001
Dell mass market edition / September 2004

Published by
Bantam Dell
A Division of Random House, Inc.
New York, New York

Library of Congress Catalog Card Number: 00-065039

ISBN 0-440-24210-X

Manufactured in the United States of America
Published simultaneously in Canada

OPM   10 9 8 7 6 5 4 3 2 1

To the creative writing students
of Mount St. Mary's College,
Los Angeles

HOME KILLINGS

PROLOGUE

I'm twenty-eight, Latina, and a southerner. Atlanta was my hometown. Now Nashville is where I hang the few skirts I own. I'm a bona fide rookie homicide detective, having made the cut only six months ago. I've only seen three murdered bodies in my life, the latest one being this young guy Diego Sáenz. Still, I'm good at this. I know I'm good because I think about murder all the time. I have that right. My big sister's killer gave me the right six years ago. He also gave me obsessive vengeance, though I've learned to keep that in check, hidden away from my superiors. I've played the game, followed the rules, jumped every single hoop. I rarely show my rage. I put the anger toward the cases before me like a thin stream of gas on an open flame. Used sparingly, anger is the best fuel. But once I find the man who took Catalina away from my mother and me, I'll throw the whole tank into the fire.

CHAPTER ONE

My first thought that night: I hate gunshot wounds to the head.

I leaned forward, placing my right foot ahead of the other and bending my right knee so as to hover over the dead man's face. This was uncomfortable. Still, I didn't use my gloved hands to balance myself against the red Honda sedan that stood two feet from the body. An old rule from academy days marched through the rear of my memory: "Always keep your hands behind your back when first approaching the crime scene."

I didn't need to hear that. I knew it well enough. Still, the rule played along, reminding me that this was my first case in this new city that I barely called home. Better to hear recordings out of the rule book. Rules helped me distance myself from the killing, but not for very long. This exit wound, right through the top of the skull, an inside-out, crumbly, bloody cradlecap topped with disintegrated brain tissue, shortened the distance between the victim and me real quick. But the killing didn't let the pistol in the man's hand escape my sight, the first thing that was wrong with this picture.

"*Carajo*," I muttered, "what a mess."

"What's that you say?" the voice came from one side. It was a southern voice, one of the common twangs I heard throughout Nashville. I looked up at an older man. He crouched next to me. He was the medical examiner. His name escaped me. I hadn't worked any big case since arriving here from Atlanta four weeks earlier, and up to now had had no need to meet the examiner. The dead man's doughnut head promised to bring that old guy and me together for a while.

"Oh. Nothing. Just a Spanish word," I chuckled, tossing my hair over my shoulder as if catching it on a hook. I sounded embarrassed. It wouldn't do to translate *carajo* to a stranger. Bad manners, my mamá would remind me with her scolding voice.

He didn't respond. For the moment he seemed too preoccupied for introductions. He had sliced a small opening into the victim's abdomen and was now shoving a digital thermometer into the slit. Then he crouched there, holding the thermometer still. "Gonna be hard to get an accurate reading," he muttered. "Too much blood gone from that head wound. The bullet must have sliced through the edge of the carotid. The blood pulls away the heat more quickly." He wrote a note in his pad regarding the incision.

Bulbs burst about us from the two uniform cops who took pictures of the area. They lit up the early-morning darkness with their silent flashes. While the doctor pushed the thermometer deeper into the man's gut, I walked away to look at the car. It was a small Honda, sporty red. The driver's door was open. The body itself lay in front of the car to the right side. The car straddled two parking places, covering one of the lines with its midsection. It appeared that the victim—if he had been the person driving—had pulled in quickly, paying little attention to the lines of an empty parking lot.

The short, buzzing sounds of an unhooked telephone chirped in the grass. I was surprised no one had noticed that. Perhaps the scene-of-crime technicians had decided to leave the cellular phone there, waiting for Prints to come by and dust it. I shined my handlight into the grass. The thin, new cellular was the type that fits easily in a breast pocket.

Behind me, the M.E. pulled the tiny, thin rod away from the man's abdomen. He had to stand to hold the thermometer up to a streetlight and read it. He turned away from me momentarily. The man was much taller than I, and skinny.

I wasn't sure if he wanted to know me or not. He seemed busy, too busy to take time with me. Yet I walked as if I had no place here. I was one of two or three women in the area. Perhaps that was what made me hesitate to take my position—which was the main position—at the crime scene.

Then there was the kill itself. I couldn't keep my eyes on the wound too long. I had to stand again and take a couple of steps back. Beyond the Honda, in the background of my vision, a large riverboat floated in the Cumberland, its ornate bridge protruding above the flood wall. On the other side of the river stood the black outline of old buildings, a small, antique skyline that had been overshadowed by the new skyscrapers standing on this side of the water.

Two police officers wrapped the area with yellow tape. I kept my hands in the small of my back and walked toward them. They muttered to each other about how strange it was to find a suicide in this part of town. "Right downtown, on River Park, in the middle of the night. Can you figure that?"

I introduced myself as the primary detective. Actually, I was the only detective, but I wasn't about to tell the uniforms this. One of the cops turned and looked down at me. I could feel his eyes float quickly down my body, which made no sense, considering I wore a long black trench coat that covered me from my neck to my ankles. These cold November days demanded such protection. The cop seemed familiar. Then I realized it was his eyes. They had floated over me before, in the hallways of the Main Police Squad downtown. One day the previous week I had walked by. He had looked me up and down, then had whispered to his partner, "Check out the lady in red."

My mother would not have liked that statement. Yet she would not have scolded the officer for his soft, lewd comment, but would have berated me instead for wearing my favorite color. "*Demasiado* sexy, *hija*," she would have said. "You are giving messages that do not befit a lady."

As always, she was right. And yet I never had the desire to send ladylike messages. I was a homicide detective, not a damned debutante who waited on her fifteenth birthday at the church doors for the perfect man to come by and sweep her away. I'm Latina, but damned if I'll be that Latina.

"I'm Detective Romilia Chacón, officer. And you're..." I looked down at his nameplate and almost chuckled, "Officer Beaver. First name?"

"Henry."

"Mind if I call you that?"

He didn't answer.

"One of the other blues tells me you've got the notes on this. What can you give me?"

The beaver walked away from me and the tree branch where he had been tying the yellow tape. He approached the car. "Pretty cut and dry. Suicide."

"Why do you say that?"

"Because of the gun in the man's hand, Detective." Beaver looked at me with that Some-things-are-just-too-obvious-look. I wanted to give him my Go-screw-yourself-up-the-ass-with-your-own-nightstick look, but decided to turn my attention to the body. He continued, "It's a forty-five caliber. Once we lift it, we'll check the numbers to see if he owned it. I got his wallet from him, got his name and address. That's why they called you, Detective." His voice was deadpan.

"What's his name?" I asked, knowing that it was a Spanish name, and ready to see how this gringo cop was going to butcher its pronunciation.

He had to flip through his notebook to read it phonetically. "Diego...uh...Diego Sinus, something like that."

"Sáenz," I corrected, looking over his shoulder at the spelling. "Diego Sáenz." My clipped Salvadoran accent made his very voice sound stupid.

"Yeah. Whatever. Not like we need to practice our Spanish here in Nashville." He closed his notebook. "Anyway, Prints will dust the weapon and lift it in a minute."

"His name sounds familiar. What about legal time of death?"

"It's 3:11 a.m. I arrived here at that time and called it in. I had driven through here an hour earlier, but hadn't seen the car, so he killed himself sometime after I moved on. I came back around, and here he was."

"You got an estimated time?"

"You'll have to ask Doc about that."

"Right. By the way, what's Doc's name?"

"Jacob Callahan."

Before dismissing him, I asked Beaver for any other information on the victim. He gave me the rundown: Name: Diego Sáenz. Age: twenty-four. Weight: one hundred sixty-five pounds. Race: Hispanic. Height: five feet, nine inches. Eyes: brown. All of this was from his driver's license, of course. It told me very little.

"I also found two credit cards on him. VISA Gold and MasterCard Platinum. Oh yeah, also a press card."

So Sáenz was a reporter. "May I see the card?" I asked Beaver.

He handed it to me. It seemed legit: Sáenz worked for *The Cumberland Journal*, the second-largest paper in Nashville and the surrounding areas. This wasn't going to be a commonplace killing among a few drunk migrant workers. I bet my boss McCabe didn't expect my first case to be a victim who carried around ten grand in plastic money.

I gave the press card back to Beaver. He took a step away, blatantly ignoring any chance of my dismissal, not even remaining by my side for a "Thank you, Officer Beaver." Maybe he would appreciate "Up yours, Officer Beaver" more. He angered me. But he also emptied a hole in me. I had a sudden urge to call home, wake my mother, and ask her how my son, Sergio, was. She would tell me, of course, that he was asleep, he was fine. Yet she would understand the lack of logic in my phone call, and would assure me that my *hijo*, my *querido*, was safe. It would be enough to fill the edges of this hole.

Beaver walked back to his tree branch. He said nothing, though I could hear the other uniform walk up to Beaver and whisper something through a barely controlled, manly giggle. Something about ladies wearing red, perhaps? I had spiked platform shoes back home that could slice their quick erections right down the middle.

I walked back to the body. Dr. Jacob Callahan leaned over Sáenz. He moved his gloved hand over the head, then pulled back, as though he had merely waved the dark air between him and the victim's wound to clear out an opening where he could see. He wrote notes onto his pad.

I offered a rubber-gloved hand and a fairly large smile to the squatting man. "Excuse my bad manners. Here we are working together, and I haven't introduced myself yet."

Callahan stood up. With his full height it looked, from my point of view, like the lone streetlight was just beside his left ear. He gave me his gloved hand. "Jacob Callahan," he said. "Most call me Doc, even though it's not a very creative nickname. And you should excuse me," he said, chuckling. "I got right to work without saying hello. Just wanted to get the temperature. Not good to wait around for that."

Though it was dark out, I could see parts of his figure. His graying hair was once honey brown. He kept it short. Wrinkles tried to cut into what was once a perfectly smooth, tanned face. Callahan looked very good for his age, even handsome. His jaw was a strong one, and though the years had caused a slight sag in the muscle and skin, the jawline still looked like well-sculptured marble. Doc smiled. It seemed sincere enough. "You're new in the unit, aren't you, Detective?"

"Just a few weeks old. A babe to the Nashville scene."

He liked that, grinning a little more. "Welcome,"

he said, motioning his hand like an emcee, back toward Diego Sáenz.

We approached the small car together. "Did you get an ETD?" I asked.

"Yes," Doc said, his Nashville accent turning to a get-down-to-business quickness that I appreciated, sensing that the elder southerner was ready and willing to work with me. "The loss of blood concerned me. But there was still enough heat in his abdomen to get a reading. Then I compared notes with Officer Beaver. Sáenz's body had dropped two degrees. With this cold night and the blood loss, I'd say the estimated time of death to be 2:15, 2:30, more or less."

"That's pretty accurate."

"I'll shoot for the best I can."

"By the way, what day is today?"

Doc held his watch up to the light. "Let's see... November second."

"Ah. *El día de los muertos*," I said, mumbling it.

"What's that, Detective?"

"The Day of the Dead. Yesterday was All Saints' Day. Today's All Souls' Day, or The Day of the Dead."

"Oh. I see. So you're a religious person."

I laughed. "Oh, yeah. I never miss a Christmas or Easter mass."

The air felt colder. I wrapped my coat tighter around me and leaned over again, staring into the man's still-intact face. Another uniform cop approached Doc Callahan and gave the examiner a flashlight. "Thanks, son," Doc said, then flicked the light on and shined it down over my right shoulder. A spark reflected off the victim's left ear. Sáenz sported a diamond earring. Then the light fell upon the full of the wound. It was too much for me to say anything in either of my languages. I tipped, and almost placed my left fingers on one of the blood spots next to Sáenz. After several seconds of composure—still not enough, as I could feel my voice quiver—I asked, "What do you make of this?"

"Well, lots of suicides stick the barrel in their mouth. That's usually pretty efficient. They either shoot upwards, at an angle, and blow out their brains like this young fellow appears to have done. Or they shoot straight back, missing much of the brain but destroying their esophagus and the whole upper region of their respiratory track, drowning or bleeding to death. This fellow's way of doing it worked pretty well. He apparently put the gun underneath his chin, tucking it right up against his Adam's apple, aiming upward. I'd say the bullet destroyed his sinuses, then cut through the brain, probably slicing up the medulla oblongata before ripping through the cerebral hemisphere and exiting here, between the frontal and parietal bones, right through the coronal suture."

"So he literally blew his brains out."

"Exactly."

One doubt dangled over me. "You think it's a suicide, then?"

He grinned slightly. "Notice I've said the word 'apparent' about a dozen times. Though I'm willing to bet it was."

"Strange area of town to do yourself in."

"Maybe he liked fishing," said Doc, motioning to the river, "and they weren't biting."

"Then what about the gun in his hand?"

Doc knew exactly what I was referring to. "It's a sure bet that his was an instantaneous death. His hand muscles were in work at the moment of death. He could have had a cadaveric spasm, which is like a pinch of early, quick rigor mortis. When that happens, the victim's hands clutch whatever they were holding, permanently."

I raised my eyebrows, then shined my flashlight over to the body, directly at the hand. Even in the night I could tell that the back of the hand looked somehow stained.

"What are those blotches on his hand?" I asked.

Doc looked over at it. "I'm not sure." His brow furrowed. "I'll need to make a note to check that..."

I stood up and looked around, my eyes falling back upon the car. I looked at its driver door. "By the way, was this door open when you got here?"

Beaver, who had walked over to us, answered, "Yeah. It was open. I guess Sáenz left it that way when he got out of it."

Which means he was in a hurry, I thought. I studied the positions of all the objects. Car parked over two spaces, as if done quickly. Door opened. Body found on the right side of the car, just two feet from the front passenger wheel. Cellular phone found directly to the left of the car, just before the front driver's wheel. He either dropped the phone while walking over to this side, or flung it behind him once over here. Maybe he flung it the moment he shot himself... but that gun in his hand, it was all wrong.

Doc asked Beaver to help flip the body half-over. "I just want to see if there are any other opening wounds in the dorsal region," he said. The men turned Sáenz forty-five degrees, resting him on his right arm and pelvis. Though Beaver cradled the right side of Sáenz's head, the skull tipped slightly, showing me once again the smaller hole in the tuck of his neck and mandible. A bulb flashed almost directly in my face. The cop with the camera had just taken another shot of the body, then moved away. "I don't see anything...

Okay, that's good. Let's put him back," instructed Doc. He and Beaver lowered the dead man onto his back again.

A man and a woman, the ones from Prints, separated and took different parts of the car to dust. The woman took the phone. The man worked on a door handle. He aimed a flashlight from various angles upon the handle, then twirled a fluffy fiberglass brush between his palms. He dipped it into a fine, black powder, then brushed the dust delicately over a print. The woman did the same with the phone.

I asked her for the phone once she was done with it. Cradling it carefully in my right hand, I hit the "redial" button with my left forefinger. The weakened phone barely chirped out three tones: one high and two low. The last two were the same sound.

Nine-one-one.

I walked away to give them more room. Doc followed me. We walked beyond the yellow boundaries of the plastic police line. I pulled the thin, tight rubber gloves from my hands. Doc did not, as if accustomed to functioning most of his day with them on.

"So, you're not so sure it's a suicide?" he asked.

"I'm sure it's not a suicide. This dude was murdered."

"Really?"

"Yep." I let my bravado sink in a good five seconds before telling him about the last call Sáenz made. "Why call nine-one-one if you're ready to kill yourself?"

Doc shrugged his shoulders. "Maybe he was reaching out, looking for anybody to talk with. From his point of view, it was an emergency."

"Maybe. But I bet those blotches on his hand will tell you differently."

Doc raised his eyebrows at me. He smiled politely. Then he excused himself. "I'll have a report for you in a few hours. If you want, I'll give you a call when it's done."

"Great. I'd appreciate it."

He folded his tall body into a Jaguar and drove away. I turned back to the scene, where Beaver was telling a few of his fellow uniforms to wrap it up because this suicide case would be quickly closed, and they would be leaving the area soon. My pleasantries with Doc ground into hot anxieties as I watched this jerk hand out orders that were mine to give. It was time to show him the size of my spiked heel.

CHAPTER TWO

Beaver, this is no suicide."

Though he called me "ma'am" and "Detective," his voice sounded as if it hissed through a boiling tea kettle.

"I don't know why you feel you've got to say that, Detective. This is a cut-and-dry case, as far as I can see."

"Yeah, but you're not the primary, are you? No. You're a uniform, and that means that I'm in charge here." Beaver shut up. His silence gave me room. "Look at the gun, Henry. Is there something wrong with that picture for you?"

He stared at Sáenz's hand. After a good ten-second look, he turned back to me. "No. What's the matter with it?"

"It's still in his hand."

Beaver looked at it again. Though I began to explain, I could see the shadowy light of realization come over his eyes. "If he's blown his own brains out, don't you think the shock to the body and the impact of the bullet would have made him drop the gun, maybe even fling it? But it's still nicely packed between all his fingers." I, of course, said nothing about Doc's theory on cadaveric spasm.

"You think someone put it there, after shooting him."

I nodded my whole head affirmatively. Then I told him about the last number that Sáenz dialed. "Put those two together and you've got yourself a complete murder."

The sun was just coming up. Doc's forensic workers and two cops were picking up the body and preparing it for transport, leaving only the chalk line as a reminder of Sáenz's last place on earth. "I think we've got to do a more thorough search, Henry. We can take advantage of daylight before the area gets busy with people going to work."

"Yes, ma'am," he said. It didn't sound so insincere. He walked away from me, instructing some of the others to comb the area. I followed my own advice, and began to wander.

This day was good to us. Though cold, it promised to be a bright, cloudless morning. Yet no matter how welcoming the first moments of dawn were, they still left a murderous edge to the scene. No matter how I looked at it, and no matter at what time of day, I was standing in an area where a man's head had been mutilated by a piece of lead. Murder was still a new enough concept for me that it ate at my intestines. There were cops who had seen years of homicide, only to build up a callus in their stomach and their brain, smoothing down the callus each night with thick whiskey or drugs.

I hadn't gotten that far down the road yet. There was some consolation in being a rookie.

Still, the new sun helped, for it showed me the difference in tones of the two colors of red in the bricks. First there was the red of olden days, bricks that had been baked one hundred years ago, now placed here as part of a tourist attraction. Then there was the tiny red, those dull, blotty stains that you could mistake for either mud or grime left by an animal or vagabond.

Or they could be bloodstains.

They trailed away from the chalk-picture of Sáenz. I counted four of them. They made a line toward the grove of trees. Daylight now penetrated that small grove. Through the low branches and the trunks of evergreens, I could see the floodwall and, just beyond it, the Cumberland River.

"So you ran," I spoke to the perp. "You ran, but you didn't realize that you stepped your shoe into Sáenz's blood..."

I followed the crimson trail. It disappeared once I got to the grass. "But you left enough of a beeline to show me where you went." With that, I stopped walking and jogged into the shade of the evergreens.

There was nothing here except more grass. No parking lot nor sidewalks. The city had left this area of the tiny park in a somewhat pristine state, offering tourists a little place to picnic and watch the tops of boats float by. The floodwall blocked a full view of the river. About three blocks away stood another small parking lot. "Maybe you parked down there and made your getaway from there afterwards."

Stopping to make a mental list of my next steps, I leaned against the floodwall. "Better scrape some samples of those stains on the bricks, take them to Doc, verify if they're Sáenz's," I muttered. They could have

been the perp's blood, especially if Sáenz had had a
chance to wound the killer before dying. This, at least,
could give us the killer's blood type. I rested my elbow
on the floodwall, right next to another stain.

This one was more apparent, as the floodwall's cement top was white. It wasn't much, but it was enough
to catch my eye. I looked through the grove of trees
and back to the Honda parked in the brick lot. The
bloody beeline was consistent: the killer had run across
the lot, through the grassy grove, and to this wall. I
looked over the wall. There was nothing but river.

"I'll be damned," I said. "Did you jump? *Ay Dios.*"
This could mean that our killer was dead, and we'd
need to call for a river search, which was a mess of a job
to do. For that reason only, I hoped my killer was alive.
"But what kind of guy jumps into river water at this
time of year?" I remembered how cold it was last
night, though it was not freezing.

There was too much here to leave behind. The
parking lot offered a line of bloody spots that made a
trail. The floodwall gave me another stain, showing me
the possible end point. It was the grove of trees and its
grass that had yet to give me something.

I got on my hands and knees. In a few seconds I
heard the low chuckles of the men who looked at me,
wondering what the hell I was doing. Screw them.

Luckily, it had not rained in several days. The
ground was dry and soft, almost cushiony with the mil-
lion pine needles that had fallen through the years. It
made for a nice bed where lovers could spread blankets
and eat sandwiches and drink wine, where children
played while their touring parents from Cincinnati or
Davenport sat and drank beer in a hot Nashville sum-
mer afternoon. There were samples of those days still
here: a cola can ring that had, no doubt, been snapped

off by a nervous lover or a kid who wanted to make it
into a toy. A wadded paper napkin from McDonald's
underneath the pine needles. Cigarette butts galore,
small enough that, while walking through here, you
would not notice them until you got on your hands and
knees and stared into the needles and counted far too
many ends of smokes. Extinguished matches, flipped
into the air, only to land in this thick bed. Though
clean, the pine needles hid a lot of garbage. Only
someone searching, with his head down low, about
four inches from the pine-needle bed, would be able to
see the tiny filth of the area. Yet I was not judging this;
I was searching, and the more trash I saw, the happier I
was, for trash meant possible leads. Trash could mean
answers. Trash, such as that cellophane piece of wrapping that still had the ribbon used to strip it from a new
pack of cigarettes, the one caught between three pine
needles, barely flapping in a slight breeze ten inches
from my nose, with a very clear smear of bloody print
upon it, meant hope.

   "*Veníte vos*," I said to it. Come to mamá, honey. I
pulled a small plastic bag from my coat, opened the
bag, and wrapped it over my left gloved hand much
like another glove, then reached down and picked up
the cigarette wrapper. With my right hand I lowered
the bag from my fingers and closed it over the piece of
evidence, careful not to smear the print. "And not only
a print, but a big one at that!" I said. "You, *hombre*,
must have very big hands. You also must be very stupid, lighting up after killing someone." Yet stupidity in
killers is always welcome.

   Though I continued looking over the grassy, pine-
needly area, I was too excited about this cigarette
wrapper print to pay the same careful attention to the
remaining ten feet between me and the rim of the

parking lot. Yet I did look and saw that the area just around the wrapper had been disturbed, as if someone had either fallen harshly or had wrestled with something or someone.

I brushed my knees and got to work, scraping the bricks and floodwall as carefully as possible, putting each sample of brick and blood mixtures into separate bags, then tagging each bag with basic information: "Stain #1, found approx. five feet from victim, first of five stains." "Stain #2, found approx. nine feet from victim, second of five stains," all the way up to the final stain on the floodwall.

I gathered my collection of evidence bags, now filled with scraped stains and a cigarette wrapping, and walked to the car. A strain of adrenaline shoved itself through my limbs, torso, and brain.

Obviously, Beaver had watched me work. His voice was much more conciliatory and curious. "Hey, Detective, what'd you find?"

I barely waved the bags at him. "Evidence, my friend. Evidence of a murder."

CHAPTER THREE

Though excited about my find, I also knew what it meant: that blood-crusted cigarette wrapper was about to keep me separated from home for a while. I still had not lost all the loneliness that working with assholes like Beaver can create. I was still new to the city, new to the department, and about to open my first murder case. The ambition to find out, to get ahead, though strong in me, had never been enough to fill completely that certain void. I called home.

And the conversation happened just as I thought it would. "What's the matter, *hija?* What time is it?"

Mamá and I spoke in Spanish, as always. "I just wanted to know if Sergio was okay."

She yawned. "Let me check, just wait a minute," and her voice trailed off as she placed the receiver on the end table. "I'll go see if the *zipitillo* carried him away..."

The *zipitillo*, El Salvador's rendition of a troll hiding under a bridge, ready to eat passing children. Her sarcasm was ready even at this early hour.

"He's fine. My little heaven is dreaming about Big Bird or whoever it is he watches on television. Little king."

That's what I wanted to hear. My mother calling my son *mi cielito, mi reinito*, all the diminutives of a pure love that somehow put me right next to him, standing over his bed, listening to the rhythm of his breaths.

Then she surprised me. "What's the matter?"

"Matter? Nothing. I'm working on a case." She already knew this; I had whispered my goodbye to her before leaving the house a few hours earlier. "I just thought I'd check in."

"You'll be all right, girl. You will do well."

That was all she said. But it was more than enough. She knew me. Knew that I feared failure perhaps more than death—failure in two areas, as a detective, as a mother. We moved toward the end of the conversation; she told me, "*Te quiero mijita. Cuidáte vos.* I love you girl. Be careful." I promised I would, then listened to her simple words once again, that I would do well; I hoped she meant for both my callings.

Though his driver's license told me little about this case, it quickly explained why I was the detective put on it. Sáenz was Hispanic. People like Sáenz were the reason the Nashville Homicide Unit hired me. In the past few years more Latinos had moved into the Nashville area, many of them migrants working on the horse farms surrounding the city. Others worked the usual crops: tomatoes, tobacco, a few corn crops. Construction crews had also brought numerous Latinos into the city. The necessary equipment for survival—*taquerías*, little Mexican markets, immigration paper selling— brought in the workers' relatives. Whole families left Guanajuato and Monterrey and Usulután and El Petén to settle down in little towns called Crossville, Carthage, Clarksville, Shelbyville. As in any community, murder was bound to become part of that growing group of people sooner or later. Before I arrived, my boss, Lieutenant Patrick McCabe, dealt with a case involving drunk Mexicans and Guatemalans who had gotten in a fistfight that ended with a bloody knife in the gut. The man died after dragging himself through an acre of a nearby tobacco crop. McCabe and his small retinue of southern white dicks had found their deductive reasoning and acumen stunted by their inability to speak Spanish. Take the smartest monolingual gringo in the world and put him in a roomful of Spanish speakers, and you'll have yourself one insecure, frightened, regressive, pissed-off, stupid-feeling individual. It only takes a couple of cases in which language differences become an issue in order for someone like McCabe to throw up his hands and beg for help. So they hired me.

Sometimes I'm still not sure why I came. I was relatively happy in Atlanta, having grown up there all of my life. I had just moved into rookie-detective position there, and had recently solved my first case. There's a whole big extended family of Latinos in that Georgia city, much larger than the one in Nashville. On weekends, when I wasn't working as either a cop (in earlier years) or as a homicide detective, I'd lose myself in my own people, like I'd stepped over the border without having to carry a passport.

My mother never left that internal country, not until I had jerked her out of it and brought her to Nashville. I still wasn't sure if she'd forgiven me for that. Even when I reminded her of the reasons, that the violence and the gangs were getting too difficult to deal with back in Atlanta, and that my boy Sergio, her only grandson, was destined in ten years either to join one of those gangs or get killed by them, she would only shake her head halfheartedly.

This, of course, was no time to think about life decisions. My first case was opening. It was a little different from what I had expected. As far as I could tell, there were no drunk migrant workers around here taking the blame.

From the moment Officer Beaver tried to pronounce it, Diego Sáenz's name had sounded familiar to me. I had read Sáenz's work in the office. Though I had a subscription to *The Nashville Banner* at home, the Homicide Office received both papers. I perused the Spanish supplements that both papers offered once a week. McCabe had not told me to do this. It was my own way of getting to know Nashville and its surrounding areas, both through the eyes of gringo Nashvillians as well as those of the new Hispanics coming into the region.

The fact that both papers offered Spanish supplements meant that they recognized the growing Latino population and wanted to take advantage of it. I suppose they thought that migrants who could read would be hungry for written Spanish words. As far as my house was concerned, they were right. Though not a migrant, Mamá always waited eagerly for the Sunday paper in order to pull the supplement out. I would bring home the supplement from *The Cumberland Journal*. It was not long before she took a pencil to the pages and corrected the grammar. "Who did they hire to write this, a fifth-grader?" she would complain. I didn't think there were that many mistakes, though perhaps I gave the papers some slack. Even if the reporters themselves (such as Sáenz) were writing correct Spanish, the typesetters had a time of it typing in a language that was not at all familiar to them. Missing accents was the biggest felony, according to my mother.

Then again, we were no doubt more picky than most. Even our friends back in Atlanta made fun of how bookish we were. Scattered over our coffee tables, kitchen tables, cabinets, toilets, and bookshelves were books that we had bought while vacationing in Mexico. There were books in English as well, though they were all mine. Mamá spent little if any time picking up literature in English. She had finished reading *Paula* by Isabel Allende the week previous. I knew I would have to read that soon, considering how it had affected her. She had closed the book with tears in her eyes, then came over to me and hugged me like an old bear, whispering into my ear how much she loved me. I didn't know what the hell was going on, so I just patted her back and told her to calm down and have some coffee with me. She explained that the book was about Allende's daughter, who was in a coma. It was the great Chilean writer's nonfiction testimony to her girl, in the hopes that the telling of the family tale would wake her up. That was enough to explain Mamá's sentiments, as well as her admonition, "I don't want to see you in some hospital bed, *hija*, because of a bullet that some *carbón* has put into you!" She was good at jumping, every chance she could, at the opportunity of talking me out of my job. Isabel's book was just the latest endeavor.

For every book of poetry by Neruda found on a desk or coffee table, or collection of short stories by Carlos Fuentes or Allende on the toilet tops, you'd find

a work by the master himself, Gabriel García
Márquez. We were true, die-hard Gabi fans. All the
copies, of course, were in the original, delicious Spanish. *Leafstorm* lay upon a pile of old *Newsweeks*. I had
just finished *Of Love and Other Demons* and left it in the
kitchen for Mamá once she finished *Paula*. Mamá always had *Love in the Time of Cholera* at her bedside, like
a Bible that she referred to from time to time. My favorite, and the Novel-of-the-Gods, of course, was *One
Hundred Years of Solitude*. I had read it so many times
that every single page of my copy snapped off the spine
in the last reading. I had to hold it together with rubber bands.

Books were one main fountain of conversation for
us. I never felt alone with a novel or a collection of poetry in my hand. Since we had moved to Nashville,
Mamá had spent even more time reading. There was
no one around her to speak with, except her grandson,
Sergio. When I came home, she was ready to go.
Though she was tired, so was I. After I wrestled with
Sergio on the floor for a while, Mamá and I always
spent an hour together with coffee before we got
around to making supper. Bottom line, she was my best
friend. I know I was hers, too, though I was now a trai-
torous friend. I had yanked her out of her home, had
dropped her down into a Latino-less neighborhood.
She wasn't about to forgive me quickly for that.

At times I worried over how much she read, the
hours she was keeping, the insomnia that, in these
days, seeped back into her life. That was always cause
for concern.

Of the two newspapers, *The Cumberland Journal*
had better coverage on Latino issues. Sáenz was also a

better writer than the guy over at *The Banner.* "At least he puts his accents where they should go," she said.

She and I had gotten to like Sáenz's articles, mainly because they were written by an insider, rather than some foreign (be it gringo or Latino) reporter coming in to investigate the local Latino scene. Sáenz once wrote a leisurely piece on shooting basketball with the local Hispanic youth on Sunday evenings while the mothers cooked up the usual of beans, rice, *mole, tortillas.* He had written it in both languages, I suppose to make sure that the entire population of Nashville could get a sense of life among our own. This made both Mamá and me like him and respect him, without even knowing him.

The scene of the basketball article was over on Nolensville Road. In the few weeks that we had lived here, I quickly learned that Nolensville was the place where many of the Hispanics hung out. McCabe had told me this when he had hired me. "You'll be spending most of your time over there, I'm sure," he had said. He probably meant that I'd be talking with drunk Mexicans who had witnessed a barroom brawl. This first case, the violent murder of a newspaper reporter, made sure that I would be looking at the Nolensville community from a different angle.

I called *The Cumberland Journal* from my car phone. It took a while for the night reporter to pick up. She had not been informed yet of her colleague's death. As she worked through her initial shock (as well as, perhaps, her own angle on how to cover the story), I asked for the editor's phone number.

Tony Stapleton was dead asleep when I called. He was not happy. Once I told him I was the primary detective covering the death of one of his reporters, he shook the thick, concrete sleep from his head and asked the necessary questions.

"Jesus, who was it?"

"Diego Sáenz. I just came from the scene."

"Where?"

"River Park. Down from the Market Street Brewery."

"Oh, my god ... what was he doing there ... how was he killed?"

I told him, as neutrally as I could. But it's hard to clean up the image of somebody's head being turned into a doughnut.

"But, that almost sounds like a suicide."

"We have enough evidence to show it wasn't."

He didn't speak for a moment. I could hear him breathing, then whispering to his bed partner.

"Could I see you to ask a few questions?" I asked.

"Of course, yeah. I'll meet you at the office, if you like. Or you can come to my home."

"Let's do it at your newspaper," I suggested. This was not to respect his privacy. I wanted to have a chance to see Diego Sáenz's desk.

He agreed. We hung up. I drove toward the office building of *The Cumberland Journal*.

Tony Stapleton was a small, portly man in his mid-fifties whose hair was waning and whose waistline was not. He fiddled with the belt loops of his pants numerous times as we sat in his office and talked. Beforehand he had asked a woman—no doubt the night reporter whom I had talked with to get Stapleton's number—if there were any fresh coffee made. He had brought in two cups. I drank mine straight. He added four packets of sugar and a dollop of cream to his.

"I thought all Latino people liked a lot of cream and sugar in their coffee," he said to me, smiling.

"I've been in this country all my life," I answered. "Bitter is better."

"Tell me, Detective, did they put you on this case because of Sáenz's ethnic background?"

"Yes, as a matter of fact, they did." No need in lying. My looks and name gave me away.

He chuckled slightly, the small laugh breaking through his shock over the murder of one of his reporters. "So the police department is trying to become more diversified..."

The way he slurred out "diversified," I could tell he had his doubts. Being a newspaperman, he probably knew more about my own department than I did. Then he became serious again. "You know, Diego Sáenz was as American as I am. Or, no doubt, you. He was born in Muscatine, Iowa. He spoke Spanish like someone from Mexico City. But he spoke English like Tom Brokaw." Then Stapleton turned away, as if to hide his eyes for a moment. He looked for a seat, taking longer than it should for an editor to find a seat in his own office.

Books and magazines were organized in small piles on the floor, haphazard endeavors at putting some order in an orderless life. He probably made these piles with the idea of reading each and every one of the pieces of literature, knocking them off one mound at a time. He was a good three years behind, just from looking at all the books on newspaper histories, local Nashville interests, psychology books, copies of *Newsweek*, *Time*, *The New York Times*, *Knoxville Journal*, *Atlanta Constitution*, *The New Yorker*. There was, at least, some order in the wall hangings. Pictures of friends and acquaintances, everybody from Nashville's Mayor Thomas

Julians to a visiting Ronald Reagan back in the mid-eighties. The newspaper's awards and his own private journalist awards were also displayed in a nicely organized manner.

Obviously, newspaper reporting was Stapleton's life, no matter how disheveled it was.

"So, what do you know, Detective?" he asked while handing me the styrofoam cup of coffee.

I brought him up to date, then asked, "Do you know why Mr. Sáenz was out on the river early this morning?"

"I have no idea. Unless he was working on a story."

"What kind of stories was he working on?"

"Diego had his hands in a lot of things all the time. He was good at juggling them all. He made sure the Spanish supplement was ready for the Thursday issue. That kept him busy much of the week. A lot of those were human interest stories. Then sometimes he would do what he called 'catch-up' work. Like the Benny Bitan killings. We had already printed articles on Bitan's capture and the way he killed those two people. But nothing had been written about it in Spanish. So Diego did a big synopsis piece—much like a magazine article—that covered the entire case. It was a feature in the Spanish supplement."

Although those murders had occurred right before I moved to Nashville, I knew just about as much as any other Nashvillian did. Detective Jerry Wilson of homicide had arrested Benjamin "Benny" Bitan for killing a retired family practitioner who lived in Bellevue and a nurse who worked at the Vanderbilt Hospital. Bitan had made front-page news throughout the country due to his methods of killing. In early October he had slit open the doctor's throat on both sides, cutting the two carotids before plugging his chest with a bullet. He did the same to the nurse two weeks later.

Detective Jerry Wilson had found Bitan with his last victim. Benny had curled up next to the dead nurse and had fallen asleep. Wilson had found in Benny's pockets the key that linked the man directly to the two killings: a plastic bag of costume jewelry. The fake jewels, according to what Wilson said to the press, looked like jade pyramids no bigger than a thumbnail. Two of the pieces of jewelry had been found in both victims. During the autopsy Doc Callahan had found them pressed against their palates, on top of their tongues.

This, of course, became the stuff of tabloids. Everyone wanted to know what kind of sick man slit people's throats and shoved costume jewelry into their mouths. It also gave Detective Wilson immediate entry into local stardom. Every paper in the state and from other southern states gave the detective his moment of glory as the man who cracked a set of serial killings after only two known victims.

I had yet to meet Wilson. Considering his newly acquired fame, I was not sure I wanted to. I was new here. Why would a famous detective like him have reason to hang around a rookie like me?

Stapleton interrupted my thoughts. "I think I know what got Diego killed."

"What's that?"

"Drugs."

"You mean he was marketing drugs?"

"No, no, no. He was doing a story on drugs. Just a couple of weeks ago he did a piece on little kids and junior high students who were given free marijuana cigarettes on the school playgrounds. It started out from his Hispanic angle, you know, how migrant kids are getting approached by some dope peddlers looking for a new market. They get the kids hooked, then before you know it you have them stealing from Mom and Dad to buy more. Then Diego found out it wasn't just Hispanic kids. These peddlers are going around to just about every junior high in the city. It was a bigger story than he anticipated. I know our office got a lot of calls from parents who were panicking from his information."

"So you think that story got him killed?" I asked, a bit incredulous. Reporters had run riskier articles than that and had survived drug-cartel reprisals.

"I'm not sure. Diego was starting to take off from the office more than what we were used to. He made sure everything got done, mind you. He liked to talk with the typesetters whenever they sat down to get his Spanish supplement ready. You know, help them out with the language. But then lately he was cutting out more. I asked him what he was up to. He just said he was doing some follow-up on the drug-playground angle, that something big looked like it was coming over the horizon. When I asked what that something big was, he wouldn't tell me."

"Why didn't you pressure him?" I asked.

"I don't know. He's been working here for two years now. Really dependable guy. Got all his work done, performed excellently. Won a couple of awards for his reporting and his Spanish articles. You have a young guy around like that, you start to trust his instincts. Diego was a real bulldog. He said he was working on a bigger article, and asked if I could give him another week to get it together. I said sure. It's busy around here. I didn't get a chance to pin him down on it."

"But it was about drugs?"

"I presume so, yes." Stapleton studied one of the legion of periodical piles surrounding us. I wondered if he had slipped into an "Oh, how I wish I could get around to more reading" trance. But he was thinking. "Diego spent a lot of his time over on Nolensville. He was very involved with the Hispanics. I think he did some volunteer work, too, teaching English as a Second Language to kids in the grade schools. You may want to go over there to find out more."

"I will. I just wish I had a contact there, someone who knew Sáenz personally..."

"Wait a minute, wait a minute." Stapleton snapped his fingers in the air between us, trying to recall a name. "Oh, you're going to see how bad my Spanish is...Damn, I can't remember it. But he had a friend there, some kid with a nickname...that's it: Cat."

"*Gato?*" I asked.

"Yeah, but something else...Black. *Negro*, right?" His face lit up, as if he had just won a point on a Spanish Wheel of Fortune. "*Negro Gato*...something like that."

"*Gato Negro?*" I corrected his grammar.

"Perfect! Yes. Diego had a friend named Gato Negro. Some kid over on Nolensville. Diego used to shoot hoops with Gato Negro and a bunch of other boys. Some kind of youth group. When he was writing the drugs-on-the-playground piece, he told me how Gato Negro helped him with some of the information."

I wrote that down. The first contact on Nolensville. "Can you tell me, Mr. Stapleton, about this new drug operation? Is it small time, or do you think it's an organized effort to bring drugs into Nashville?"

"You sound like a reporter, Detective." I could tell it was a compliment. "Drugs are already here, of course. You can get grass or cocaine if you want to. Heroin, too. And this is a town composed of mostly blacks and whites. So if you're following certain drug leads, it'll take you into those two markets. I don't know how organized those markets are. But everything Diego did, he did it from a Hispanic angle. The population is growing; as you probably well know, it's becoming yet another entity in the face of the city."

He did not seem displeased by this. I was sure not all his fellow Nashvillians shared his enthusiasm over the new influx of immigrants. "So you think Mr. Sáenz was following a story on an organized Latino drug market?"

"Maybe. Yesterday morning he walked by my office door and said that he had something big he wanted to talk to me about. I had two phone calls coming in at the time and two other reporters in here, chewing my ass about who was going to do some front-page copy. I just said to Diego for him to get back to me, I was really busy."

"How did he respond to that?"

Stapleton looked as if he was trying to recall the moment. "That was the last time I talked with Diego. I probably sounded a little impatient at the time. You know, with the phone calls, the other reporters..." Guilt leaked out with his words. Then he raised his eyebrows with the following phrases that sounded more confessional than anything. "Yeah. He looked a little downtrodden. He said, 'All right, *jefe*, that's fine. I'll catch you later.' He called me *jefe*. You know, boss. It was kind of endearing. Ah, damnit. I can't believe he's dead."

After a moment, I asked, "Would you mind if I got a look at his desk?"

Stapleton stood up, welcoming the change in conversation. "It's out in front."

Sáenz's desk was much more organized than his boss's. Just a few periodicals were stacked in one corner. A Spanish-English dictionary was shelved along with a regular English dictionary. A computer and terminal took up much of the desk space. As much as I had an aversion to computers (always fearing that they would be the death of books someday), I knew I would need to get into Sáenz's and find out anything in there that would point me toward his killer. The department must have had a computer technician. Or a partner who was also a computer nerd would have come in handy in a case like this. "Can we get into Mr. Sáenz's computer files?"

Stapleton shook his head in doubt. "I can give you permission, of course. But I'm sure Diego had a password to get into his own files. You'll have to figure that out."

"I was afraid you were going to say that." Ignoring the computer momentarily, I looked at the few photos that Sáenz had leaning on his desk. "You know these people?"

Stapleton leaned over. "That's a picture of his family and him, up in Iowa. His mom and dad, a bunch of brothers and sisters. This is a shot of him when he won a UPI award. This one, I don't know who it is."

It was a picture of Diego with a young man, perhaps eighteen or nineteen. Ball in hand, they were leaning against a basketball pole. Diego was smiling. The boy was looking tough, his arms crossed, the one hand showing balled up in a fist with the word "Loco" tattooed over his knuckles. I wondered if the other hand displayed the word "Vato."

I also wondered if that was Gato Negro.

Stapleton told me that Diego was not married, nor, as far as the editor knew, was he dating anyone. "I think he had a lover back in Iowa, but he dumped her or she dumped him. That was before he came here."

I leaned over the desk again. "He was a good-looking guy," I said, thinking back to the body, remembering how death has a way of taking beauty away.

"Yeah," said Stapleton, "some people wondered why he didn't try out for a local television news show. He had the looks."

"That would have been something."

"Yeah, but he lacked one thing to be a television anchorman."

"What's that?"

"Stupidity."

A real newspaperman, I thought, looking at Stapleton.

The editor picked up his own words, as if afraid that maybe I had a relative in the television business. "Diego was one of the smarter people I knew. He went to Loyola in Chicago, graduated in journalism with honors. This job opened right when he got out of school. I was hesitant at first to take someone so young, without any experience. But he just wowed me during the interview. I hired him on the spot."

Stapleton allowed me to look through the desk drawers. Nothing in particular helped move me toward any conclusions. Only pencils, clips, Wite-Out, press cards, tape, calculator, stamps, pins, *The Cumberland Journal* stationery. "Do you know if he kept a notebook on him, Mr. Stapleton?"

He thought a minute. "Yes. He kept a small one, usually in his shirt pocket. I remember, because he was the only reporter on the floor who owned a Mont Blanc pen." Stapleton chuckled.

"How does a reporter own a Mont Blanc?" I asked.

"It was a gift from his mother. She gave it to him when he graduated. Oh, god, I've got to be calling her..."

With that, I left him, thanking him for his help, and assuring him that I would be in touch. Stapleton shook his head in understanding, though the heavy thought of having to tell parents such news had invaded most every corner of his mind.

Then his news-mind flicked back on, slicing through the mourning. "Detective," he called out as I walked through the door. "What I've given you is privileged information. The name Gato Negro and all. I'd appreciate it if that data stayed between you and me, until I decide to print it."

I half-promised him it would, though there was no energy behind my words. The lilt in his voice revealed his readiness to take issue with me regarding whose rights were primary, his as a reporter or mine as a homicide detective. This sudden tension was necessary, I suppose. But I had felt it before, from reporters in Atlanta. It didn't make for fast friendships.

CHAPTER FOUR

Before leaving the offices of *The Cumberland Journal*, I used one of the front desk phones to call Doc.

"I'm sorry to bother you in the middle of your work."

"That's fine. I can talk," he said. The flat echo of his voice made it clear he spoke into a speakerphone. An assistant made periodic comments in the background.

"Did you find a notebook on Sáenz? Perhaps in his shirt pocket?"

"Nope. Nothing."

"Really?"

"It surprised me, too, considering he was a reporter."

"What about a pen?"

"Oh, yes. A Mont Blanc. I always wanted to have one of those. But no notebook. If he had one, looks like your killer lifted it."

"So you're thinking it's a homicide now?" I asked. This surprised me, as I had yet to tell Doc what else I had found after he left the crime scene.

"Yes, I'm a believer. Remember those blotches on his hand that you pointed out to me? Sáenz's right hand was bruised. The back of it. There are marks all around, under his knuckles. Also slight bruising over the central phalanges of his middle, ring, and pinky fingers. Good work, Romilia."

"Damn." The image became clear immediately in my head of how Sáenz had died. "So somebody grabbed his hand while Sáenz held the gun?"

"Yep. Then they forced it under his own throat and had his finger pull the trigger."

"The perp overpowered him."

"I'd say. Your killer is strong. Looks like Sáenz's hand was in a large vise grip."

"I take it there were burn marks around the entry wound."

"Indeed. He was shot up close. The barrel was pushed up hard against his skin."

The image crystallized, all except for the face of the killer. The murderer somehow got close enough to Sáenz to restrain him, grab the gun in the reporter's hand, and force Sáenz's hand and pistol up under his head, then squeezed his fingers enough to have the gun go off.

With the image, questions came to mind. Was Sáenz aiming the gun at the killer? If so, how could the killer be so quick as to grab Sáenz's hand? Did he come from behind or in front? Why was a news reporter carrying a gun?

"This brings up a lot of stuff, Doc," I said. "I'd like to come over and visit you sometime today, after I check on this Nolensville Road lead."

"Mi casa es su casa," he said through a horribly accented Spanish. Then he laughed.

Though a fairly large southern city, Nashville was not Atlanta. Even in the early-morning hours Atlanta can offer some movement, even if it is only composed of drunks and the homeless. At seven a.m. there was very little happening down Nashville's Nolensville Road. The four-lane highway that pointed north and south from the center of town to its edges was desolate. Few cars drove by. Nolensville collected Nashville poverty. Numerous old businesses lined the roads, used cars, a tire shop, ubiquitous pawnshops, a very old McDonald's that still had the original neon "M" that showed the lightbulb tube running through its yellow background. There was no gas station here, nor parks, nor churches. And, of course, no banks. The pawnshops had control over any loan and investment transaction. Toppled trash cans on the sidewalks spilled out several days' worth of garbage. This scene was a lifetime away from the streets of Bellevue in the west or the little town of Franklin just to the south, where the real moneychangers lived. The only similarity between Nolensville and those two posh communities was that it was now shrouded in the calm of early morning, and seemed as tranquil as the most peaceful place on earth.

It took a few minutes of driving before I saw something that offered me a possibility. A sign upon the wall of an old wooden building said *"Taquería,"* with an arrow pointing up a side street. It was not a large sign, perhaps the size of a small windshield. It had few adornments on it save the colors of the Mexican flag: red, white, and green. *Taquería* was not a word that a Latino would use in order to cultivate a gringo clientele. This small sign was obviously meant to attract local raza.

I took the side street and pulled away from Nolensville Road. One half block away, a light burned through a fairly large picture window. A crack ran down one of its corners. A woman moved around inside. Though passing the window only once, I could tell she was older, perhaps in her mid-fifties. She moved around, placing objects upon shelves.

I parked the car and walked to the front door. A streetlight that offered no glow buzzed above me, its constant electric crackle cutting through the silence of early day. The sign hanging in the window of the door said "*cerrado.*" I knocked.

The woman turned and looked at me, a certain harshness penetrating her stare. Undoubtedly, a number of her children and grandchildren had been on the receiving end of such a stare whenever having done something wrong. What I now did wrong, most assuredly, was break the rhythm of her early morning, taking her from the first moments of a workday.

She moved to the door. Perhaps my being a woman allowed her to do that. Yet she did not open it until asking in thickly accented English who I was. I introduced myself in Spanish, saying I was with the police and showing her my badge and ID. She stared at it, then with no hesitation unlocked the door and opened it wide. The cold air rushed in, making her show me a curt courtesy, "*Pásese, por favor, pase adelante.*"

I thanked her and walked in. The odor of a hundred bags of *masa harina,* the flour used for *tortillas, tamales, pupusas, flautas,* and every other corn-based food, whipped into my nose. That had not happened since Mamá and I had left Atlanta. This woman's shelves held a cornucopia of Latin foods: cans of processed refried beans, both pinto and black; red cascabel peppers, dried and packaged in crinkly plastic sacks; bags of sweet breads piled high in a wooden trough; three troughs filled with tomatoes, jalapeño peppers, serrano peppers, banana peppers, green *tomatillos* in their husks, cilantro, onions, garlic. A trough to one side displayed at least one hundred CDs and cassettes of *rancheras, corridos, cumbias,* Gloria Estefan, Selena, Los Tigres del Norte, Los Bukis. Another wooden trough held a legion of videocassettes. A large refrigerator with glass doors displayed pounds of cheeses from both cow's milk and goat's milk. Bags of premade tortillas were also stacked in there, waiting for a working mother to come by before rushing home to make dinner for a hungry family. Posters lined the walls: Selena standing beautiful and voluptuous, a photo taken just weeks before her murder; another of a Latina woman whom I did not know, but who stood in a pose that barely allowed for her arms and thighs to cover her nude breasts and pubis; right next to her an old, large poster of Our Lady of Guadalupe. Below the posters, upon rough wooden shelves, sat two huge stereo speakers. She had yet to turn them on. They sat like fat, black mouths, ready to belt out a round of sad *corridos*.

This place was different from Nolensville Road. Out there, on the street and during the day, most assuredly the population was predominantly African American and White. That street really had yet to begin to speak two languages. Yet here, just a half block away from the daily rush of Nolensville, stood an almost breathing edifice of *raza*. I had found the pulsing heart of a very small yet growing Nashville Latino barrio.

"What can I do for you?" she asked in Spanish,

though her eyes looked me up and down. She was about ten inches shorter than I. "You're a cop, you say?"

Chota was the word she used for cop. Mexican. I shook my head at the not-flattering term. I offered my hand and gave her my name, but did not tell her yet that I was with homicide. She gave me her one hand, but in the other she held a sack of white onions. She held them in a way that requested I get to my point. Yet I waited for her to introduce herself. She did not. "And you are . . . ?"

"Marina. Doña Marina Osegueda, at your service." The courteous words came out automatically. I doubted them. She just stared at me, waiting. Her dress was simple enough, a pattern that looked as if she had bought the material at a sewing store and had sewn it herself. She had tied her steely hair into a bun to keep it out of her face. Her aging eyes were quick to dart about. They had been darting ever since she spotted me through the window of the door. "What do you need?"

"I'm looking for someone."

"What's his name?"

"They call him Gato Negro."

Marina's piercing eyes quit piercing me. They rolled upwards as she turned and carried the bag of white onions to a bin. "What's Nelson done now?" she asked, placing the onions carefully into the bin.

"That's his name? Nelson?"

"Yes. Nelson García. But he likes to be called Gato Negro."

"Why? Does it mean something, like a gang thing, or . . ."

"Because he hates the name Nelson. Thinks it sounds like a queer gringo."

I shook my head at this logic. No doubt Doña

Marina, the local distributor of Latino food, was also the conduit of local gossip.

"So you're finally coming around to make him stop busting out those streetlights?" she asked, motioning her face toward the window and the pole outside.

"Well, no ... did Nelson do that?"

"Yes, when he was fifteen. About four years ago. I called the police, but you never came."

"I see. No, I'm here on other business. Do you know Nelson well? Is he a relative?" I asked that to see if she would be calling Nelson's home after I took off in my car.

"No. He and his family came here just a few years ago. When he and his sisters were just kids. Nice family. But Nelson is a little wild."

"Do you know where he lives?"

She walked over to the window. I followed behind. She pointed beyond my car toward a house that sat alone in a patch of yard. A couple of bicycles lay in the dry grass. A dark blue pickup truck in relatively good condition was parked just in front of the house.

"Right there. But they're all asleep right now. Hey, what's this all about? You don't look like a regular cop, *hija*."

She called me "daughter," which made me feel the mother in her. It made me want to ask more about herself, her own children and grandchildren, how long she had lived here and what had brought her to Nashville, a Latino-less town, in the first place. I wanted to introduce my son to her, just to hear her go on about how cute he was. All that would have to wait, I hoped, until another visit, one during off hours. But most assuredly I would be telling Mamá about this place. Marina's store would make my own mother feel more at home. Perhaps it would help her insomnia.

"Oh, it's nothing really. I'm working on a case. I think Gato Negro could help me out on it." I smiled, hoping to disengage suspicions.

"Is it because of drugs?" she asked too suddenly.

"What about drugs?"

"Oh, that boy. I hear he's been smoking that stuff. The grassy stuff, you know." She did not have any sense of the lingo in either language. "But he really is a good boy, officer. I've known him since he was just a little *chamaco*."

"Don't worry, Doña Marina, I don't think he's in any real trouble yet."

She heard my *hasta el momento*, my "yet." She looked at me.

"You know," she said, "I've never met a *chota latina* in this town before." She kept looking at me. I could not tell, from her forced stance of neutrality, whether she gazed at me with respect or with a necessary distance.

I tried to break her eye lock. "You have a wonderful store here," I said. "I would like to come by during the day and pick up some things for my mother."

The compliment—as well as the reference to mamá (yes, I was actually born unto this world, not hatched in the *Chota* Department)—seemed to lighten her demeanor. She actually smiled. "You like it? I built it seven years ago. Well, my boys built it for me. At first there was very little business. But now I can't keep up with the demand. I even have *gringos* and *negros* come in here and buy food!"

We chatted a few minutes longer. Yet I was anxious, now having a real name to follow up on. I wanted to wander over to that house and get a chance to talk with the boy. I hoped that, arriving at this early-morning hour, I could catch him sleeping, which would help get more honest, crude answers from him. But I said none of this to Doña Marina, wanting to keep her from picking up the phone or walking over to the García home to warn them. Perhaps she would not. Then again, how much appeasing could I do, given the fact that I was out so early in the morning looking for a guy named Black Cat?

I cordially said goodbye and walked out. Her eyes pushed through the window and lay upon my back. I turned and smiled one last time. Doña Marina slapped a quick smile upon her own face and waved back. I pulled away from the curb, certain that her smile lasted for a very short while.

Instead of walking up to Gato Negro's house, I drove the half block away from Doña Marina's store. It was a last-ditch attempt to have her stop looking at me. Maybe she would believe I had left the neighborhood, and thus would return to preparing her store for the day.

I walked up to the faux-brick-covered building. Some of the façade had begun to peel. The roof shingles were uneven. Though poor, the porch and small yard were kept tidy.

A woman in her mid-forties answered my knock. She had obviously been up for a little while. "Yes?" she asked in clear English. It was clipped with a Mexican accent.

I introduced myself, showing my badge. "Is Nelson García around?" I asked in Spanish.

She hesitated, then said in Spanish, "No, he's not here now. He comes in later."

"Oh. From work?"

"Yes. Of course."

"What time do you expect him?"

"I, I am not sure. He comes in at different times."

"I see. Where does he work?"

A quick lie could not come to her. What place would be open this early in the morning where he could be working? A place where a cop wouldn't take the time to check out?

"I am not sure. He has changed jobs."

"I see. You his mother?"

"Yes."

"And you don't know where he works?"

She said nothing, only looked down at the door frame.

I sighed testily. "Look. I just need to ask him some questions. Something's happened to a friend of his named Diego Sáenz. I was wondering if Gato could help us find out what occurred."

"Something has happened to Diego?" She blurted out the question. "What?"

"He's dead." I said nothing more, excused myself from the home, and left, planning when my next surprise visit would be. Again, I felt a set of eyes upon me and my Taurus, fearful eyes, ones that had just learned that someone she knew had passed away, yet ones that scrambled to find reasoning within the chaos of such news.

Right as I pulled away, I felt and heard something hit the side of my car. In the rearview mirror I saw a young man who had looked as if he had just bolted awake. He stared at me in the mirror, then made his way to my door. I rolled down the window.

"I'm Gato Negro, man," he said. "Nelson." Though he spoke in English, his accent was strange. It was not

Mexican. He did not give me a chance to say anything.
"What you mean Diego's dead? What happened?"

"We found him murdered last night."

I thought Gato was turning to throw up. But all he
did was whirl about one time with the news. He cursed
lowly. Tears started to punch out from his eyes.

"Why did your mother lie for you, Gato?" I asked,
getting out of the car.

"I don't know. She sees cops, she automatically
lies, know what I'm saying? Shit, I'm not even on pro-
bation anymore."

"But you were?"

"Yeah, for a shoplifting bust. But I'm clean now,
officer...what's your name?"

I introduced myself.

"So you are *raza*. And a cop. Damn."

I got out of the car. "Why did you run out to stop
me?" I asked.

"Diego's my friend. My mamá ran back and told
me. I jumped out of bed. Dang, I can't believe he's
dead..."

It was then that I could pin his accent down. Dang.
Though he spoke in both languages, his English was
most definitely southern. It seemed strange, having
such a twang come out of a Mexican American's
mouth.

"So who do you think would want Diego dead,
Gato?"

His watery eyes glanced at me a couple of times.
His black hair, still matted from a night of sleep, hung
halfway over his left eye. "Is it worth anything?"

I pulled a twenty-dollar bill from my purse. I held
it until he spoke.

He looked left and right down the street before
saying, "You ever hear of a guy called Tekún Umán?"

The name was familiar to me. But not here. Its memory wove back to my days of living in Atlanta. I said this to Gato.

"Yeah, well, he ain't livin' in Atlanta now. He's set up shop here."

"What kind of shop?"

He lowered his head, obviously avoiding my question.

"Come on, Gato, what do you know about his business?"

"You're homicide, right? So I guess you don't keep up as much with narcotics."

Not only was Gato street-smart, but he also knew the basic ins and outs of the police department. "So Tekún Umán is involved in drugs?"

Gato started to walk away. "I don't know much. But I got approached on the street a few weeks back, with a good offer. They said this guy was good, he'd take care of you if you took care of the street market for him. I told 'em no. Like I said, I'm clean." He made sure I heard that a couple of times. "Read the papers, man. You'll learn about him."

I wanted to stop him, but I knew I had no real reason to. Then an obvious question came to mind: "Hey, wait a minute. What kind of name is Tekún Umán? What's his real name?"

He was already at the doorstep of his home when he answered me. "That's some Indian name from Central America. I think his real name's Murillo." That was all he would tell me. His door was now closed.

CHAPTER FIVE

There was only one Murillo who had made the papers the past few days. Rafael Murillo was a gentleman from Atlanta who was the founder and CEO of Southern Homestead, a new nonprofit organization that planned to work for the resettlement of refugees from all over the world. Having founded a number of nonprofit groups in the Atlanta area, Murillo had recently moved to Nashville because, as the paper wryly quoted him, "I just love country music." He went on to explain seriously that he had visited the capital of Tennessee a number of times on business trips, and gradually fell in love with it. "I've been able to do my nonprofit work in Atlanta for ten years. Those organizations are doing fine on their own now, they don't need me. It was time for a change in my life. Nashville was most attractive. So here I am!"

There was a photo next to the article that was

headlined "Atlanta Philanthropist Plants Roots In
Nashville." The picture was of Murillo and one of the
City Council members shaking hands. Murillo smiled
casually, accustomed to having cameras thrust in his
face. The white council member was much more enthusiastic. Reading the article, I knew why: Murillo
had the reputation of bringing a lot of jobs into each
area that he opened up, starting with the construction
of the building that was to house his nonprofit program. Instead of renting an already standing building,
Murillo liked to begin fresh. "I have a soup kitchen and
homeless shelter in Atlanta that will compete in looks
and furnishings with any Sheraton or Radisson. But
those hotels can't compete with my prices—it's all free.
I believe that poor people and the homeless should enjoy, even for a transient time, some of the comforts
that we all want and strive for. It helps to build their
dignity."

When asked how he managed to fund such projects—ones that did not bring him back any money—
he answered, "Funders have been good to me. And I
have been blessed with an ancestry that has worked in
lucrative fields back in my father's home country."

That home country, the article said, was
Guatemala. His father's family owned a large coffee
plantation there. His father met his mother—a white
woman from Chattanooga—while both attended Vanderbilt University forty years ago. Rafael Murillo was
their only child. "Mamá and Papá spoiled me. So I
think it's my duty to spoil others," he was quoted as
saying.

"He seems to be an intelligent bullshitter," I muttered, flipping through the newspaper to find the end
of the article. Then I thought of young Gato Negro,
the boy who had given me this lead this morning. "Out

of the mouths of babes." Gato Negro knew something. How, I had no idea. But according to the teenager, Murillo was not the generous savior come into town that the paper had made him out to be.

I flipped back to the first part of the article and studied the face. He was young, perhaps in his early thirties. He wore a beard that was cut fairly close to the skin. His thick black hair was well groomed and combed. Though Latino, you wouldn't know it from his skin. It was, according to this picture, very light, lighter than my own. Then I reminded myself, we come in all shapes, sizes, and shades. There was no real defining the look of Latinness.

Nashville's first impression of Murillo, due to this article, was a good one. I folded the paper up and dropped it on my desk. "Now it's time to see if the impression is real or not."

Just then my boss, Patrick McCabe, walked in. He barely said good morning to three night detectives who were just going out the door, ending their shift. A number of day shift cops had already walked into the office. McCabe looked over at me and quietly signaled me to join him at his desk.

I obeyed. My boss straightened his tie in a small mirror in one corner of the room. He smoothed back his thinning brown hair, then hunted around his desk for a white cup that looked like it had not been cleaned in months. "You want coffee?" he said. I thanked him, but declined. He excused himself and walked out, poured his first helping of the day, and returned. His smaller, fifty-odd-year-old body was not pudgy, nor was it thin. He was somewhere in the middle, as if he could never make up his mind whether or not to exercise. As far as I knew, his only vice was too much coffee, all day long. He did not smoke, and made sure that anyone who did saw the "No Smoking" sign on his desk.

"Murder down at the river," he said to me while straightening out the papers on his desk. "A newspaperman. Shot in the head, made to look like a suicide. What else have you got for me, Romilia?"

I smiled politely, though I don't know why. "Seems like you've got just about as much as I do." That was the wrong thing to say. I knew that the moment it came out.

"I certainly hope not." It was the first time this morning he looked straight at me.

I told him what I had found so far, emphasizing the cigarette wrapper and the bloody trail toward the river, then the connection with Gato Negro and the possible drug lead on Murillo.

"Murillo...that name sounds familiar," he muttered.

"Maybe you read it in the papers," and I handed him the article I had just read.

"Ah, yes. That's right. So. You've got this philanthropist as a possible suspect. I'm certainly glad you've got this case, and not me."

"Why is that?"

"I hear Murillo will be meeting with the mayor sometime this week. He's very popular with the bigwigs in town. You better have a solid foundation before you go poking around in his expensive underwear."

Just then McCabe's face fell slightly and his eyes rolled upwards after glancing through the large glass of his office into the main area of the Homicide Department. I turned. Detective Jerry Wilson had just walked through the door.

"Oh, god," muttered McCabe. "Here comes Mr. Hollywood."

I wasn't sure what he meant by that. A puzzled look must have crossed my face, for McCabe explained to me. "He was on the television show 'Sunrise over Nashville' this morning. The media's still flocking around him like a bunch of dogs in heat. Just because he happened to stumble onto Bitan sleeping with that nurse. A lousy piece of good luck like that, and he's Super Dick. He'll probably have my job someday..."

Obviously Wilson was a lot on McCabe's mind. My boss was venting too much frustration out to me, his newest detective. I had not known, until now, that Wilson's collaring of the killer Bitan was one that came out of pure luck. I asked, "I thought Wilson followed him out of a bar until Bitan led him straight to the nurse's body."

"That's true. But Wilson was in there having a drink himself. No investigative work. He just happened to sit next to Benny, who was fooling around with a woman's locket. I have to give him some credit. Wilson wondered what a drugged-up derelict like Benny was doing with a woman's necklace. Then Benny started talking crazy, about how dirty she was, and how he wanted to protect her before they found her. He was stoned out of his head. So Wilson followed him and found him bedding down with the victim. The locket was the nurse's. Still, it was damned luck. You know how difficult it can be to track down a serial killer? Damned impossible."

I knew this was true. Out of all murders, serial killers are the most difficult to trace. Unlike domestic or professional killings, where there is motive and some sort of relationship between killer and victim, a serial killer usually has no connection with his prey. The killer may hunt down three or four or five people in one city, then disappear to another city at the opposite end of the country before the authorities catch up with him.

I looked out through the same window. Other detectives were slapping Wilson on his shoulders, telling him he looked good on TV. He did look good. Perhaps in his early thirties, he had white skin that was fairly tan from obvious regular trips to the booths. His short blond hair grew thick over his skull. His was the type of handsome that let him get away with not combing that hair perfectly, but allowing for a slight lump here and there, as if he had just taken off a hat. He was a looker. He made me look.

Trying to look sincerely humble, Wilson smiled at his colleagues. Then he turned toward us and saluted McCabe, waving at him through the window. McCabe waved back, smiled halfheartedly, then mumbled, "Okay, okay, you little shit . . ." Then he turned to me, as if suddenly remembering that I was there. "None of what I've just said leaves this office."

"Of course." And I would keep my word.

McCabe snapped his attention back to my case. "Call narcotics in Atlanta. See if they have any trail on this Murillo guy. If they do, look him up and give him a visit." I could tell, the way he clipped his words, that he was dismissing me.

"He's a goddamn snake."

The woman on the other end of the line, a narcotics detective named Dunn, did not mince words.

"He's got cocaine running in from Guatemala every month. Heroin through some connection in Haiti. He's the Kroger of the drug trade here in the south."

I almost wanted to laugh at her reference to the

well-known grocery store. "So you've got proof on this guy. Why haven't you..."

"Then the bastard sets up all these service organizations as fronts, but they're real organizations, you know? They really help people out. The soup kitchen is a regular Olive Garden, handing out free food twice a day. The homeless shelter is, well, shit, it's nicer than my house. Everybody loves the man. Nobody will give him up, especially his 'beloved poor and oppressed,' as he likes to call them."

I finally got a question in between her rantings. "Then why haven't you picked him up yet?"

Though I thought it was innocent enough, she turned defensive. "Why do you think? I've told you, he's a damn snake! He just slithers through the cracks. We've tapped his lines, put surveillance on his house and his office, everything. But he's got this code with his people, uses the stock market to talk about his business. When they say to him over the phone, 'Sales on Martha White is up,' then he's probably talking about coke. When they say 'Buying on Sweet'n Low is happening,' then it's smack. That's what we think. But we haven't been able to make a bust yet. Then that no-good son of a bitch up and leaves Atlanta. Now he's going to start the same shit in Nashville. I just can't believe it..."

It went on like that for a good ten minutes, mostly me listening to her angry rendering of all that they had done, in vain, to catch Mr. Murillo. I asked her about his nickname, Tekún Umán. She knew nothing about that, which told me that, no matter how much surveillance they thought they had done, somehow a street kid like my new friend Gato Negro knew more about Mr. Murillo than did the entire narcotics division of Atlanta P.D.

I thanked her and hung up, leaving her still breathing heavily.

Murillo's temporary office was an old school building that sat two blocks away from Centennial Park. As I walked to the doors, I glanced over to my left and saw, beyond the parking lot, the Parthenon that sat in the middle of the park. I had yet to visit that tourist site. Mamá and my son, Sergio, would get a kick out of seeing it. They said it was an exact replica of the great Parthenon in Athens. Why such a building was put in Nashville, I was not sure, until another detective on the floor said that this city was once nicknamed the Athens of the South. Then again, I'm not sure why it got that name either. I was a newcomer, and knew little of this place I cautiously called home.

Murillo's building had yet to be renovated. It was an old school, built several decades ago, perhaps closer to the beginning of the century, long before all these other office buildings grew around it. Though mostly squared off like the other buildings in the neighborhood, it had one corner that was rounded. From the outside it looked like the lone tower of a simple castle. Windows had been built into the round structure, allowing me to see a large office on the first floor. "Must have been the principal's office," I muttered, seeing it as the apparent seat of power for the entire building.

Inside, it looked old and abandoned. Though the halls were well swept and mopped, and the garbage kept in receptacles at the end of the hallways, I sensed that it had not been used in a long time. Large stains that someone had tried to scrub still clung to the off-white walls. The ceilings were high, built long ago, which probably meant that the building was not cost-efficient when it came to heating and cooling. Then again, perhaps Murillo didn't pay so much; it was damn cold in the hallway. Dark, too. "This sure doesn't look like a Radisson Hotel," I muttered.

No lights were on. The only way I found the way to a door marked "Office," where a bright light shined out its opaque window, was with the help of a few windows scattered over the north wall.

The door was open one inch. Music from a local country radio station played through the crack. Voices also made their way through it. I opened the door partway and heard Spanish. One of them, the fatter gentleman, chuckled over what the thinner man with the mop had just said. Then the corpulent fellow looked up from his paperwork at me and smiled, saying, "Yes, may I help you?" in a clear, pleasant English.

I introduced myself. "I'm looking for a Rafael Murillo. I understand this is his building."

The English speaker chuckled. "This is his building all right. But you won't find him here much. Hi. I'm Francisco Colibrí, his assistant. They call me *Pajarito*."

Teeny-weeny little bird. What a hell of a nickname. I guessed it was due to his last name, as well as a bit of irony regarding his portly size. He then introduced the man with the mop as Miguel Martínez. Miguel said nothing, though he smiled shyly and waved.

"So," I asked, "why isn't Mr. Murillo in his office much?"

"Oh, he doesn't care for the decor. Or the lack of it. He only comes in whenever he has a meeting with regional authorities or when I have to get him to sign some papers. Once they demolish this building and build a new one, then you'll find Mr. Murillo here more regularly."

"I see. By the way, isn't he also known as Tekún Umán? That's quite a nickname."

Both men just looked at me, as if I had said some curse word.

"Well, isn't that his name?" I asked again.

"Uh, yes. Yes, it is. I believe that's right, isn't it, Miguel?"

Miguel shook his head negatively, not willing to commit.

"Yes. I've heard some people call him that." Chico then quickly changed the subject. "But, as I said, I'm sorry, Mr. Murillo is not in right now."

Just then the janitor Miguel piped in, "*Díle que seguro el jefe anda ya con una de sus señoritas, pero a saber cuál.*" Tell her that the boss is no doubt out with one of his girls, but who knows which one?

"*Ay, entonces, es un mujeriego, pues,*" said I. So, he's a womanizer, then.

"*¡Púchica!*" exclaimed Miguel. I had no idea what the word meant, but it sounded like some form of emotive surprise. He went on to say that, though I looked it, he wasn't expecting me to speak in their native tongue.

From then on we spoke in Spanish. I easily picked out the parameters. They probably had only monolingual, English-speaking people come by the office. To have somebody like me come in was a surprise. I suppose they somehow saw me as more gringa than Latina, though I'm not sure why. Pajarito seemed to be Tex-Mex; his skin and his cheekbones showed his strong Mexican descent. We talked, falling into a casualness. I had yet to tell them my profession. Perhaps they saw me as one of the many ladies who sought out Mr. Tekún Umán's sexual attention.

Miguel was from farther away than Pajarito. His

skin was much darker than either of ours. His soft features, especially his eyes, revealed a certain Indian background to him, perhaps from southern Mexico. His shy smile that broke large over his face before he ducked his head down to hide it revealed a friendly yet subservient demeanor. He was the one who kept these old, abandoned halls clean as a whistle. Though it was obvious that Pajarito was Miguel's boss, they enjoyed a friendly relationship.

This was all picked up in a matter of minutes, for finally Pajarito asked me, smiling, "And may I ask what business you would like to speak with Mr. Tekún—Mr. Murillo about?"

"I'm a homicide detective. I need to ask him some questions."

"*¿De veras?* Has something happened?" he asked, his smile dissipating.

"There's been a murder. Diego Sáenz. We found him dead this morning. Did you know him?"

At the moment I said *asesinato*, both of them focused their attention upon me. Miguel put his head next to his mop handle. He seemed to clutch it. Then he turned away. Pajarito's eyebrows downed, trying to furrow together. "Sáenz, Sáenz . . . no, I'm not sure that I did."

"There was never a Hispanic newspaper reporter who came in here and asked for Mr. Murillo?" I asked.

"Newspaper reporter? Oh, yes. I do believe there was. A young man, right? Black hair, spoke Spanish and English. Yes, if it's the same man, he was in here a couple of weeks ago. He said he was from the paper and wanted to do an article on Mr. Murillo's nonprofit company. I told him that the paper had already done a very big article on him the week previous. But the young man said he was doing some sort of follow-up article. Either way, I told him he could find Mr. Murillo over at the bookstore."

"What bookstore?"

"Daniel Childs Bookery, over on Hillsborough. He's always over there on Mondays and Thursdays. Stays there for hours. The day the young reporter came here, it was a Monday. So I told him he would find Mr. Murillo there."

Today was Monday, too. I knew where to go. But I needed directions. Pajarito drew me a quick map on a small piece of stationery with "Murillo Enterprises" written neatly in the upper corner.

I took the map and thanked him. Then I went quickly to the door, closing down our casual conversation. I caught a glimpse of their faces. I was not sure if they were shocked over the news that I had just brought them and perhaps worried over how their boss had anything to do with this, or if they were confused by the way I fabricated an informal conversation with them, only to depart quickly, like a gringa, the moment I got what I wanted. Perhaps it was both.

CHAPTER SIX

Hillsborough Road took me to a nicer area of the city. This was my first time here. Shopping malls with some of the more opulent stores and churches with well-kept lawns fell in line on each side of the road. Three Mercedes drove past me. There was not a piece of trash to be found alongside the street.

Daniel Childs Bookery stood prominent among these buildings. It was larger than the other stores next to it. A large, easily readable clock face stood prominent upon the brick front of the building, displaying the time: 10:24 in the morning. I had been on this case for about six and a half hours. As it began in the early morning, with one of the night-shift dicks calling me around 3:30 to inform me that a Hispanic had been killed, I now felt a certain weariness wash through me. Then I remembered what Pajarito said, that this place had a coffee shop. I planned to make use of it.

I parked my lackluster Taurus right next to a new, dark, emerald green Jaguar. Next to it was parked a red Lexus. "Jeez, this city is crawling with rich people." Two large tables stood in front of the store on the sidewalk. They were covered with remaindered books, their prices marked down to practically nothing. I glanced over the piles quickly, wondering if I would find a lost gem. Nothing there except old O. J. Simpson courtroom books, first novels, and confessional memoirs of unpopular movie stars, written by ghost writers.

Inside was a different matter. It was the largest bookstore I had ever seen. To the right an enclave as big as half my house displayed the latest in fiction and nonfiction. I could not count the books. Before me was the first of three long halls made out of bookcases that reached to my shoulder. Along the walls of the room (the main room itself was the size of a city auditorium) stood bookshelves that were twice my height. A children's section took up the entire back wall. Sergio would have run straight toward it. Individuals milled about casually, sitting on benches and reading while barely listening to the classical background music piped in: Bach, no doubt. A concerto.

Then there was the upstairs. On the second floor stood a whole other world of books. A thin, waist-high balcony allowed one to stand on the second floor and look down casually to the first. There was a section that had no books, only chairs, tables, and what looked like some type of food bar in the back. That had to be the coffee shop. A good place to start the search for Tekún Umán. Before walking upstairs, I glanced around one more time at the legion of literature and made a silent promise to myself to spend a few hours here some evening with my son, once this case was closed.

Case closed. The words bit at me. Six hours old. How many hours would pass before I closed it?

The coffee shop was like any other coffeehouse in the country, which was just fine with me. Though they offered a variety of flavors and strengths, everything from decaffeinated latte to raspberry chocolate Guatemalan, I'd head straight to a strong, simple Colombian. But I did not order yet. I had to find my suspect before walking about with a cup of coffee in hand. And I didn't picture myself sitting with the suspect with a hot cup of java while drilling him with a few subtle yet pointed questions. My coffee would be to go.

He sat alone at a small table that stood right next to the balcony. This allowed him to glance up from the book he was reading and casually look about the first floor of the bookstore, appreciating the scene of women and men meandering slowly between bookshelves, pulling books and glancing through first paragraphs. Then he would return to his book, reading another page while carefully, adroitly bringing the cappuccino to his lips and placing it back, without looking, upon its saucer. So careful and formal was he, the cappuccino did not leave a foamy moustache upon his black one.

He wore a dark blue pin-striped suit, obviously very expensive. His shoes were black wingtips, shiny as if he had just bought them. Then there was his shirt. It was a white pullover shirt, no doubt a fine brand, but a pullover nonetheless. This had been a fashion for a while among men, a style that I had always found attractive, wearing a fine suit with a thick, well-made T-shirt.

The newspaper photo had not done his skin justice. What I had seen as white was really an olive color, not as dark as my own, but swarthy enough to show he had Latin blood in him. His well-trimmed beard and thick hair were both black, with only the slightest reflection of silver to the side, which could have easily been the light reflecting off it.

There was no one else at the table with him. No one, except that one larger man whose back was turned to Tekún Umán, sat nearby. Most all the other tables around him were empty. As I approached Tekún Umán's table, the man behind him shifted, turned his head slightly toward me, then placed his hands upon his table. A bodyguard, no doubt. My next step was at first careful, then angry. Screw him, I thought. Screw them both, the bodyguard and the man who felt the need to hire a protector.

As I drew nearer, Tekún Umán's face lifted from his book with a smile. He looked straight at me. "Ah, you must be Detective Romilia Chacón. A pleasure." He stood up. The bodyguard relaxed, pulling his hands away from the table. Though I could not see the full breadth of the guard, I could tell from his frame that he looked recently departed from some special training, one that cut his muscles deep into his shirt. "I'm Rafael Murillo," he continued, giving me his hand. "Won't you please sit down?" He motioned to a chair.

I sat. "I take it Pajarito is quite a singer. He got to you before I did."

"Well, yes, I must confess, he did just call me." Tekún sat back in his chair as if to get a better, slightly distanced look at me. The bodyguard tucked himself closer to his own table, giving his boss room. Tekún stared at me. "He was right."

"Who?"

"Pajarito. He said that a very beautiful woman was about to call on me."

I tried not to react.

"But he wasn't right about everything. He called your hair brown. 'Brown' sounds nice for skin color, but your hair deserves a better description." He paused, studied me, and said, "A thick chiffon of golden auburn."

All right, that's enough. My eyes dropped down to the table to avoid his kind yet solid stare. I saw what he was reading. *Cien años de soledad. One Hundred Years of Solitude.* Gabriel García Márquez.

He was a Gabi fan. And in the original Spanish, no less.

I held back surprise and elation and focused upon the task at hand. "Did Pajarito also tell you why I wished to speak with you?"

"Yes. You work with the police department, and you're investigating the death of that young reporter." Tekún leaned back closer to the table, a sincere look of concern flashing through his brown eyes. "Tell me, how did he die?"

"He was shot in the head."

"Oh, goodness." Tekún pulled back again. "Murder? I hate hearing about such things..."

I cleared my throat. "Yes, and I'm the primary on the case, so I'm just beginning my canvass of leads."

"I see. Coffee?"

I looked at him and his offer. "Oh, uh, no. I'm fine, thanks." I must not have been very enthusiastic nor did I sound convincing, for Tekún lifted his hand and his gaze up to the workers at the coffee bar. One young woman with red hair and glasses jumped away from the large copper espresso machine and trotted our way.

"I may be wrong, but you don't look like the

specialty coffee type," Tekún said to me as the young white woman waited by his side for the order. "Colombian or Guatemalan seems more your style. Am I correct?"

"Well, yes, as a matter of fact, Colombian is my fav…"

"Excellent." He turned to the waitress. "One large Colombian, please, Martha."

Martha walked away. It all happened relatively quickly. It shouldn't have been a big thing in my mind. The man was just ordering me a coffee. But I felt the weariness of the day hitting me. I turned and said to Martha "I'll get it," but she was already out of earshot. I made a note to myself to pay, first thing after questioning this guy. "I didn't know these coffeehouse places had real waitresses. I thought you had to go up and get your own order yourself."

"You do. But I've got the reputation of being a good tipper. They delight in serving me at my table. And I hate waiting in line." He looked straight at me, then after a few long seconds of studying my face, said, "You seem a little tired."

"I've been up awhile." Until the coffee came, I felt the need to get back on focus. García Márquez was the closest buoy around. "I see you're a Márquez fan."

"Oh, of course. No greater novelist than he. Can you believe I've read this book at least a dozen times, and I still come around to flipping through it again? I don't know, there's just something so very true about this crazy story." He laughed. I wanted to laugh with him.

"Yes, I've read it. A few times," I said.

"You have? Really?" Tekún placed the flat of his palm upon the book, like a judge ready to take an oath. "So I take it you're familiar with the very first line,

'*Muchos años después, frente al pelotón del fusilamiento, el coronel Aureliano Buendía...*'"

I interrupted him by finishing the quotation. "'...*había de recordar aquella tarde remota en que su padre lo llevó a conocer el hielo.*'"

Tekún grinned, then burst into a delighted laugh. "Isn't this wonderful. A police officer who enjoys good literature. And in the original language, no less."

"I don't know if that should be so surprising. Anybody should be able to read Márquez."

"Very true. You have me there." He shifted slightly in his seat, getting more comfortable. "Who else do you like?"

I rattled off a list of favorite names: Allende, Fuentes, Suárez, Francisco Goldman, Puig. Once I said Neruda, he interrupted me with another quote, "*Ay, lo que yo soy siga existiendo y cesando de existir.*"

He smiled at me. I beat him to the punch. "That's from *Residence on Earth*, right?"

"So you know your Neruda. Impressive." He grinned again. His teeth were perfect.

Behind him, the bodyguard lit up. It was a strange sight. The cigarette was brown, not white, yet slim, not like a cigar. I thought back to my smoking days, when a very eccentric friend of mine in college smoked similar cigarettes. Though I could not remember the brand name, I did recall how elegant the brown cigarette looked.

This brown cigarette was dwarfed by the bodyguard's huge fingers. It seemed an anomaly for that reason as well: a hired gorilla puffing on a thin, elegant fag. The manager of the coffee shop, a young white fellow who looked like he worked here between college classes, also caught wind and sight of the smoker.

"Excuse me," he said as he approached the bodyguard's table, "but you can't smoke in here."

Godzilla from Guanajuato just looked up at the manager. "I am smoking in here."

"Yes, but it's against the house rules to smoke anywhere in the bookstore, which includes the coffee shop..."

"I really don't give a shit, kid." His voice was low and gravelly. It had its effect on the manager, who began to twitch from nerves.

"I'm sorry, but I can't let you..."

Then the bodyguard stood up and looked almost straight down at the boy. The boy's face seemed to regress into childhood. His jaw dropped. I think I heard a wheeze come out.

Tekún Umán interjected. "*Raimundo, no te preocupes, compa.*" Raimundo sat back down slowly. This did not appease the young manager's quaking. Tekún turned to the manager, "Please, if you would allow for my friend to enjoy his smoke, he will be much happier." With that, Tekún shook the youth's hand. I saw a green bill slip into the boy's palm. He looked at it. It must have been a large note, considering how the fear in his eyes mixed with the surprise of the gift. He muttered half a dozen thank-yous, either for the money or for keeping him from having his face ripped off his skull. Then he left us alone.

Tekún Umán smiled at me. "Sometimes serenity overcomes violence. Sometimes not. Today it did."

My coffee came. I waited little time for it to cool, sipping from it carefully. "This is all very nice. There's nothing I'd rather do than talk about García Márquez. But I'd like to get back to work, if I could, please."

"Ah, yes. The death of that reporter." Tekún Umán bent toward the table, ready to work.

"He came looking for you a couple of weeks ago. Why?"

"Yes. He came here. Sat right where you're sitting now. He said he wanted to do a follow-up piece on the article that his paper had done on me the previous week. I was a bit puzzled at this. *The Cumberland Journal* had done a fine piece on me, very thorough and correct. Nice picture, too. So why, I asked myself, would the same paper send someone out to do another article one week later? It made no sense to me, and I told him this. 'Save your column space for more relevant news,' I said to him."

"And did he interview you? Or did he just leave?"

"We talked awhile. He was a fairly intelligent young man, though not well read. I advised him to catch up on reading some of the very authors you've just mentioned. He didn't seem interested. Though he spoke good Spanish, I could hear it fall into some of the street slang, too. You know, *vato*, then using *chingado* with a stranger. Such manners. At least he didn't try a *tuteo* with me. He addressed me as *Usted*, which was, you would agree, appropriate. But he was a crusty young fellow, I'll give him that." Tekún chuckled.

"How do you mean?"

"Oh, he just insisted on doing the article."

"And you insisted on not doing it?"

"Yes. I really didn't want any more publicity than what I already had. It's embarrassing." Tekún picked up a small spoon and began stirring the leftover cream of his cappuccino into the final sips of strong coffee underneath it.

I tried to word my next question carefully. "Did Mr. Sáenz ask you any questions regarding information on new drug markets opening up in the Nashville area?"

"Drug markets? What kind of drugs? Pharmaceutical, or illegal, or what?" Though he glanced up at me, he still casually stirred his coffee.

"Illegal. Marijuana, cocaine, heroin. Did he ask you anything about that?"

"Why in the world would a reporter ask me about drug markets?"

I quickly covered my trail. "Mr. Sáenz was doing a report on the growing market of illegal contraband to children in the local schools."

"Oh, yes. I had read a couple of his pieces. 'Getting High in the Playground.' Something like that. Not very original."

"You don't think so? Handing out grass to kids on school property is a pretty interesting, and depressing, subject. It's good to see it in the papers."

"Yes, but Mr. Sáenz did not do a very good job of writing about it. Especially in the Spanish supplement. He needs to work on his syntax. Or, I should say, needed to."

I thought back to the Spanish articles I had read. I hadn't found them to be too bad. But Tekún seemed to have a very critical eye.

He interrupted my thoughts. "Still, I ask you: Why question me about such things? I'm a nonprofit CEO, not a drug runner."

"Yes, by the way, I had a couple of questions about that, Mr. Murillo, or should I call you Tekún Umán?" It was my turn to smile, mollifying my acerbic use of his nickname. I hoped it would break through some of the bullshit that he was feeding me. "By the way, what does that nickname mean?"

"And where did you learn about that name?" he smiled, obviously curious.

"A little cat told me."

He stopped stirring his coffee. He put the spoon on the saucer.

"So what does it mean?" I asked again.

"It's an old Indian name from Central America. Tekún Umán was a Quiché warrior prince in the Mayan nations of Guatemala. He died in hand-to-hand combat with Don Pedro de Alvarado in the early 1500s. He's an old folk hero to the Guatemalan people."

"Oh. And you're Guatemalan, right?" I asked.

"Half. My father. My mother is from Chattanooga, Tennessee."

"What a combination."

He smiled, somewhat humbly. "I am what you call a true Latino southerner."

"But then why the nickname?"

"It came about in Atlanta. I suppose the folks call me that because they appreciate the work I do for them. The homeless shelters, the soup kitchens, the renovation of poor barrios. They see that as heroics. I just see that as my duty. My obligation." He sipped from the coffee. "I must admit, it's the first time I've heard the name come out of the mouth of a police officer."

Which told me I had won a point somewhere, inching closer into the inside of his world. "And how do you come to pay for such a duty? It's pretty expensive to remodel an entire barrio."

"As I said to the newspaper, my family was blessed with a great deal of monetary wealth back in the old country. Coffee plantations. I am, you could say, one of the sons of the oligarchy in Guatemala. I've never felt comfortable with that. So my philanthropy work, which pretty much takes up all my time, is my way of dealing with that heritage."

"I see. So did the coffee plantations back home buy you that Jaguar outside?" I knew this was a guess. But the Jaguar was the most expensive vehicle that I had seen in the lot. It was also very close to the door. He could have bought his way into a handicap parking space.

His stare was losing its kindness, though not its solidity. "The Jaguar, and the Lexus next to it."

I was obviously confused.

"The Jaguar is mine. Raimundo drives the Lexus. Though he is my gentleman's gentleman, I have never given up the love of the road. Raimundo just stays right behind me, wherever I go."

Was this just bragging over opulence, or a warning, that he was always protected? I was starting to get tired of the games. "So, you wouldn't know of any information regarding Mr. Sáenz's drug investigation?"

He paused, then said, "Obviously, you think I do."

"I didn't say what I think, Mr. Murillo. I just asked you a question."

"Yes. A question that you've asked me twice within a very short conversation. To be honest, I find the allusion insulting."

"I don't mean to be insulting, Mr. Murillo. I'm just trying to do my job of finding who killed Sáenz." I took a sip from the coffee. It was delicious. I had finished about half of it. I wondered if it was the caffeine that made me tense, or this heated curve of our conversation.

"May I suggest, then, Detective, that you be a little more careful with your questioning. Perhaps do some preliminary investigation before tossing out inappropriate questions to people."

That was enough. "Mr. Murillo—or Tekún Umán—

or however you like to be called, you are part of my
preliminary investigation."

He sat back. He obviously heard the anger in my
voice. I heard it, too. Part of it was the rage I had vicariously felt from the woman in the Atlanta narcotics
division. They had been trailing this man who sat before me for the past two years. They had come up
with enough information to paint an almost thorough
picture of a drug king whose moat was the world of
nonprofit organizations. They had just not gotten a
complete enough portrait to hang him up on the wall
before he left town. Now here he was, sitting pretty,
starting a satellite kingdom in my new hometown.

But not all the anger was from the woman in
Atlanta. Anyone who knew me well enough knew how
my rage was a silent contender hidden in the folds of my
brain, always waiting for the right moment to flick out.
Sometimes it was appropriate, though not the easiest
beast to ride. It seemed appropriate now. There was no
need to beat around the bush with him. Going directly
through him seemed to be the only way to rip through
his façade. "Look, Murillo. I know who you are. Atlanta
has your file. You're always interested in the stock
market, buying Martha White Flour and Sweet'n Low
Sweetener. Now you've come to Nashville to spread
your 'philanthropy.' Don't bullshit me, Murillo. I'm
not in narcotics. But I am looking for a killer. I don't
give a damn how many city council members you know.
I'll ask you any question I need to, and I'll expect
straight answers."

I had almost said "I'll find out if you had anything
to do with the killing," but a last-second judgment call
told me not to. Yet knowing what Gato Negro had
alluded to, and what the narcotics cop in Atlanta had

screamed to me about, I had no time to put up with
this man's lies.

He said nothing. He only stared at me. His eyes
were locked onto my face. Raimundo, the bodyguard
behind him, shifted, stretching up in his chair, showing
me the full height and bulk of his cobra-shaped back. I
stood up, leaving the coffee unfinished. Following pro-
tocols, I gave him my card. "Here. If you think of anything that you believe is relevant to my investigation,
I'd appreciate a call."

"I see. Is your home number on here?" He looked
up at me without smiling.

"There's my beeper number, if you want to get
hold of... You just call if you've got something to say,
¿me entiendes?" I don't know why I said that to him in
Spanish, except to show him that I could deal with him
in either culture, and that I was willing to.

"*Perfectamente*," he answered.

"Good. Waitress." I turned toward the coffee bar.
"I need to get this, please. How much for the coffee?" I
was searching in my purse, but I could still barely see
her signaling to me. Then I heard Tekún's voice behind me.

"No, Detective. I've already bought you."

"What?" I turned on him, ready to slam him for
such an insult to my profession. "What the hell do you
mean you've bought..."

"I mean I already paid for the coffee. I bought it
for you."

I said nothing, but just walked away, feeling the
eyes of the waitress, Murillo, and Raimundo, all
upon me.

CHAPTER SEVEN

One of Doc's lab assistants left me a message on my phone recorder, informing me that the blood samples I had found on the parking lot and the floodwall were A negative, the same as Sáenz's blood type. If the killer's blood was any type other than A negative, the killer was probably not wounded during the killing moment. This could mean that there was no struggle.

The blood from the print on the cigarette wrapper was also A negative. Doc had the print delivered to the Fingerprints Department to see if it matched with anybody in the Automated Fingerprint Identification System, or AFIS. I wouldn't hear from Fingerprints until tomorrow morning, as it usually took overnight to verify a print with both the local file and with the FBI's much larger database.

The blood type proved enigmatic. It did not groove completely with other information Doc gave me regarding Sáenz's gun-toting hand. It was bruised all around, as if the person who had held it needed to squeeze hard in order to keep Sáenz's hand controlled. In his last moment of life Sáenz probably knew what was happening, and he did try to struggle free.

The only thing I could make of this so far was that Sáenz did know his killer or killers. He may have even been aiming his gun at them. Somehow they were able to take control of the gun and turn it on him. They shot him. Was it an accident, one that made them panic and thus create a cover-up, making it look like a suicide? But the place where the bullet went through, straight clean through the man's head, looked too well placed, too strategically positioned, to have been an accident.

Then the thought came over and over again. Sáenz knew Tekún Umán. And no doubt his bodyguard. Raimundo looked tough enough to force someone to plug his own skull. He could have also held Sáenz's other hand at bay, clutching it so that Sáenz could not fight back.

Another message on my phone recorder, left there by the dispatcher, said that ballistics had tried to trace the gun found in Sáenz's hand. It was not registered to anyone. There was no way to find out if it had belonged to the victim.

"A reporter toting an illegal gun . . . and he was just twenty-four years old. Where does a guy that young, working for a well-established newspaper, get an unregistered gun, and why?"

That certain panicking feeling came over me, regarding the possible dissipation of leads. Tekún Umán was not about to share much more with me. There was Gato Negro, but he was just a kid. How could he have anything to do with this? "Watch yourself, Chacón," I admonished myself. For the sake of thoroughness, and perhaps a need for detachment, I needed to put Gato in the mix, right there with Tekún.

The phone rang. It was the photo lab downstairs, telling me the pics from the crime scene were ready. I thanked them and said I would be right down. "Well, there's something to do," I murmured, but I didn't really believe that anything would come out of looking at a set of one hundred–plus photos. I had been pretty thorough down at the crime scene, something even the young Officer Beaver would have to admit.

I grabbed my purse and checked the tightness of my ankle holster. The weight of the nine-millimeter parabellum dragged the leather down. It had a way of digging into my ankles when it got loose. Then I walked toward the front door.

Detective Jerry Wilson came in again for the second time that day. I had heard a couple of guys in our makeshift kitchen say he had gone for a radio interview around noon. "That guy is a local celebrity," one of the detectives said. It was not in a praising voice. Some wondered how long Wilson would be kept in the limelight and how it would affect his job. Others thought it would do nothing but enhance his career possibilities. He certainly wasn't doing anything to hinder such professional goals.

I got a better look at his light brown suit and silk tie, both of which were no doubt very expensive. His blond hair was still just slightly mussed, much like a mole on a woman's otherwise perfect face. He was a good four inches taller than I, thin, as if he ran a few times a week. His eyes were bluer than Superman's. I wondered if he used tinted contacts. Fine with me. His smile broke wide over his face, showing a nice set of pearly teeth. I guessed that his age was even closer to mine, but still over thirty. Perhaps thirty-one.

He was still riding the wake of his success. The local newspaper and television media had yet to tire of him, inviting him onto talk shows, interviews, and newspaper pieces. I had read, a couple of days ago, the most recent article about him. He had been quoted as saying, "All this attention has been wonderful. But it's time for me to focus on the next case. I'm still a young investigator. I don't want to sit on any laurels just yet." His modesty, whether or not it was sincere, certainly caught the attention of the wider Nashville audience. Still, others wondered if he would, in the future, be shooting for higher positions, such as head of homicide, assistant to the district attorney, or perhaps the DA itself.

Yet if anyone on the homicide floor was jealous, you wouldn't know it by the handshakes and backslaps that the other men gave him.

I was just about out the door when he stopped me. "Excuse me, aren't you Romilia Chacón?" His voice was suburban southern. I guessed it was Tennessean, then remembered that his desk had a UT Volunteers banner on it. He was probably from Knoxville.

"Yes," I said, turning to him with a smile. We shook hands.

"Hi. Jerry Wilson. I'm sorry, I've meant to introduce myself earlier. You've been working here, what, a couple of weeks now? I feel bad that I haven't gotten to know you until now."

"Oh, that's fine. You've been a little busy, Detective."

He chuckled, rubbing his thick jaw with his left hand. "Please, call me Jerry."

I said nothing, but smiled in appreciation of the

informalities, uncommitted as to whether or not I
would use them. I wouldn't mind using first names
with the guy.

"I hear you're on your first case," he said. "That
reporter fellow, Sáenz. You've put together that it's a
homicide, right?"

"Yes. At first it looked like a suicide, but it didn't
take long to see that the perp had left some pretty blatant clues." I filled him in on what those clues were: the
gun in the hand, the call to nine-one-one, the tiny,
stained trail of blood to the river.

Wilson raised an eyebrow, then it dropped down
again quickly. "Sounds like a real neophyte killer, leaving so many mistakes."

"True," I said, not thinking about it in that way.
Though unsure why, I felt an insecurity rising. Perhaps
it was the man's local popularity. Or maybe it was his
quick insight into my case. He had a few more years on
the job. I put the focus on him. "Hey, you've really
done well lately. I know I'm at the end of a long line to
say this, but congratulations on the Bitan case. Serial
killers getting caught are, well, they're always the long
shot."

"Yes. Thanks." He pretended to look up and down
the room, as if to see that no one was eavesdropping. "I
must say, it was about ten percent deduction and
ninety percent pure luck." We both chuckled politely.
"But more than anything, I'm glad he's collared."

"I hear he was a pretty ugly bastard," I said.

"He is. He is. Sad case. Two people who were
really good folks, and who had nothing to do with
Bitan, die just because he got it in his sick brain that it
was their time."

"God knows what makes up a serial killer's brain,"
I said.

"That's the truth, because I sure don't. But now he's in jail, thank god. And now, to be honest, I'd like to get this attention away from me!" He undid his tie slightly, smiling as he blew out some exasperation. "McCabe's going to have my ass in a sling if I do any more interviews."

I thought back to McCabe's conversation with me that morning, when he told me he hoped I would have more information for him by the end of the day. His was a voice that did not mince words. "He's pretty much a hard nut to crack, isn't he?" I said, as we both glanced over at McCabe's large-windowed office.

"Oh, he's all right. Well, no, you're right. He's great at subtle demands, and lousy with praise. But then, he's the bossman."

I made my way to the door. Wilson shook my hand again. "Hey, if there's anything you need to help you settle in more, or if you need a hand on this case, just get hold of me. I'm a little bit freer right now."

I thanked him. We departed, him leaving me with that kind smile.

I walked down to the photo lab office and picked up my packet of pictures, then returned to my desk to spread them all out. McCabe left his office and stood next to me, coffee in hand. "Isn't it time for you to head home, Romilia?"

"I'm afraid I don't have much to offer you, Lieutenant," I said, obviously embarrassed. "So I guess it's not day's end." Then I filled him in on my cup of coffee with Tekún Umán. I didn't tell my boss how the bastard alluded to "buying me off."

"So, all that happened with Mr. Murillo is that you got angry and he felt insulted."

"I still think he's involved in this somehow."

"Maybe. But what you think doesn't mean dog

droppings until you've got evidence. You can still ride Murillo. But be careful. He's the new sweetheart of Nashville's City Council."

"Right. So you see, boss, I don't have much."

"Yeah, but you've been up since three-thirty. It's already three o'clock. The city's going to have to pay you four hours of overtime, and they don't like that." He sat down on a chair that was next to my desk. "You won't be worth much if you don't get some rest."

"You're telling me to go home?"

"Sounds like that, doesn't it?"

"The leads could get cold."

"What leads?"

I raised my eyebrows, wondering if he was angry, or if he was merely stating a fact: there were few, if any, leads.

"Those are the pics?" he asked, motioning to my packet while raising his cup to his lips.

"Yeah. I was going to study them, see if I missed anything."

"Then take them home," he said, standing from the chair. "No more time on the city's bill. Get some rest, Romi. Give me some news in the morning."

He just told me not to waste the city's revenue. He called me by my nickname. He demanded information within seventeen hours. He was both quietly endearing and constantly demanding. Though I felt jumpy whenever talking with him, I had to admit to myself that I liked him—in a leary, bossman sort of way.

CHAPTER EIGHT

I drove home. My new house stood in the north part of town above the Capital Center. I lived in Germantown, a small neighborhood near the interstate, well into the borders of Nashville. Germantown was considered one of the older areas of the city, where some of the ramshackle buildings had been recently renovated. Whoever moved into the neighborhood had to sign an agreement to overhaul their home to conform to Nashville's Historical Society norms. The city had hoped to save Germantown from becoming a poor ghetto. Then came the eighties, and Nashville suffered the same sickness as the rest of the country in regard to housing: nobody was buying. Germantown sat stagnant in its own half-development. Now slum apartments, where drug busts happened weekly, stood not fifty yards from dapperly reconstructed homes that proudly displayed bronze plaques drilled into the hundred-year-old bricks by members of the Historical Society. For Sale signs were stuck in tiny front lawns everywhere.

Then there was my mother and I, living right in the middle of it.

I had bought at a good time. Mine was one of the smaller houses, though well kept, with a porch that had been remodeled and the whole outside covered in cream-colored siding only a year before I moved in. A new roof had been put on as well. Though the neighborhood seemed caught between new progress and old poverty, I felt good about buying here. It was the first home I had ever owned.

Mamá had a different opinion. "*Y ¿por qué aquí?*" Good old Doña Eva Chacón had asked me that two months previous when we had first looked at the house before buying it. She and I had stood in front of the little home, staring at it while waiting for the realtor to show up. I had tried to keep my three-year-old from running into the street. "Why did you pick this neighborhood, *hija?*" Her voice was concerned, and not a little perturbed.

"These are good homes, Mamá. They're in great shape. I always told you I wanted to buy a nice house someday for Sergio, and not some piece of crap that's ready to fall apart."

"*Cuidáte, vos,*" Mamá admonished me. "Don't be throwing dirty words at me."

"Mamá, 'crap' is not so bad."

Mamá did not answer. She looked around at the neighborhood. An old man, slightly bent as if from working hard jobs most of his life, walked on the other side of the street. He was African American. "I don't know, Romi. You're going to have us live in a barrio of *mollos?*"

I hated that Spanish term for blacks. "Mamá, this is a nice neighborhood. And it's going to get nicer. The market is just a little slow now. It's a great time to buy. And look," I said as I motioned south, toward Nashville's skyline, "we're only a few blocks from the center of the city. They're building a beautiful mall park there. We're almost walking distance."

"You won't catch me walking around here, *hija*." She sighed heavily, a familiar, motherly sigh. "Why couldn't you find a place in town where there are more Latinos? I heard there's a place somewhere called Nolensville Road with lots of Hispanics."

I'm sure I rolled my eyes, knowing that my mother had memorized the name of that street. "Yeah, and it's got some of the worst housing in Nashville. That's why the Latinos move there. It's the only place they can get. Mamá, you're going to have to face the fact that Nashville isn't as filled with our folks as is Atlanta. But it's still a nice city."

Mamá rattled off several phrases in Spanish. Then she looked away and muttered, "Sergio will not be happy here." As usual, her grandson was her final weapon.

I turned and looked for Sergio. Then I smiled and said, "Oh, he may be happier than you think."

Mamá turned. I pointed with my lips toward my son, who had met a small boy about his age in the house next door. The African-American neighbor and he were following a line of ants back into a hillside home. They both squatted over the hill, staring as the army of insects did their work of carrying food underground. Then they made a game of putting small sticks in front of the line to watch the ants circle the barrier, then continue on their trek.

Mamá did not argue with the scene. She only said,

while staring at the house, "It will take a long time to make it home."

I put my arm around her. "You said that thirty years ago when you first left El Salvador and went to Atlanta."

Yet my own statement had concerned me. Such drastic changes were not good for my mother. I knew this. I realized that moving to Nashville meant opening up a Pandora's box of memories for her. All I knew to do was buckle down and get ready for the storm. It was a silent storm, one made up of insomniac nights, when I would find her sitting up in bed, rocking, breathing irregularly, unable to get words out of her throat, staring at the walls as if a group of green-clad ghosts were trying to break them down and get to her. Sometimes I wished that the fits were louder, unleashing some of the collected hell inside.

That conversation had happened almost two months ago, when we first started house hunting. It had been September. The leaves were just turning, leaving all of the south's mountains and ridges in a beautiful array of lingering gold, red, and mauve. All that had now fallen, making its way into the cold rot of winter.

Sergio now tackled me at the door, like Dino bringing down Fred Flinstone. I did not complain in the least.

"*¡Ey, mi cipote!* How are you doing? Did you miss me today?"

He looked up at me, still hugging me at the knees. "Mamá, why didn't you eat breakfast with *abuelita* and me?"

"Because I went out working early today, *mi'jito.*"

"Did you catch a bad guy?" he asked, his three-year-old voice articulating an idea that he had yet to understand.

"Not yet," I chuckled, "and you and my boss will keep asking me that until I do, won't you?"

He just giggled and hugged me tighter. I picked him up, wanting to hold him as well as keep him a certain distance from my ankle holster.

Our house, even though separated from a Latino world, was a place where Spanish ruled. That rule was set down by my mother. My kid was fairly bilingual. I carried Sergio in while announcing my presence to Mamá. She was in the kitchen. I could hear her putting clean pots away.

She leaned against the door frame and crossed her arms. "Not even a note telling me where you were."

"That's why I called you. I had to go quickly, Mamá. There was a murder."

"So I heard." She had the television playing, and had probably seen the local news. Though she never spoke English, she fooled the gringo world by understanding just about every common word. "Some young Latino boy. What was his name?"

"Sáenz. Diego Sáenz."

"Sáenz..." She pondered the name. "I knew a Sáenz family in Houston once. Does he have family there?"

I thought about how many Sáenzes lived in Houston, not unlike Jones or Johnson anywhere else in the country. "No, I believe he was from Iowa. But you've seen his name before. He wrote for the paper."

It took her a moment to put it together. "The man who wrote the supplement?"

I nodded my head affirmatively.

"My god. What happened to him?"

I waited until Sergio ran into another room and picked up his Hercules doll. I half-whispered, "Somebody shot him through the head."

She raised her eyebrows, then rolled her eyes. "¡*Ay Dios!* What else does this city have to offer? You said it would be more peaceful here than in Atlanta, and look what's going on. First, they catch that guy under the bridge, sleeping with a dead nurse, and now this."

"Come on, Mamá, it's not always like this." I didn't want to get too deep into the conversation. Whenever we got into my work, she had a way of trying to talk me out of my job and into a marriage with anybody who would have me.

She made me a mid-afternoon meal that looked more like a breakfast: eggs, beans, rice, and some left-over tortillas from last night's meal. For Sergio, she wrapped a tortilla around a hot dog. He sat in his booster seat, dipping the tortilla-dog into ketchup and biting huge hunks. At first I was not sure I could eat, having seen Sáenz's mutilated head just a few hours earlier. Now, however, both sleep and hunger turned on me. I hadn't eaten a real meal since last night at around six o'clock. I had been up since three-thirty, which meant my body had done more work than normal during those hours. I was hungry. I knew that, soon afterward, I would be sleepy.

But then there was that packet of pictures. And I knew I would not go to sleep just yet.

After our meal, in which we took some time to catch up on her day, I helped my mother clean the table and wash the dishes. Then I opened the packet and spread the pictures out on the dining-room table, where we had just eaten. Mamá walked by. Though I tried to shield her sight with my own body, she peered over my left shoulder. I could almost hear, or feel, her face contort into horror. "Girl, why do you bring such things home?"

Though angry, her voice was not self-righteous. It

was, however, a voice that asked a question rooted in a country from twenty years back. Unlike other detectives whose mothers could not believe what their child was having to contend with in their job, my mother had seen such violence before. And much worse.

"I'm sorry, Mamá. But I've got to study these photos." Then my voice turned, showing my own nervousness. "I'm afraid I'm almost a full day into this case, and I don't have one really strong lead."

She walked away. Then I heard her words down the hallway, sad and true: "I just wish you could have taken another road..."

I sighed and tried to put my attention back upon the photos that I was still spreading out over the table in some sort of order. "You know why I do this work, Mamá," I said, more to myself than to her. My mother was no longer in the room. My son was watching Nickelodeon in the television room. I was alone except for the portrait on the wall, the one that most certainly stared down at me now. My older sister's smiling face could not make me forget anything. In the corner of that large photo, my mother had stuck a small snapshot that someone had taken at Catalina's funeral. There we were, my mother, myself, Catalina in the coffin, her hands crossed over her breasts, a white dress with a full collar closing up over her neck, hiding everything. We posed in Salvadoran fashion, with no smiles, looking straight into the camera so as to never forget our beloved dead.

My mother's Salvadoran past pleaded that I renounce this job. Our shared past in Atlanta demanded that I become what I was. And in some ways, Catalina was the only reason Mamá could endure my occupation.

"Everyone knows full well why I'm in this line of work."

With that statement, made to the empty air of my dining room, I shook my head of personal memories and placed my sight upon the murder of Diego Sáenz.

The good thing about the uniform cops who took these pictures was that they took too many. Better than too few. I had to choose from about eighty photos the ones that focused on the specific scene itself, especially around Sáenz's body. This left me with about twenty photos spread out on the table. I stood over them, my palms pushed against the edge of the table.

I had tried to place them in an order, a quasi-panoramic view of the murder scene. I placed the photos in two lines, ten pictures in each line. From the left corner of the first line I scanned over toward the right, staring at the shadowy mast and top decks of a riverboat, the floodwall that kept the Cumberland River from flowing into downtown Nashville, the red Honda Civic, the top of Sáenz's body lying faceup, a small grove of trees, and one lone streetlight that threw soft light upon the brick parking lot, then more trees to the right that created a dark area, thus making the long, thick floodwall disappear into the night.

The bottom line of photos showed more of the parking lot. It had a round curve to it, encircling the area where the murder had taken place. There was the full shot of the car, then two shots of Sáenz's body, then a couple more shots of the empty parking lot. I could see the bottom half of the trees, their thick trunks that the camera had flashed into view. The camera's bulb, however, could not light up that obscure cave of darkness just beyond the trees, where I had found the cigarette wrapping.

There was a whole other set of pictures that I had placed to one side. I would flip through them like huge playing cards while still glancing at the panoramic view. The set showed a few shots of the cellular phone (upon which Prints only found Sáenz's fingerprints), various angles of the body, and shots of the car's interior.

In practically all of the photos, especially in the panorama, stood cops, Doc Callahan, the fingerprints technicians, and myself. We wandered in and out of the scenes, sometimes blocking the photographer's view. Though I had selected the ones with the most view to them, the living still moved around in this broad portrait of the dead.

I stared at those photos for a good half hour before I realized that I was not seeing them anymore. Either sleep, or the lack of inspiration, was seeping into me. I walked to the hallway where my mother had gone, then ducked into the bathroom. "This would be a great time for a cigarette," I muttered, remembering younger days and bad habits.

After the bathroom, I glanced into Mamá's room. She was lying down, her glasses on, a book above her chest. She did not see me, so absorbed was she in the tale, a way of escaping the photos that she had just glanced at, ones that burrowed quickly into her history of death squads and political persecution. I walked away.

I stared down one more time at the photos. It was Doc flipping the body over to check for other lesions, then flipping it back again, that held me. This was the second full photo of Sáenz's body. The first photo was of Sáenz himself, alone, with Doc barely visible in the background shadow, holding up the thermometer in order to read the degrees. I asked myself why I had chosen two photos of the same angle and the same subject and put them side by side. "Must be way too tired for this," I muttered. It was then I saw the green spark.

It was a tiny spark. Someone may have mistaken it for a piece of glitter that had fallen onto the print. I rubbed the photo to make sure. The spark was part of the picture itself. It barely glistened from a crack between two old bricks of the parking lot.

This was the first time I really stared at the parking lot itself. It was not asphalt, but old brick, much like the cobblestone roads in cities of the previous century. This was part of the River Park's motif, to have an automobile parking lot made of these same lovely red stones. I remembered how the wheels of my car had made a pummeling sound when I drove onto them. The bricks were rounded enough to create long, even grooves throughout the lot.

A reading end table in one corner of the room had some supplies that I could use. But my magnifying glass was not there. "Sergio, *hijo*, where is my glass?" I asked, knowing immediately that he was the only suspect in the house who would have taken it.

I was right. One minute later he walked into the dining room with the handle of the glass in his hand. "Here you go," he said. He knew he could have been in trouble, and his suddenly quiet voice showed this.

"Just be careful with it, okay?" I asked.

"*Vaya pues*," he said, lingering on the words while walking back to the afternoon show of "Blues Clues."

The glass was no help. I glanced at the first photo, of Sáenz alone while Doc checked his thermometer. The spark was not there. Although the photo had been taken from almost exactly the same angle, as if the photographer had not moved, there was no glitter.

I stared at these two shots for a long time. But it was not time wasted. I didn't finish my coffee.

"Oh, shit," I said. I took the two photos again, one in each hand. The one in my left hand was taken before Doc had moved the body to look at its backside, checking to see if there were other wounds. The one in my right hand was taken right after Doc had moved the body.

No spark in the first one. A spark in the second.

"Oh, shit. This is not good, not good at all . . . But it can't be . . ."

I dropped the glass onto the table, snatching up the two photos and leaving the rest there. I donned a coat. Down the hallway I projected my voice, "Mamá, I'll be right back. I've got to check something out."

She rose from her bed. "*Hija*, you just got home. Where are you going?"

"I've just got to check something, Mamá. I promise I'll be right back." But both she and I knew I was lying. She rolled her eyes and once again said something about my profession, as well as my enigmatic obsession with it. I'm surprised she didn't say anything about me promising to be back soon, when we both knew I would not. Perhaps we both had gotten accustomed to my usual set of *mentiras benditas*, my holy little lies.

I got in the Taurus and drove across town, driving faster than I should have.

It was now five o'clock in the afternoon. Traffic was at the point of deserving curses. Yet I was going downtown, which should have been emptying out of cars at this time of day. It was. By the time I got to

Market Street, I was one of two or three cars on the road. From the Market Street Brewing Company I could see the yellow tape still strung over the area. A cop stood to one side, casually watching the area as he had been ordered.

I flashed my badge at the cop. He relaxed, seeing I was a detective. I crossed under the yellow line and stared at Sáenz's chalk line to orient myself. Holding the photos up, I compared them to the scene. Finally I stood in perfect position, almost replicating with my vision what the photographer had seen while shooting these two shots.

The sun was barely shining. The darkening shadow from the microbrewery kept the dim sunset from hitting here.

"At least there's the brick," I muttered, and walked toward it. Then I remembered necessary procedure.

My car was parked a few feet outside the police ribbon. I walked back, opened the trunk and pulled out my evidence collection kit. Rummaging through large, medium, and small paper and plastic bags, evidence tags, paper-coin envelopes, small vials that pharmacists use to dispense tablets, and plastic containers with airtight lids, I found my tweezers. A tissue paper-shaped box of disposable rubber gloves was beside the kit.

I put on a pair of gloves first, to not get my own fingerprints on the insides or outsides of the bags. Then I took the tweezers and one small bag, closed the trunk and walked back to the chalk line.

Leaning over the crack in the bricks, I opened the plastic sack and held it in my left hand, then took the tweezers in my right. It took a few times to snare it, but I finally did, pulling it out of its gritty hiding place.

"Oh, shit," I said, for the third time today.

"What have you got there, Detective?" the young officer said, walking over to me.

I stared at the gritty, stained jade pyramid, its point and its base clipped carefully between my tweezers.

"Trouble. I've got me a load of trouble."

CHAPTER NINE

Though I now had a lead, no one was very happy about it. Including myself.

Lieutenant McCabe leaned over his desk in prayer position. He wore no tie. His shirt collar was unbuttoned. His elbows pressed upon the desk, his fingers were clasped together in a hand-wringing or petitioning fashion. A couple of times he squinted his eyes. I could tell, right then, that McCabe was more than a coffee man. Perhaps it was the slight odor of fresh whiskey on his breath that gave it away. It was past his working hours. He had probably made it home, had kissed his wife while making himself the first of two Manhattans or some other stiff drink. He was not drunk right now. He had probably been moving toward a daily ritual of relaxation, and had been one half a drink into it when I called.

We sat in his office, waiting for Jerry Wilson. I

wanted to ask, "What does this all mean, especially for Detective Wilson?" But I knew that would be an inappropriate question. Both my boss and I knew what all this meant. Still, my boss made telling statements regarding his other subordinate.

"Wilson will be about as much fun to play with as a paranoid cobra. But he's got it coming to him..."

Picturing the man whom I met earlier today, the handsome young gentleman who kindly welcomed me to the force, as either paranoid or a snake, did not readily work. Then again, first impressions are not always the truest ones. That second statement pricked at me, that Wilson had it coming to him. Had what coming to him?

"I can't believe this," McCabe continued. "I mean, this is Nashville, for god's sake. It's not like we're living in Chicago or Houston. Then again, I guess geography isn't a relative factor anymore..."

I was not exactly sure what he alluded to. He buried his eyes in his palms, resting them there. Sometimes he asked me a question about the crime scene, making sure he understood the entire scenario. But he understood everything from the moment I had called him at home and told him, "I found a jade pyramid right next to where Sáenz's body was."

"But you found it next to his body, not on him," McCabe now said to me. "Not in his mouth. That's not the same MO as Jerry's serial killer. The pyramids were always found on the bodies of the victims, right on their tongues."

I again explained to him the photo sequence, having already laid them upon his desk. "I really think that the jewel was planted on Sáenz. It probably fell out of his mouth when Doc turned the body over..."

Just then Jerry Wilson walked into the office. He did not knock.

He looked straight at me, without offering his hand. I felt so very rookie-like. I also felt my age, twenty-eight, and for some reason being twenty-eight felt like one year below the legal drinking age.

"So," he said, "I hear you've found something interesting on the Sáenz case." He just stared at me for about ten seconds after saying that. Those blue eyes, which earlier today seemed heaven-sent, were now piercing, like a sharp product manufactured by United Steel. Then he turned those eye-blades to our boss.

McCabe did not stand from his desk. He leaned over and picked up the green jewel in the tiny plastic bag. "Romilia found this."

Wilson carefully took the bag by the paper index card that had the data and my and McCabe's initials signed on it. He examined it, holding it barely five inches from his nose. The tiny green pyramid seemed to float within the bag's clear folds. Jerry then set it carefully back on the desk. "This is not good," he finally said.

"No, not at all." McCabe leaned back in his chair and rubbed his left palm over his face.

No one spoke for a long moment. It was too long for me, so I decided to fill it. "The way I see it, there are two general possibilities: There's either a copycat killer out there, or the real killer is still free."

"Bitan killed those two people," Wilson snapped at me. "We caught him at the second crime scene."

I pushed my fingers through my hair, letting the tips of my hair fall against my left shoulder. "I hope that's true. Then that means we've got a copycat killer on our hands."

McCabe spoke. "We would be more sure of that if

somebody had not decided to tell the press about Bitan's little jewelry motif." He stared straight at Wilson.

Wilson's smooth face boiled quickly into a discolored red. "The investigation was over. Bitan was in jail, Pat. The press was hounding me, I had to give them something . . ."

"You didn't have to give them shit," interrupted McCabe. "Bitan's still up for indictment. You should have funneled everything through me to decide instead of whoring it out to the media. If no one knew about the metals, then we could focus this investigation on just a few individuals, like people who were Bitan's friends, the bums who slept under the bridges with him. But now, thanks to you, anybody could be the killer. Every twenty- to forty-year-old guy who masturbates too much while obsessing over his mother who beat him with a cast-iron skillet could get in line as a suspect."

McCabe's sudden, very articulate rant shut the room down. This, I figured, was what Wilson had coming to him. I now saw that our mild-mannered, coffee-drinking boss also had a temper, one that could take control of harsh words until they sliced. I hoped never to get under his verbal blade.

I waited until the wave of shamed blood passed through Wilson's face before asking him, "Detective Wilson, what was the exact MO of the killings themselves, of the doctor and the nurse?"

"Totally different way of killing. Bitan cut their necks open with a sharp blade, then shot them in the stomach with a twenty-two. Then he'd stick the jewel piece into their mouths. Doc was the one who found the jewels."

"That is very different," I said, hoping that my agreeing with Wilson would mollify both his shame and, somehow, our boss's anger. "Sáenz was shot through the head with a forty-five. At first it looked like a suicide. But it quickly became apparent that it was a homicide."

"Precisely," said Wilson. "You see, Bitan made no bones about it. He killed these people by cutting their throats, then blowing a hole in them. It was a blatant homicide. But whoever killed your Sáenz was trying to hide something. First he makes it look like a suicide. Then he plants a jewel on or near the body. He's not too good with this profession, if you ask me, making it look like one thing, then another. Did you even check yet to see if this pyramid matches the others?"

"We haven't had a chance to do that yet," I answered. "I want to take it to Doc, too, find out if it has any samples of Sáenz's blood on it."

"See? There are still a lot of unanswered questions." Wilson stared at McCabe. "Until you get answers, you could easily see this as a copycat crime."

"Or maybe it is the jade pyramid killer," said McCabe, "and he's just changed his methods a little. Wants to throw us off, make it look like he's somebody else. Wants to have homicide cops get the jitters and talk in circles. Just like us."

Wilson could almost not stand to hear this. "I'll bet good money that Bitan is the real one, Pat," he said, pointing out the window, I presume, to the state penitentiary where Benny Bitan now spent his nights and days.

"I don't know whether to hope you're right or not, Jerry," said McCabe. "If Bitan's guilty, then that means we've got another nutcase on our hands. If he's not, then our serial killer's more elusive than you previously imagined."

Wilson said nothing to that.

"Either way," continued McCabe, "I want you both on the case. Go back and visit Bitan over at Rocky Mountain Pen, see if he's got something different to say, then . . ."

"Wait a minute," interrupted Wilson, and he leaned slightly over McCabe's desk, his hand out in front of him. "Both of us? You mean she and I, as partners?"

McCabe hesitated a few poignant seconds while staring up from his desk at Wilson. "Yes, Jerry. That's exactly what I mean. No more Lone Ranger Syndrome for you. You've got to work with someone."

"Pat, I haven't worked with anybody in two years. I don't think it's a good idea to start."

"I think it's a great idea, Jerry. It's not good to work alone."

"Yeah, but, but she's just a rookie, for chrissakes." He did not even look at me while his voice ground into a useless whisper, one that pretended I was not present.

"A rookie who was dogged enough to go back to the crime scene and find an important piece of evidence before it got washed away by rain or the city's janitors. Listen to me, Jerry: this is not a suggestion. It's an order." Then McCabe turned to me and twisted his silent knife deeper into Wilson by saying, "Romilia, as the primary, I want you to check with the FBI. Call their Behavioral Science Unit in Quantico. We never got around to doing that when Bitan was captured, and I've regretted that, now even more. Check and see if they've got any information on other killings in the U.S. where jewelry was left behind on the bodies. Specifically, little jade-like pyramids. But also other jewels. Maybe the killer was into pearls or diamonds beforehand."

Calling me the primary was not lost upon Wilson.

This time he did not interrupt. He laughed, his head shaking back and forth in an incredulous manner. "Pat, I just can't believe you're doing this. How can you make her the primary? She's raw! And the serial killings were my cases."

"Sáenz is her case, Jerry. She's the primary."

His voice was final. No longer did he need to rely on his anger to get a point across. His authoritative decisions were enough.

Jerry said no more, though his turning and slamming the door as he departed seemed to say quite a bit. The slam itself crawled up my spine and popped it like a tuning fork.

McCabe only smiled as he sat back down in his chair. I could not tell if the grin was in recognition that Wilson was an asshole to work with, or in satisfaction for finally being able to pin Wilson's ass to the wall.

The difficult part of all this was he used me as the pin.

"Don't mind him," McCabe said to me. "He'll be fine. It's just a little embarrassing for him, you know? Getting all that limelight for his work, only to find out his work has come down to being worthless." Then my boss chuckled. He chuckled for longer than what I was comfortable with.

Finally he composed himself. "You'll do fine, Romilia. You've done great so far. Remember, you're the primary. That means you make the decisions."

I thought about how impossible this scenario seemed. "Wilson is right, Lieutenant. I'm new here. Doesn't that give him preference as primary?"

"Not necessarily. You're both the same rank."

I leaned over slightly, shaking my head, feeling my hair hit the sides of my face. "You know, boss, he looks pretty mad. I don't know if this is gonna work."

McCabe just sat back in his chair. He wove his fingers together before his face and smiled ever so slightly. He looked as if he were envisioning his Manhattan that waited for him in the fridge back home.

"Don't worry, Romilia. You'll be fine."

I left the homicide office and walked down the hall. I had to turn a corner in order to take the elevator. Wilson was waiting for me there. He took me by surprise, his face above mine the moment I turned the corner, his blue eyes looking down at me, larger than I had ever seen them. His hair seemed even more mussed. Now, however, it did not seem so much like a beauty mark, but a warning, that this entire face was about to whip the air in a shamed frenzy.

"I just suggest," he began, his voice low and almost a whisper, as if afraid someone would turn the corner and find us, "that you give me a lot of room. I'm going to solve this case. I'll catch the son of a bitch who killed your Sáenz boy. I'll put him right beside Benny Bitan."

Though it frightened me, it also pissed me off. In the moment I allowed my anger to come forward, I could also see that what he was doing, this silent form of threatening, was really very childish. He was a man who had been raised to public heights, now brought down into inevitable shame and, possibly, mockery by the press. No man that I have ever known handles this very well. He was in the throes of a temper tantrum. Still, he was bigger than I, something to consider.

I walked carefully, though directly. "Detective, I suggest that we start from square one. Cover all the bases. Make sure we're looking at everything. Otherwise, you know how we could blindside ourselves, thinking only one way. It could keep us from seeing another angle."

He didn't say anything for a moment, perhaps surprised that I would dare say something back to him. I continued. "Since you were the primary on the first two killings, why don't you call the FBI at Quantico? You've got a better sense of those killings than I do. You'd be better prepared to talk with them." Then I had to find something to give myself to do. "I'll...go back to *The Cumberland Journal*, see if I can get into Sáenz's computer, though I know shit about computers. I wonder if the department has a computer technician who could help me. Then maybe you and I both could go and visit Benny Bitan, see if we can get something out of him."

The fact that I suggested he get to the Feds seemed to calm him somewhat. He breathed out, almost lowering his body away from me. We both got into the elevator. We remained silent for about three floors, then he spoke.

"You don't need to bother the department's technician. I know something about computers."

I looked up at him. "Really? We should make the newspaper run together."

"Fine." He added, "We should meet early tomorrow. Seven o'clock."

"Sounds good."

We said nothing more. At the bottom floor we separated. I said back to him, "Good night," but he did not respond. No doubt he was deep in thought about how much his face had been in the newspapers and on television. He would hit the front pages again, though now for different reasons.

When I came through the door of my home, I expected my mother to be there, either berating me for coming in so late or giving me the cold shoulder for the same reason. But she did neither. Mamá smiled from the kitchen. "How did it go?" she asked.

"Oh, okay. How are things here?"

"Sergio is in bed. He wants you to go in and give him a kiss before he falls asleep."

"And so do I. Hey, what's that smell?"

"I made some *chuco*. You want some?" She brought me a cup of the sweet, hot corn drink.

"That sounds great. The temperature's dropped a few degrees outside." I walked to the living room, still confused. She should not have been so chipper.

I gave my boy two kisses, one on his forehead, the other on his cheek. He did not stir. I tried a third on the other cheek, but no luck. He was sacked out for the night. I returned to the den. Sitting down and cradling the cup in my hands, I set my head back on the couch, trying to force some relaxation into my skull. Work would begin early tomorrow, with a man whose demeanor could explode, given the wrong egg I would accidentally step on. This *chuco*, I thought, would be even tastier and more effective with a shot of whiskey in it.

Mamá spoke to me from the kitchen. "By the way, you got a phone call from a nice young fellow."

"Really? Who?"

"I can't remember his name. But I wrote it down here somewhere. He says he would like to take you out to dinner. We spoke for a very long time. I bet I was on the phone about an hour with him. Such a gentleman! And his Spanish is so eloquent. We talked mostly about books. He's a García Márquez fan, too! He quoted some lines to me from *Cólera*, and I thought, 'Well now, this young gentleman is as romantic as that book is!' Let me see here, where's that paper? Oh, here it is. Yes. Mr. Rafael Murillo. He said that if you didn't remember his real name, then perhaps you'd recognize him by his nickname, Tekún Umán. Wasn't that the name of that Indian back in Guatemala?"

I sank into the couch.

"He said he so enjoyed having coffee with you today. Why didn't you tell me you met someone? I think he's smitten with you, *hija!*" My mother's voice giggled away.

CHAPTER TEN

The *chuco* did not help. I could not sleep.

I was not sure what bothered me more. There certainly was a growing list. I was brand new to the force and working on my first case. Not only was my first case a homicide that had been poorly masked as a suicide, it was a murder left with the marking of a serial killer. Detective Jerry Wilson, once Nashville's Man of the Hour, now had to face the world with the possibility that he had put the wrong man in jail. It was a sure thing that—for doing my duty—I was placed high on his mental shit list.

And now I was getting phone calls from a drug runner who had the hots for me.

"How did he get my phone number?" I asked myself aloud while rising out of bed. My private number, like that of most homicide detectives, was unlisted for security reasons. It wouldn't have taken a CIA agent to figure it out. Still, he had to go to some trouble to find it. "I wonder if he's got somebody on the take inside," which made me think about what he said to me when we had coffee—his reference to buying me.

"That prick." Yet though I called him that, my thoughts continued to call up his face. His smile. The copy of *Cien años de soledad* next to his coffee. He also wore a nice cologne.

But what did he and my mother talk about for an hour? I put my hope in their love of literature. Perhaps they only chatted about Márquez. I thought about that awhile, studying the tiny crack in the ceiling of my bedroom.

"If you're not going to sleep, then make yourself useful." With that, I tried to swat away his images.

Mamá always saved the daily newspapers in a pile down in the basement. Why, I do not know. She said she wanted to have them recycled, but that's one thing she never got around to putting in the recycling bin. She believed firmly in recycling; she just never remembered to fill the bin up and put it out on the sidewalk for the collectors to gather it on Wednesday mornings. It was kind of like me being Catholic but only going to Christmas and Easter mass. The papers sat on the cement floor in a perfect pile, just underneath the stairwell. Put a gallon of gasoline next to them, and you would have had the perfect picture for a "Home Safety" book, showing how to torch your house properly.

Though I had gotten on her for stacking them so high, I now was thankful for her inability to become accustomed to the ways of the environmentally conscious. I lifted up a large chunk of the pile and carried it upstairs.

HOME KILLINGS   113

   They were in almost perfect order (I had to give
Mamá credit for that). They dated back four months. I
didn't need that much. I needed only to go back two
months, when the first victim, Dr. Lawrence Hatcher,
was found dead.

   Hatcher, a white southerner from Atlanta, Georgia,
who had graduated from Emory University twenty
years earlier, had been practicing family health for almost two decades in the Nashville area. He shared a
practice with three other doctors in the Hillsborough
District. He was known for his concern for the poor and
his activism with nonprofit groups, having gone
on medical delegations to Nicaragua in the eighties as
well as refugee camps outside of Bosnia in the early
nineties. Hatcher had recently been developing the
People's Health Institute, a nonprofit clinic that would
offer first-rate medical services to the rural poor surrounding the Nashville area.

   The first clinic was built just outside of Nashville,
in the town of Shelbyville. Hatcher had received some
criticism for spearheading this project, as he had decided to focus the clinic upon the rural poor rather
than the urban. Critics said that a clinic would be able
to reach more people if founded within the city limits.
Hatcher had disagreed, saying that Nashville offered
enough services to the indigent. The countryside was
in need of a response to the growing population of
poor people.

   No one criticized Hatcher once he was found dead
on the morning of October seventh in Percy Warner
Park, where he always did his early-morning jog. His
neck was slit on both sides, cutting right through both
sets of carotid and jugular arteries. A superfluous bullet
had been lodged behind his heart, entering the body
through the lower thorax and cutting through the

cardiac organ before stopping right on top of the vertebrae. There was no mention in the article of a jade pyramid, though I and the rest of Nashville now knew that the first jewel had been found on the doctor's tongue.

The articles did not say much else, except to state that Hatcher's death left a forty-seven-year-old widow with three grown children as survivors, as well as a few quotes from investigators (the main one being Jerry Wilson) saying that they were following up on all possible leads.

According to the paper of October sixteenth, Ms. Pamela Kim was a Californian of Korean descent who had moved to the Nashville area two years ago. Twenty-nine years old and single, Kim was a registered nurse who worked at Vanderbilt University Hospital. The article showed a fairly large picture of her. The shoulders of two other people, perhaps friends who posed with her, could be seen on the edges of the photo. She was lovely, with a ready smile and long black hair that fell over both shoulders. Though not much was known about her, the article did state some perspectives her colleagues had on her. She was a devoted Catholic who had, six months earlier, made a trip to Lourdes to visit the site where supposedly the Virgin Mother Mary had appeared. Kim was also known to work one night a week at a local soup kitchen. Though she was a newcomer to Nashville, the article on her was actually longer than the one on Hatcher, due to the fact that she was killed in the same fashion and was found with her killer clinging to her like a lover.

To the opposite side of the article was a picture of Benny Bitan, a thirty-eight-year-old white male originally from Newport, Tennessee, who had been living in homeless shelters for the past three years. It was not a flattering photo. Benny's mouth was open, slack-jawed. His eyes bulged as if he had not slept in a week. His black, thinning hair was matted either by sweat or by the thick, heavy dew in which they had found him and the body. The article itself told the whole story, how Detective Wilson had followed Bitan from a bar to the body. It was on the east end of town, off of Old Hickory Boulevard. Wilson had to follow Bitan for a good hour before the derelict finally lowered into the shadows underneath the old railroad bridge and snuggled up to Kim's two-hour-dead body. Though the newspaper alluded to Wilson's bravery, I read into it a certain level of either machismo or stupidity. To arrest the suspect, Wilson had gone under that bridge alone without backup. That was a good thing to know about my new partner.

Later articles reported on Bitan's life and how it no doubt helped to create a killing machine in him. Both his parents dead, he had been raised in several foster homes. He had a history of alcohol and drug abuse. He had been known to start fights in the homeless shelters, once pulling a knife on another man. Though no weapons were found on him, in his drugged stupor he had muttered something to Wilson about having dropped both the knife and the gun in the Cumberland River after killing Pamela Kim. Though they dragged the river, they found neither (I wrote a mental note to myself, right underneath the question about the weapons in the river, "Get a Nashville map"). A few hours later Doc Callahan had found the green jewel on top of Pamela Kim's tongue.

The article talked of Wilson's triumph over finding the serial killer. Though it was a tragedy that two people had died, there was also some consolation in the fact that he had been stopped before creating any more havoc. This I knew to be true, if it was true that Bitan was the killer; some of the most notorious serial killers in the country had left a trail years long and littered with literally hundreds of bodies. They were also known to change their killing methods. If the two medical professionals' deaths were Bitan's work, then he had been stopped very early in his career.

Then, of course, there was an obvious note of difference between the first two killings and Sáenz's death: Diego Sáenz was not a medical professional. He was a reporter. "If Bitan is innocent, maybe the killer's not only changing his MO, but also his type of victim," I muttered, writing that down as well.

There were other responsibilities, ones that I did not really care to do, for they meant reopening the Hatcher and Kim cases. One, obviously, was to visit Benny Bitan in prison. But another was to interview once again the people who knew the doctor and the nurse. This meant visiting Hatcher's family and stopping by places to get to know more about Kim's life, such as making a visit to the soup kitchen where she volunteered. I also had to visit the Evidence Department and study the two jade pyramids found on Hatcher and Kim, and see if they matched up to or differed somewhat from the pyramid I found next to Sáenz's chalk line.

I looked up from my kitchen table. It was past midnight. "God, girl, you better get to bed." I dragged away, turned off the light, and walked down the hall.

I crawled into bed without even brushing my teeth. I was just about to fall asleep when I heard a sound at the bottom of my bed. It thumped away at the baseboard. I jumped. The stories from the newspapers whipped around my head. Then I knew. "*Hijo*, what are you doing up?"

Sergio did not say anything, too sleepy to respond. From the night-light I could see him rubbing his face with one fist. Usually I would have taken him and led him back to bed, or carried him back when he was too asleep to make the trek himself. But not tonight. Though I tried to brush away the articles that I had just spent the past hour with, they still pricked at my skull. The thought of Diego Sáenz's bloody head also kept me awake. "*Veníte, mi corazón*," I said, asking him, my little heart, to come to me. He crawled up in bed and laid his head upon my biceps. I pulled the covers over both of us, then pushed my nose a couple of times through his thick black hair. It was perfect; he helped me move toward dreams.

CHAPTER ELEVEN

Though I was already up at six-thirty, the phone's ringing made me jump. My body reacted without my permission, protecting itself from the high probability that this was Tekún Umán calling. Then there was something else, sliding right alongside that defense, a thrill that was not exactly unwelcomed.

I barely said hello when my boss McCabe ordered me, "You better get down here."

"What's going on?"

"You need to put a rein on your new partner."

"What? I can't..."

"The news media is down here. They've got fire shooting up their asses, with one of their being the latest Jade Pyramid victim. They want to talk with the primary."

"Is Wilson down there now?" I asked.

"No. Just the media. Jerry's not shown up for work

yet. But I'm sure he got a call from the papers last night once the story on Sáenz broke, and he couldn't keep his mouth shut."

I left home without eating breakfast. But I did kiss my son and mother good morning.

I could barely get through the front door of the department. Once someone asked me if I was the primary on the Sáenz killing, and I said yes, they looked ready to eat me alive.

"Is it true that a jade pyramid was found on Sáenz's body?"

"Was Sáenz's throat slit like the other two victims?"

"There is some speculation that this was a strange form of suicide. Can you confirm this?"

"Have you been put on the case because you are Latina?"

"Can you speak Spanish? Did you read Sáenz's work in *The Cumberland Journal?*"

"Where are you from, Detective? Are you new to the Homicide Department?"

"Was Detective Jerry Wilson's investigation of the Hatcher/Kim murders a failure? Have you been put on this case to take Wilson's place?"

I recognized only one person in the crowd, the young woman whom I had seen in the offices of *The Cumberland Journal* while speaking with Tony Stapleton. The only thing that I could tell them was that we were in the preliminary moments of the investigation, and that we could not release all information at this time. At least, that's what I think I said. I always thought reporters were in competition with one another. Now I began to think differently. Though they let me pass, the gaggle of reporters also seemed to work together to keep me within their crowd long enough to get those questions out.

Before leaving the house, I had remembered to grab my city map from the closet. At my desk I quickly studied it. It only took about thirty seconds to see that the distance between the bridge on Old Hickory Boulevard and the nearest curve of the Cumberland River was a good three miles. And in my mind, that made Benny Bitan innocent of Pamela Kim's murder.

"Lieutenant," I said, walking into his office with this information without even saying hello. Mamá would have certainly frowned on that. "I'm surprised nobody saw this earlier. Here is where Bitan was found, with the body. Here is the Cumberland. Supposedly, he killed Kim, then threw the weapons into the river. But there's three miles between the bridge and the river. How could he have done all that within two hours, and also get a few drinks knocked down at a local bar? That would have been a six-mile trek, a difficult hike for a drunk man. I think we should get over to the prison and question Bitan again before we ..."

"Bitan's dead," said my boss.

"What?" Then I noticed that, from the moment I had walked into his office, McCabe was trying to tell me this information. His face looked fallen, as if he hated to give me this news.

"The prison called me right after I called you. They found Bitan in the middle of the night, hanging from his neck by a bedsheet. Wilson's heading over there now."

Strangulation packs too much color in a dead man's cheeks. I knew Benny Bitan only from the newspaper photos. He looked rough then. He looked like pure horror now. I hated to think that, if there were an afterlife, he was heading to it with this face. He may have ended up as ostracized there as he had been here.

Doc was already present. He spoke quietly, as if not to disturb the air of the gray cell. "It's impossible to tell, from the rigor mortis, how long he's been dead. He was a strong man, though not necessarily in good health. It could have come on early, but, as you can see, it's still got him."

I could see. Yet I could not determine any expression of horror or pain or fear in the man's face. Some believe that a quick, violent death has a way of freezing the victim's face into its ultimate emotional demonstration. Not true. Before rigor mortis sets in, the body relaxes for a while. Whatever Benny Bitan was feeling in the last moments of his life, the emotion was lost in the relaxing minutes after death. Death, I reminded myself, took away everything, leaving the living only with a carcass whose skull was crammed with trapped, cooling blood.

We examined the area, but the scant details pointed to suicide. There was no one in the holding cell but Benny. Three cement walls made up most of the cell. His body was hanging from two feet of taut bedsheet. The other end was tied to the metal weaves of the top bed bunk. He truly must have wanted to die, for he had to have thrown himself from the top bunk, dropping the full of his weight to the floor in order to snap the consciousness out of his head and allow death by suffocation to begin.

We walked away. Wilson and I did not talk until we got outside.

"What's that old phrase 'Dead men tell no tales'?" he said to me as we walked to our cars.

I didn't know how to respond to that cliché.

"Have you eaten yet? You want to have some breakfast?"

I looked over at him as he got in his car. "You're going to eat breakfast? After seeing that?"

He glanced over at me. "You can't let something like that bother you, Romilia. Unless, of course, you're new to this line of work." He got in his car.

This was too much. I walked directly to his driver's-side door and banged my middle knuckle against the glass.

"What?" He stared at me as he lowered the window.

"As the primary on the Sáenz case, I'm asking you not to talk with the press anymore."

He actually chuckled. "I see. You want all the glory for yourself now. I can see it: 'Rookie Dick Saves Nashville from Serial Killer. Wilson Seen As Idiot.'" He started the engine.

"Don't be stupid, it's not about glory! You're telling the whole world how our killer works, don't you see...?" If he did see, he wasn't telling me. I had to move back a step once he shoved it in drive and left me standing.

I walked in a small circle, my hands on my hips, my eyes taking in the prison's tall razor fence, the forest to one side, the desolate road ahead of me.

Knowing that a bulk of the reporters would be heading toward the prison at this time, I returned to my office, hoping that a clear space would exist between my car and the front door.

At my desk someone had left a note from Prints. It said that the latent fingerprint had been run through the FBI's regional files, and that no matches were made. This killer's prints were not on record, at least not in the southeast region. It also said that the blood type on the cigarette wrapper was A negative. Sáenz's blood type.

Just then Doc called. "Listen, while we were at the prison, one of my assistants got the blood type on your jade pyramid," he said.

"Great. What is it?"

"A negative. Sáenz's, no doubt. That's a pretty rare type."

"Anything else?"

"That's all she told me. She's got a report on it, if you want it. Also, Fingerprints found nothing on the pyramid. Just like the other two murders, the killer was probably gloved. Either that, or the blood covered over any print. But I suspect he or she was gloved. Fingerprints said they didn't find any other prints except Sáenz's on the phone, the car, or the gun."

"Thanks again, Doc."

"Anytime, Romi." He hung up.

I began to think it out. Same blood type on the cigarette wrapper as the victim's. No prints—except Sáenz's—on the pyramid or the gun. Benny Bitan hanging from his bedsheet. I checked the list that I made last night around midnight: There would be no interviewing Benny Bitan this morning. Scratch that. But Wilson and I could visit Hatcher's family as well as Kim's acquaintances at Vanderbilt Hospital and the homeless shelter where she volunteered. There were also the other pyramids found on those two victims. Then, of course, there was Wilson to contend with, my partner, who now ate a casual breakfast somewhere between here and Benny Bitan's hanging body.

The phone rang again. "I better get away from this desk if I'm going to think about this quietly." It was Tony Stapleton.

"Detective Chacón. How are you this morning?"

"A little spent already. What can I do for you, Mr. Stapleton?"

"This Bitan death over at the penitentiary... Got any ideas for a headline story?"

"Not really. Except to say that it was suicide."

"Everybody knows that, Detective. But why did he do it? Or did he really commit suicide? Do you have any doubts? You know, if he had learned what you learned yesterday about Sáenz's murder, maybe old Benny wouldn't have chosen to hang himself. What do you think?"

I tried to chuckle, though it would not come out. "I really don't have any theories for you, Mr. Stapleton."

"Please call me Tony. And remember, Detective, I've helped you out recently. It seems you could reciprocate."

"Tony, I was just doing my job visiting you. My victim happened to have been one of your employees. If you were a trucking company manager, I would have done the same thing."

"Yes, but I'm not a trucking company manager. I'm an editor. And as an editor, I dig for information. So don't mind me while I keep digging, all around you." His own chuckle tried in vain to hide his caustic statement.

"Dig away," I said, my own way of saying "up your ass, *pendejo*."

We hung up with cordial goodbyes. I barely took my fingers away from the phone when it rang again. "Jesus!" Then I answered it with a fairly loud "Homicide. Chacón."

"Goodness, sounds like you've started your morning off a little tense, Detective."

It was Murillo. Tekún Umán.

"Yes, Mr. Murillo. How may I help you?" I kept my words as guarded of breath as possible.

"Did your mother give you my message that I called last night?"

"Yes, she did, as a matter of fact."

"I was wondering why you didn't call back. Though I know you're quite busy and all."

"Yes. But I didn't call back because your call seemed more personal than it did professional. Considering that your desire to go out to eat had nothing to do with this case, I decided not to follow up on it."

"Oh. I see. I take it then that any possible personal encounters between us are nil."

"That's pretty accurate, Mr. Murillo."

"Please, no 'Mr.' That makes me sound old. Feel free to call me Rafael."

"Fine. Or how about Tekún?" I offered a chuckle.

He did not chuckle. "I suppose you could call me that, if you choose."

"Either way, I don't think we should be getting together, considering our different lines of work."

"Why can't crime prevention and charity work blend together? I think we could create some interesting proposals between the two."

"I'm not interested in any proposals right now."

"Romilia, I really would like to get together with you. Now your mother seems open to having lunch today. She invited me to your house. It wouldn't be *buena educación* for you to stand up a guest in your own home."

"Now wait a minute," I said. "You know where I live?"

"No, your mother said I should clear it with you first. But I don't see any harm . . ."

"Forget it. No lunch."

"Doña Eva will be disappointed."

"I can deal with that." Though I wondered if I could. My mother seemed hot for this guy, a promising son-in-law, come to whisk away her daughter from the tribulations of cop-life.

"Then how about a cup of coffee, Romi?" Great. He had talked with Mamá long enough to get my nickname out of her. "Listen, I know you suspect me of some strange foul play. But I promise you my name is very clean. I'd like to prove that to you. Besides, maybe I could be of some help with your case."

I looked around the office. My new partner was nowhere to be seen. No doubt munching down some waffles at a Cracker Barrel somewhere. Not much I could do now without him. Maybe I could clear some things with Tekún, both personal and professional.

"Fine. Coffee. No more."

He hung up graciously.

CHAPTER TWELVE

Though he had insisted on seeing me, I had insisted on paying for the coffee and for picking out the place to meet. It was fifty degrees outside, a warm spell for Nashville in November. The sun was out. Few clouds painted the blue sky. Though there were no leaves on any trees, it was an appropriate time to be outside.

So I picked Centennial Park and McDonald's coffee to go.

I handed Tekún the styrofoam cup. When he had first seen me, he had smiled from his Jaguar, closing the door and locking it with a computerized key ring that made the vehicle chirp metallically. Once he saw the big M on the side of the coffee cup, his brows knitted together. His mouth puckered slightly.

"This is your idea of a date?" he asked.

"No. This is my idea of a meeting."

"Oh. I see." He cracked open the cup's rim and

brought it to his lips. The smell stopped him. "This is awfully strong."

"It's not a latte, if that's what you mean."

"What, no cholesterol-ridden fried apple fritters?" He forced a southern accent.

"That would mean too much between us."

"Fine. Would you like to walk around a bit?"

We walked the entire perimeter of the Parthenon, looking out at other people, mostly young students from Vanderbilt University who were taking advantage of the sudden break in the weather. To our left three young men tossed a Frisbee. A woman with a double-stroller rolled her two babies along the sidewalk that stretched over the large park. The din of traffic from West End Avenue was at a comfortable distance from us. Yet there was nothing comfortable about this moment. It was ten a.m. The Sáenz case was already thirty hours old. It was now being called by the media the third possible Jade Pyramid serial killing in the Nashville area. I was having a hard time enjoying a stroll through Centennial.

I was also out of my rhythm, one that I knew kept me sane. I exercised daily, making sure I got a couple of miles in on the track at the Y before working out with the weights for an hour. Yesterday I missed going to the gym. It would have been my arms and chest day. Today would have been my legs, torso, and back. I didn't do heavy weights, but light with numerous repetitions. This daily exercise was more than ritual; it was a vice. I knew this. But it was a better vice than booze or drugs. It was an addiction that kept me sane, that kept the natural stress—or as my mother said, *los demonios*—at bay. Now two days were going to pass, on a hot case that was gnawing away at my ability to keep the tension low. A quick workout at the gym this morning would have made for a good fix.

He interrupted my thoughts. "Your mother is a fascinating and lovely woman. I could tell that from our phone conversation."

"She's something else." I grinned, though it was more chagrin, I'm sure.

"Salvadoran. I could tell that from her accent the moment she spoke. You come from strong roots."

"That's what I'm told."

"Have you ever been there?" He glanced at me from the side.

"Nope."

"Really? You should go. It's a beautiful country. Some of the best beaches in the world. Did you know that surfers from Europe travel all the way to El Salvador? They say that's where you find the best waves. I'm surprised you haven't returned to your mother's homeland."

"Returning is something that's never been a possibility for my family."

He raised his head. His jaw dropped slightly in an "ah hah" manner. I wondered if I had said too much. "You're right. It's a beautiful country. But it's had more than its share of suffering. The guerrillas and the army and all. And the death squads. The squads in your mother's country could easily compete with the ones from mine."

"Guatemala, right?" I asked. "You been back there much?"

"Oh, yes. Whenever I can. But it's been a while. Business has kept me locked up here in *gringolandia*." He looked down at the grass. I noticed he hadn't taken any sips from his coffee. He only held it up in his hand,

probably waiting for a trash can to come up in our me-
anderings.

Over to our right a red Lexus drove by. Though
the windows were tinted, I knew who was inside it:
Raimundo. I shook my head and smirked. Walking
with Tekún was not unlike taking a stroll with the president of a small nation. I wondered if the barrel of an
automatic were pointed at me.

"You have a son, right?"

Watch it, I thought. "Yes."

"Sergio. Nice name. Who's he named after?"

"My father."

"I see. Your father's dead, isn't he?"

I looked at him. "Yes. He is."

"I'm sorry. Your mother seems still affected by
that."

"My mother is fine."

"I'm sure she is. But she also misses him very
much."

My fingers pushed in the styrofoam walls of my
coffee cup. I stopped walking. He did, too. We faced
each other. "Tell me, what else did you and my mother
talk about?"

"Oh, lots of things. Books, of course. Then I was
telling her about my family back in Guatemala. How
my Tennessean mother had followed my father back to
his home country. How she speaks Spanish with a very
southern accent. Then she started talking about you
all, your father, your son. And your sister, of course.
Catalina. That certainly was a tragedy in your life. I
had read about it in the papers in Atlanta years ago,
though I had forgotten about it. They never caught
that man, did they? Never even really figured out who
he was."

I thought the coffee was going to push out of the

hole in the top. Then my fingers twitched, taking some pressure off the styrofoam.

"I see how you became who you are, Romi. Salvadoran blood that just naturally screams for justice. I mean, according to your mother, that's what your father was involved in back in the old country. And why they had to leave. I've seen that before, when a couple who's never been out of their town or country goes to another place like here. The woman usually fares well. But the man, well, I suppose we men are just not as strong. We turn to the bottle or to drugs or some other crutch. That's a sad way to die. Then the loss of your big sister to that maniac . . . It's no wonder you are who you are."

"I didn't come here to discuss who I am," I said, not even wanting to say Tekún's name. I didn't want to call him "Tekún," as that sounded too familiar. Yet I didn't want to give him the respect of calling him "Mr. Murillo" either. What I wanted to do to him would have cost me my job. "You said you could help me with this case. That's why I'm here."

"That's fine, Romi. But I think it's good for you to know how much your mother needs to talk."

"What do you mean needs to talk? We talk fine. I don't think that's your right to get into my private life. And stop calling me Romi, for god's sake!"

My thumb pushed through the styrofoam. The hot coffee poured over my hand.

He tried to help me. Before he could grab the cup from my fingers, I flung it away in a backhand toss. I felt my teeth gritting together on their own accord. My hair slapped against my face, then rolled down over my shoulders. The cup and its remaining coffee flew over to Tekún's right side and ended in a small, wet explosion in the grass. I wiped my hand against my coat, rubbing it to take away the burn. "I'm fine. I'm fine," I said to his intervention. Then I held my other hand up in a "Stay back" position. He respected that. As I cleaned the coffee off my hand with my coat, he stayed put in one place. But he did offer me a handkerchief from his pocket, which I took.

"I take it I punched some buttons," he finally said.

I did not respond. I kept cleaning coffee that was no longer there. Just the burn.

"Please forgive me. I didn't mean to open old wounds."

Bullshit, I thought—different from what I said, almost necessarily, as if it were expected of me. "Yes, well, I suppose we all have bags of bones from the past that we've got to deal with."

"Yes. But your bag seems a bit more filled than the rest of ours."

I flung my head up and looked straight at him. "You want to give me some information regarding this case?"

He sighed. After I gave him back his handkerchief, he put one hand in a pocket. We resumed walking. He offered me his coffee. I declined. After about two minutes, in which I suppose he was allowing the silence to clean out the sudden discomfort of the coffee spill, he talked. "When your victim, Mr. Sáenz, came to see me …you were right, he was working on an article about the drug market here. He talked to me about a gentleman who went by the name of Two-Bits. I understand the name fit the person. He was a two-bit drug dealer here in town. I, of course, had never heard of the man. But after Mr. Sáenz was killed, I had one of my employees, Mr. Colibrí—I believe you met him in my offices, he goes by the name of Pajarito—I had him look up some information on this Two-Bits fellow.

He's in jail now. The local police caught him several weeks ago and put him away."

"So why was Sáenz interested in this guy?"

Tekún seemed to weigh his words carefully, though not necessarily out of a need to hide anything. Then again, he was careful with everything he said, placing his words down like pieces of a chess game, always ready for a checkmate. I couldn't help but think that his supposed kind and concerned demeanor about my father and my sister was his way of wheedling into me. "Mr. Sáenz seemed to believe that Two-Bits had something to do with the deaths of that doctor and that nurse."

I'm sure my look was a puzzled one. "How? He's in jail. You said he's been in prison for several weeks. How could he have killed Hatcher and Kim?"

"According to my employee, Mr. Two-Bits was a small-time drug pusher who stayed small time because he didn't treat his drug dealings as a business. He's a rough fellow, known to be very violent. I believe Pajarito used the word 'sick' when referring to him. Two-Bits did have some people under his thumb, however, cohorts who could have done his dirty work for him. Hit men, I suppose you could call them."

He talked like a neophyte when referring to the drug world. An incredible actor, I thought, remembering back to the Atlanta narcotics detective's anger over the phone. "I see. And you think these 'hit men' are the ones going around killing people and sticking jewelry into their bodies."

"I have no idea, Romi—Detective. I'm just telling you what I know. I heard on the radio this morning the possibility that another jade pyramid had been found on the latest murdered victim, Mr. Sáenz. I thought it my duty to give you whatever information I could."

"I see. Thank you, Tekún." My previous anger had abated somewhat. Getting information that would get me farther down the road of this investigation helped to mollify that old, uncomfortable, yet necessary rage.

At first I did not notice that he had stopped, leaving me to take two steps without him. "Yes. By the way, Detective, about my nickname. You know, it's a rare person who uses it to refer to me."

"Oh, really?"

"Yes. Only very certain people know about it. Didn't you tell me a little black cat told you that name?"

"Yes, a little cat. Or a little bird. Some little animal." I laughed. Perhaps a little more heartily than I should have. Then an inner warning started to whoop it up inside me. My previous anger had, as it had before, broken down some tracking devices in my brain, ones that usually kept me in touch with clues and danger signals.

"I see." He smiled. "Well. I hope this information about Two-Bits will be of some help." He offered me a handshake, which I took. "I'm sorry about the coffee. I hope your hand will be all right." Then he turned and walked to his Jaguar. Within seconds he was gone from my side. The emerald green Jaguar left Centennial Park, with the red Lexus following directly behind.

CHAPTER THIRTEEN

My new, unwilling partner was still not back from breakfast. It was enough to have me put my thumb through another cup of coffee. Yet when I thought back on the encounter with Tekún Umán, I realized that coffee was the last thing I needed. Stimulants were not only unnecessary, they were detrimental at this point.

I used the waiting time to study the three green pyramids from the Evidence Department. After signing my initials to the data tags on each bag, I took them from the clerk in evidence, thanked her, and returned to my desk in homicide. There I placed the three bags down, sat in my chair, leaned over, and rested my chin in both palms, my sight held above the evidence bags by my elbows on the desktop.

The tiny pyramids were uniform in size and shape. Each one was about half an inch wide at the base, and that same measurement tall, up to its tip. They were all perfect and uniform, which told me they were manufactured, not handcrafted. Each one had a slight milky look to it that made it look like jade. Though both the news media and other police officers had referred to them as "costume jewelry," I couldn't see anything about them that made them look ready to wear. Perhaps they could be glued flat to a base, then hung around the neck or on a bracelet. Other thoughts came to mind regarding New Age followers who believed in the magic powers of pyramids. Put a banana in a pyramid and it'll never rot. Wear a pyramid and it'll cure your cancer. Now, stick a pyramid in an open neck wound and . . . and what? It didn't tell me much at first. Then again, perhaps the pyramid stood for some sort of cult, a Charles Manson groupie club that believed in resurrecting dead people through Pyramid Power. God knows. And He wasn't telling me much.

"What is it about you three?" I asked the pyramids. "What kind of killer is so obsessed with you—or with what you stand for—that he plants you on his victims?"

Then there was my conversation with Tekún about a drug dealer named Two-Bits. I failed to see a connection. All I could see was a Latino dandy who was a known drug lord who wanted to get a cop like me on the trail of a competitor's hoodlums. Clean out the neighborhood for him before he moved in and set up shop.

"*Ya, basta,*" I said to myself. "Too many questions. I've got to pull this in somehow."

Seeing all the pyramids together, I could tell that they were exactly the same. In my mind, the same killer planted them, and not an original murderer followed by a copycat.

Just then Wilson walked through the door. He looked ragged. Straightening out his tie, he walked toward my desk. It seemed to take him a while. Then he turned, moved toward his own desk, flung his coat over his chair, straightened out some papers that did not need straightening, opened a drawer, looked into it, closed it again, then finally made his way toward me.

"Hey," I said, "have a good breakfast?"

"Yeah. Great. Waffle House has the best pecan waffles."

"I'm glad you enjoyed them. You must eat well. Your breakfast was over two hours long."

He looked straight at me. "It wasn't just breakfast. I also made some phone calls. One to Quantico, like you asked. I also . . . turned back around to the prison."

I know my mouth dropped slightly. "What for?"

A sigh punched through his nostrils. "To talk to a couple of the guards. I didn't want to wait for the official report to come out and tell me all their diddly. I wanted to know what Benny was up to these past two weeks, since I had brought him in." Wilson shifted in his seat to get comfortable. Yet I knew the seat wasn't the problem. "They said it took him days to dry out. He went through something like the DTs, or more like cold turkey. They thought he'd bring the roof down with his screaming. They had to put him in a restraining jacket. Then he started to calm down. They thought he was getting better. You know, sobered up. Finally, Benny asked one of the guards, 'What am I in here for?' They told him. When they said Kim's name, Benny lost it again. He started howling and banging his skull against the bars. They jacketed him again. After a couple of days they let him loose. He got calm. Didn't talk with many people, though. Then they found him hanging."

Wilson shut up after that, leaving the story to sink

into me. I couldn't tell if it were a story or a confession.
I was about to comment on it. But I knew that doubts
were crushing through his brain regarding Bitan's
guilt. Earlier this morning I considered him a card-
carrying arrogant asshole. But now I saw that there was
some hope for working with this guy. Instead of making any comments, I asked, "You ready to get to
work?"

He did not look directly at me as he asked, "Have
those pyramids told you anything yet?"

"Not much."

"Stare at them long enough, maybe they'll talk."

I said nothing to that.

"I called Quantico," he said. "As far as the Feds
know, no killings of this kind, with green pyramids on
the body, are on record. They see this as our jurisdiction, and have no reason to intervene. What about
yourself?"

I told him about my string of phone conversations,
first with Stapleton and Doc, then my cup of coffee
with Tekún Umán.

"Who's Tekún Umán?" he asked. Though he pro-
nounced it well, within his East Tennessee accent, the
strange name threw him.

"He's this slick character who's not at all what he
appears to be." I filled Wilson in on what I knew about
him—his real name of Rafael Murillo, his nonprofit
fronts, his infamy with the narcotics squad in Atlanta.

Wilson thought for a few seconds. "You think this
fellow is involved somehow?"

"Definitely. But I'm not sure how. You ever hear of
a guy named Two-Bits?"

"Sure. He was a drug pusher who was put away a
couple of months ago. They collared him on an anonymous phone tip. A friend of mine who's a uniform was

at the bust when it came down. Really raunchy guy, he told me."

"Yeah, well, Tekún tells me that Two-Bits' people may be the ones involved in the killings."

Wilson grinned for the first time. "I see. He wants to get the local bullies off the playground."

"My thoughts exactly. But let's say there's something to this Two-Bits character. Why would he have a doctor and a nurse killed?"

Wilson didn't have a direct answer for that. "I don't know. Maybe if they had something on Two-Bits ... but that seems like a stretch. Why would an up-standing doctor like Hatcher have any connections with a slimy drug runner?"

I couldn't argue with that point.

In the silence, Wilson asked, "What about Doc? What'd he have to say?"

"The prints on Sáenz's phone, car, and the pistol are all his. The blood is all his. The only thing that's not his is the print on the cigarette wrapping."

"Yeah, what about that wrapping? You said it was a thumb print. But you didn't find any more prints on it?"

"Nope."

He thought about that a moment. "How could that have happened?"

"Right where I found the wrapper, the leaves and the pine needles were more disturbed, like someone had slid over them. I'm thinking the perp fell, slid in the grass, and slammed his thumb down on the wrapper. Then he got up and continued running."

Wilson nodded his head in affirmation. "Instead of having a smoke right after popping Sáenz, which would have left prints all over the wrapper."

"Exactly." Then I told him about the tiny blood

trail to the floodwall. "I think he jumped into the river."

"I'll be damned," he said, amazed. After another long pause he said, "It was cold that night."

"Down in the low forties, I'd guess. Whoever did this may have waked up with a major cold the following morning. He's either very strong or very crazy to jump into that river."

"Or very dead," he surmised.

"True. But I haven't heard of any bodies showing up downstream. One thing I forgot to ask Doc was if he found any clothes fibers on Sáenz. Did you find any foreign fibers on Dr. Hatcher or that nurse, Kim?"

He thought a moment. "No, not on Hatcher. Then on Kim, well, we probably didn't check. You know, we had Bitan, so there wasn't any need to search for miniscule things like cloth fibers. But as far as I know, there was nothing on Hatcher. You could check his file if you want."

"That may be good," I said, clicking my fingernails upon my desk. "If there were no fibers on Hatcher, and if they don't find any on Sáenz, then there could be a consistency in the killing. Maybe the killer was stripped, or he wore gloves for each killing."

Wilson smiled. It was not a pleasant, affirming smile, but a defensive, ready-to-chomp grin. "That's under the assumption that Bitan did not kill the other two."

This threw me. Wasn't this the same guy who just mournfully gave me the blow-by-blow sob story of the days before Bitan's suicide? But I shouldn't have been surprised. I've known other men who've locked onto their primary convictions with the grip of a sprung foxtrap. I decided to argue it out with him logically.

"That's one theory, Jerry. Think about it. Benny

Bitan was snuggled up to Kim like a lover. You can bet that his clothes left fibers all over her. But nothing was found on Hatcher. Don't you find that a little inconsistent?"

"Maybe that's because Benny was your everyday, all-American heterosexual killer. Maybe he didn't snuggle up with Hatcher because the good doctor was not his type. Kim was the only woman he murdered."

"Look, Jerry, I'm not meaning to toss out the window that Bitan did kill the first two victims. That may be completely legit. But I don't want to be married to that theory either, without checking out other possibilities." I stared at him. He stared back at me. This was going to be a rugged test of wills. I tried to soften the situation. Logic didn't work. Next step: an appeal to humanity. "You said yourself that Bitan was mourning Kim's death while in jail. It's not your fault that Bitan hanged himself, Jerry. And you're not going to lose face just because of all that media hype around the killings..."

"Okay, all right, that's enough." He stood up, laughing, but once again, like his smiles, it was not a welcome, cajoling laugh. It was acidic. "Don't start patronizing me, Detective Chacón. Let's just get our asses in gear and get to work on this case." He walked over to his desk, picked up his coat, then passed my desk on the way to the door. "You ready to go?" he asked, turning, holding his arms up slightly in a "what gives?" manner.

"Where do you propose to go?"

At first he said nothing. It was obvious he was not sure himself. "Well, you said something about checking into Sáenz's computer. How about going over into *The Cumberland Journal* offices and doing that?"

I nodded, recognizing that it was going to be damned hard to reel this new partner of mine in. Grabbing my coat, pad and pen, then the bags of pyramids, I walked past him and toward the door. "Let's go, then."

CHAPTER FOURTEEN

Tony Stapleton leaned directly over Wilson's right shoulder while Wilson tapped away at Diego Sáenz's computer keys. I stood to Stapleton's right, unable to see the screen. I could, however, see my partner's disgruntled side glances at the newspaper editor.

"You know," Wilson finally said, "this would be a little easier if you weren't breathing down my neck, Mr. Stapleton."

"Just making sure that everything is kosher, Detective. This is a newspaper, you know. We need to protect our informants, either alive or dead. The moment you crack open Diego's files, I want to be here."

"It may take a while," said Wilson. "This is an older computer, but you still need a password to get into it. And I can't figure out his password. Every third time I try to get into his files, the computer shuts down. So I have to start up the motor again."

I think I understood that. But I'm not a computer expert. I could tell by the way he spoke and worked at the keys that Jerry was pretty good with the little machines. I was glad I had not bothered the department's computer technician. Jerry was obviously right at home at the keyboard, whereas I shy away from even looking at the screen. It's slightly embarrassing to live in this day and age with little to no knowledge of computers, almost like the world is moving on without you.

Stapleton finally stretched upward from his crouched position, lifted his arms over his head, then said, "I do have to get back to my desk. But the moment you all find anything, Officers, please be so kind as to call me." He walked away and back to his piled-up office, leaving the door open.

I leaned in closer to Jerry. "Thank god," he muttered. "He was getting on my nerves."

"Yeah, I don't blame you." I sat down next to him. "You want some coffee or something? They got a pot over there." I motioned to the table.

"That sounds great."

"Cream and sugar?"

"No. Black."

"My type of coffee drinker." I smiled at him as sincerely as possible. He glanced at me, saw the smile, and actually reciprocated. Then he looked back seriously at the screen. "I've tried everything I could think of. But I didn't know the guy. If I had, I'd have more ideas on what kind of password he would have used."

"What have you used so far?"

"Well, I got 'Honda' for his car. Stapleton gave me the names of his parents and siblings. Then I tried his name all sorts of ways. I found one of his cards in his desk; it has his middle name, which was Enrique. No go. Then I tried Mexico, but nothing. I even tried his name backwards. Nothing. But a lot of the time I'm just waiting for the damned computer to boot back up. See? There it goes."

I looked over his shoulder and watched as the computer's screen blinked and turned black. Jerry reached back, turned off the computer, waited ten seconds, then turned it back on. He had done this at least ten times in the past half hour.

I thought of something while placing the coffee down next to Wilson's arm. "Hey, listen, I got an idea. The guy was Latino. Maybe he used some Spanish word or words as a code."

"Oh. Yeah. That's true. Jeez, nobody around here would be able to get in if he did that." Jerry glanced up at the floor filled with white and black workers, most assuredly all of them monolingual. "But god, what words would he use?"

"Let me throw a few at you."

I tossed out words that I thought would be relevant to Sáenz. *Periodista* for newspaper reporter. *Periódico* for newspaper. *Computadora* for computer.

Nothing. The computer shut down again. We tried for another set.

Since he was of Mexican descent, I tried *mole, chilango,* and *momia.*

Nothing. Shut down.

"Oh, god, this could take all day," I muttered. Jerry was also having a hard time writing the words because he did not know how to spell in Spanish. I had to spell them out for him. "Let's try some curse words; let's see, *mierda.*"

"What does that mean?" he asked while typing.

"Shit."

"Oh. Nice. *Mierda* . . . I gotta remember how to say that," he said, smiling. "No go. Give me another one."

"Oh, let's see. *Chingado.*"

"What does that mean?"

"It means, uh, well, you know. Screwing. Or screwed."

He laughed again. "You're the modest type, aren't you?"

"My mother taught me to never say those words, or the Virgin mother would come down and beat me with her crown."

"I see. Nope. No go."

"Okay. Try *jodido.*"

"What's that?"

"Same as *chingado.*"

"I see. Nope. And there she goes," he said, watching the screen go blank. He clicked off the motor, waited, then clicked it on again. "Okay. Another round."

"*Encachimbado.*"

"Spell it."

I did.

"What's it mean?"

"...the uh, the same as *chingado* and *jodido.* But Nicaraguans use it."

"Damn, you folks got a lot of ways to do it, don't you?"

"You know what they say. We're a romantic people."

"No go. Hit me again."

"Oh, let's see. Okay, *pendejo.*"

"That's got a nice sound. Another word for screwing?"

"No. But don't ever call anyone that."

"What's it mean?"

"The worst insult you could give a man. It kind of means 'pubic hair.' You can imagine from there."

"Yeah." He typed it in, but spelled it with an "h" instead of a "j."

"No, no, that's not right," and I spelled it out for him.

The computer lit up. We were in.

"Well, now!" Jerry pulled back in his chair. "Looks like this Sáenz guy had a sense of humor."

Jerry punched away at the keyboard. Within a few seconds, a whole list of files blazed in front of us. Stapleton heard Jerry's exclamation. He rushed out of his office and was at Jerry's shoulder within a New York second. "What'd you find?"

"Entrance!" said Jerry. He turned around and knocked over his coffee. The black liquid rolled toward the computer. I was starting to see a pattern in my day. Spilled coffee everywhere.

"Oh, damn," Jerry grunted. "The computer cables . . . Jeez, we could lose all of it," he said, and looked at the screen.

I ran and grabbed some paper towels from the coffee machine. Stapleton did not seem concerned. "As many times as we've all spilled coffee in here, I'm surprised the rug's not entirely brown-colored. Just make sure the computer doesn't sizzle out." Stapleton helped me clean the spill as Jerry tapped the computer keys a few times, popping around to make sure nothing was lost.

We all looked at the screen. Jerry moved the mouse's arrow around to the different files. "Where do we start, Romilia?"

I heard a bit of appreciation in his voice, as if impressed by my help in cracking the computer code. It was nice to hear him use my first name. "From the top," I said.

With Stapleton's help, we could skip over the files

that appeared irrelevant to the case. All the files from
Sáenz's first year of working at the paper did not seem
very important, nor did some of the special-interest articles that he had written earlier this year. The more
recent ones, however, looked interesting. Some were
articles, but others were draft notes that Sáenz used in
order to write his articles. He was a fairly organized
fellow. He marked all the articles with the appendage
".art" and all the draft notes with the appendage ".dra."
"Basketba.dra" meant the notes for the article on
shooting basketball with the Latino teenagers one
Sunday afternoon. "Basketba.art" meant the article itself, which was ultimately published in the Sunday
Spanish Supplement. We didn't take time to read the
articles, as we could easily grab a newspaper from the
stacks and read the hard copy. The draft files were of
more interest to us. "Perhaps those have information
that could help us out. He may have stuff written in his
notes that he didn't publish." I looked at Stapleton.
"Didn't you say he was working on something big right
before he died? Maybe he's got the info right here."

"Very possible," said Stapleton. He licked his
lower lip. God, I thought, he's hungry to find something juicy.

"Do you think so, Romilia?" Jerry asked. "I mean,
that's a lot of work, to type up a bunch of notes before
writing the article. Doesn't that seem kind of redun-
dant?"

"How's that?"

"Well, he must have had his notes written somewhere. Why would he bother to type out the notes,
then type out the article? It seems like double work."

"Not really," said Stapleton. "A number of my reporters do that. They scratch out notes in their pads
when they're out reporting. Then they come in and

bang out the notes as quickly as possible, so as not to lose them. Sometimes you can't read your own handwriting when you're trying to write down an exact quote that someone's giving you."

"That makes sense," said Jerry. "Which ones do we want to see?"

I peered over his shoulder and looked at the screen. "Here, this one. 'Bitan.dra.' That looks interesting."

He pulled it up. The screen cleared itself, then showed me what a file looked like. It was written in Spanish.

"Oh, man, great," said Jerry.

"No problem, Jerry, we're not helpless here. Here, let me sit down and give this a look." Jerry moved out of the chair and gave it to me.

"It's almost like a journal. See? He's dated each entry before writing a paragraph of notes. This one is October 18. See your name?"

Jerry stared at the screen. "Yeah. What's he say?"

I translated: "It says that you followed Bitan to the bridge and found him with Pamela Kim. You thought it suspicious that a drunkard was playing with a woman's expensive locket and talking about how he had to take care of her, not let anybody bother her."

"That's pretty much what the English articles said."

"Yeah. Looks like Sáenz took some of his information from the articles done on you around that time. There. It says 'October 20. Phone interview with Detective Jerry Wilson.' Hey, he talked with you."

"I'm not surprised. He and every other reporter in Nashville." He looked at the screen more closely. A certain look of quick mourning, or shame, passed over

his face. "From the heights of glory, one falls even farther." He glanced icily up at Stapleton.

"Hey. We're just doing our job."

Just then a reporter called Stapleton away, pointing to a telephone. Stapleton groaned, then turned
quickly to his office.

"Mean bastards, all of them," said Jerry. "Always
out for blood."

I looked at him, and in that moment felt some pity
for him. "We'll catch this guy, Jerry."

He smirked somewhat sadly. "Go on. Scroll down
some more."

I found other journal entries on the Bitan article,
but nothing that was more telling than what we had all
read in the papers.

"Let's open up another file," said Jerry. He fiddled
with the mouse and found the list of files. As he
scrolled down, I saw the word "drogas.dra."

"Whoa, wait a minute. Check that one out."

"What's it mean?" he asked.

"Drugs. Sáenz was working on stories about kids
getting offered grass in the playgrounds, ways of
getting them hooked, and starting up a market here.
Open that one."

He did. Again, Sáenz had made the file into a type
of journal for his notes. October 18, phone call to
police department for possible interviews with nar-
cotic cops. October 24, conversation with Gato Negro
(Nelson García). There was the reference to Tekún
Umán. And following right behind that, October 25,
phone call to narcotics division in Atlanta.

"Damn," I muttered, "he was onto Murillo."

Jerry leaned in to me. "You think so?"

"Yeah. I wonder if Mr. Tekún was as much a sweet
talker with Sáenz as he was with me."

"What do you mean?"

I quickly told Jerry what I had conveniently left out earlier, about Tekún buying me coffee that first day, then calling my mother and wowing her with his smoothness.

Jerry looked at me, his mouth slightly open. "You mean to tell me that a possible big-time drug runner is hitting on you?"

"Well, I don't know about that." The words sounded fake the moment they left my mouth.

Jerry laughed.

"What's so funny?"

"Your modesty. It's a riot."

I'm sure I blushed. "Look, I don't want to go into that. The guy does not have a good reputation. And god knows, he could be a suspect."

"So you think this Tekún guy did Sáenz in."

"Maybe. Sáenz was a reporter. He was hounding Tekún for an interview, and Tekún refused. When I talked with him yesterday, he got a little hot under the collar about it."

"Yeah, but would a drug runner plant jade pyramids onto his victims' bodies?"

I pondered this a moment. "He would if he's a serial killer."

Jerry shook his head. "I don't know about that. There's good money in drugs. Takes a special kind of person to get that sort of business going. You know, cruel, ruthless, business-minded, money-hungry. But not necessarily a psycho."

I did not disagree with that. I scrolled on down. Not much more was in this drug file.

"Let's find another file," said Jerry. He pulled up the list again.

The files were in alphabetical order. Several didn't sound like they had anything to do with our case. One was named "Taqueria.art," and I remembered Sáenz writing a piece on the store that Doña Marina ran off Nolensville Road. Another was marked "Sara," which was a letter to his sister back in Iowa. Going up and down the list, we tried to find files that sounded relevant to what we needed.

There was one marked "Kaibil." It had no "art" nor "dra" after it. Its last date of entry was November 1, one day before Sáenz died.

"What's that word 'Kaibil' mean?" asked Jerry.

"I have no idea."

He pulled it up. The file was empty.

Jerry tried to scroll down the page. "What gives? He opened a file, but didn't put anything in it."

I stared at the black screen. "Maybe he was going to write some information down, but then got interrupted."

"Maybe."

I muttered the word "Kaibil" a number of times. "You know, that sounds vaguely familiar to me. It almost sounds Indian."

"What, you mean like Apache or something?"

"No. Central American Indians."

"So it's not Spanish?"

"Not that I know of."

Just then Tony Stapleton came out of his office from his phone call. He walked up to us. "I think you all need to get over to Vanderbilt Hospital."

"Why?" Jerry asked.

"One of my reporters is over there now. Just called in. Remember Sáenz's friend, the black cat guy?"

I muttered, "Gato Negro."

"Right. Well, he's over there. Critical condition."

"What happened to him?" I asked.

"They're not sure. My reporter says he looks like he was put through a meat grinder. But the boy won't talk."

CHAPTER FIFTEEN

I didn't think meat grinder was the appropriate metaphor. Gato Negro looked more like he had been ribboned.

"Some farmer found him on the outskirts of town," the doctor said to me. He was a young white man who wore green hospital surgery scrubs. Before we had walked into this room, he had introduced himself as Clancy. He was a handsome fellow, though it looked as if a twelve-hour shift hung heavily below his eyes. He spoke with a soft, firm voice that meant to state the facts as clearly, yet as compassionately, as possible. "He called nine-one-one. The police and an ambulance came. They found pieces of his skin torn off and stuck to the barbs of a barbed-wire fence." Clancy shook his head slightly. "I didn't see the fence. But to hear the cop tell it, it looked like whoever did this used his body like a rag to wipe up and down the barbed wires. He lost one eye."

Though they had cleaned him up and had stripped him of his clothes, I could still see what his attackers had done. We were in the Emergency Room. I could hear the noises of other patients just outside of this small room, where a nurse worked on bandaging each and every wound on Gato Negro's lacerated body. Due to his condition, the boy had been given his own quarters before they shipped him up somewhere deeper into the hospital, where he would be cleaned and there would be fewer signs of what had happened to him. Here, however, the health technicians did not have time to clean up the room completely. Gato's shredded clothes still lay in a bloody pile in one corner of the room. Even his tennis shoes had been torn. Blood stained the new bedsheet that they had placed lightly upon him.

"They beat him as well. Those marks on his face are not all barbed-wire marks. Someone took a heavy fist to him. Or a baseball bat."

From the corner of my eye, I could see Jerry physically tremble. He did it twice. Finally he got a question out. But his voice sounded as if someone had kicked him in the stomach. Perhaps seeing living people with such scars was much more difficult on him than seeing the violence played upon dead bodies. "Is he sleeping? Or did he pass out?"

"We gave him a sedative. He needs rest. Also, we've got him on this." Clancy tapped lightly on the plastic transparent bag of glucose hanging over Gato Negro, connected to him by a thin tube in his arm. "That's the way he's going to have to eat for a while. He's going to live. But he'll be blind in one eye. We can have him fitted for a prosthetic eye if he wants, after it heals over in a few weeks." It seemed he was trying to offer all the hospital could give. "Is he a relation of yours?" he asked me, somewhat hesitantly. I supposed he was comparing the color of Gato's shredded skin to my own.

"What? Oh, no. No, he's just a friend. And a lead in a case we're working on."

"I see. The Jade Pyramid killings, I take it?" Clancy looked at me with crystal blue eyes.

"That's the one," I said. Though he was kind and pleasant enough to be around, I hoped that the tone of my voice kept him at bay for the moment. There were too many emotions burning the edges of my skull. "When can we speak with him?" I asked.

"He's on a muscle relaxant. As soon as he wakes up, you can talk with him. Oh, and there is one more thing I think you should see." Clancy carefully lifted the bedsheet off Gato, folding it over twice to let us see the boy's abdomen, clothed with light hospital clothes. Then he lifted the shirt. Underneath were a multitude of bandages, some tiny like the ones I use on my son's scrapes, others much larger, such as that big one, right in the middle of his stomach. The doctor pulled the tape slowly away and lifted the gauze. "I can't make out what it says, though the letters are clear."

My eyes fell upon the letters, which had been cut upside down upon the dark skin of Gato Negro's abdomen: *Soplón.*

Even the accent was there, over the second "o."

"Oh, Jesus..." said Jerry. Then he asked me, his voice trembling even harder, "What does it mean?"

"It means 'snitch.'"

"Damn." Jerry shook his head, almost rattling it. "Oh, damn..."

Clancy covered the word wound again, explaining,

•

"It looks like a razor cut to me. The letters are clear and defined, too much so for any knife blade." Then he covered the boy with the shirt and the sheet once again, almost as carefully as if he were preparing a sacred body for burial.

I thanked the young doctor as he left us alone. He must have seen something in me, for he left too quickly. I was glad he did. The hot rage threatened to burst from the corners of my eyes and run down my cheeks. But I would not let it. Though I knew it was more than rage; it was also shame. Shame in knowing how this happened, what words had been said for this to occur. I wanted the rage to stay inside and boil away that shame. Others in my past would have warned me about this building heat, this allowance and desire for blind anger to find its enemy, its cause. They may have been correct. Maybe.

About a minute of silence sat like a rock upon us before Jerry finally said something.

"Should we wait until he wakes up to find out what happened? Or try to rouse him now?"

"We don't need to wake him. We know the *pendejo* who did this to him. Come on."

CHAPTER SIXTEEN

"Where's your boss?" I asked while pushing through the door of Pajarito's front office. I stood before him and stared straight at him. He took a step back slightly, trying to mutter a "Oh, hello, Detective, how are you?" but failing miserably. Then he glanced over at Jerry. My partner just turned his head slightly. He didn't want to be here. He had made that clear the moment we had left the hospital, warning me about jumping to conclusions. I ignored him.

"Tekún Umán, where is he?"

"Who? Oh, Mr. Murillo. He's in a very important meeting right now, Detective. If you would like to wait."

"Shit on waiting. Where is he?"

"Mr. Murillo is busy, Detective. Please, calm down, have a seat. I'll get you a cup of coffee . . ."

As Pajarito spoke, the janitor Miguel Martínez

came out of a back room. He pushed a large janitor's dolly around, covered in cleaning rags, bottles of disinfectant, bleach, floor cleaners, dust sprays, and a large garbage can. He just stared at me.

"Where is his office, Pajarito?" I demanded.

Pajarito shyly raised his hand up and pointed his thumb to the long hallway behind him. I followed it. Jerry followed behind, although by his footsteps I could tell he trailed three paces back. As I walked down the hallway, Pajarito's half-toned voice hearkened behind me about how big a mistake this was, that it would be better to wait.

I twisted the knob as if to rip it out of the door and threw the door open. It slammed against the stopper and almost bounced back against me. Jerry put his hand up and stopped it. There was Tekún, sitting pretty at a round table off to one side from his desk. To his left and right sat two white men dressed in suits and ties. Organized piles of papers sat on the table. A young white woman sat next to the man on Tekún's left, taking notes onto a laptop computer. I figured her to be a secretary. All of them looked at me.

In those same few seconds I got a good look at this office, the one I had seen from the outside the first time I had visited here, when I thought this must have been the principal's office. Its size and shape impressed me. Constructed in the first floor of the round, tower-like corner of the building, its walls were also round, like the President's Oval Office. A few paintings hung on the walls, copies (I supposed they were copies) of Picassos, both from his early blue period and his later, well-developed cubist career. Tekún's desk sat on the opposite side of the oval from me. If he were sitting at it, there would be no doubt as to who was in power in this room. The only thing that stood between me and his desk was a large, ornate rug with a detailed red dragon painted in its middle, its tongue flicking out toward me.

Though the enormity of the office took me off guard momentarily, I regained strength in my heated anger. Tekún was not sitting at his desk, but off to one side. In that scant moment he stood slowly, looking at me with a sense of concern in his eyes. "Romilia. Excuse me, but I'm in a meeting. What is this all about?" He sounded like a lover, which did nothing but turn up the heat.

"Don't give me that shit, Tekún. You know that it's about a boy in Vanderbilt Hospital who was almost killed and who's lost one of his eyes, all because of you."

Tekún chuckled with embarrassment. I couldn't tell if it was for him or for me. "Darling, please, I'm not at all sure what is going on here."

"You bastard. I am Detective Romilia Chacón, not one of your *putas* that you keep dangling around your neck." I walked up to the table and pushed my index finger on it. "You can go ahead and play your games. All of you can build up this whole façade," I motioned to the papers, "and pretend you're doing charity work for Nashville. But I'm onto you, Murillo. If I sniff anything culpable about you, I'll drag you in." It got silent for a short moment. I decided to utilize the silence, my anger still able to guide me down an investigative path. "Just tell me one thing. What does the word 'kaibil' mean to you?"

He stared at me, sincerely confused. "Excuse me? What was that word? Detective, I have no idea what you're talking about..." But I could tell he really didn't care about its definition.

It was after finishing my little diatribe that I noticed Jerry was not right behind me. He was standing at the doorway, trying to mutter my name, get my attention, warn me in some way. At first I tried to ignore him, but his continued warnings started to whittle away at my righteous anger, like knocking the stilts out from under a cliff house. I could feel it tumbling as I glanced over at the white man to Tekún's right. I recognized him.

Tekún filled in the blanks for me. He first gestured to the man on his left. "Romilia, I'd like you to meet City Councilman Robert Harrison, and to his right, Ms. Lisa Collier, state attorney in charge of corporations." Then he gestured to the gentleman on his right. "And of course, the honorable Winston Campbell, mayor of Nashville."

The cliff house of rage fell under. A giant toilet flushed it out to sea.

I looked at the mayor. "Oh. Hello, Mayor Campbell...Councilman Harrison...Ms., uh, Ms. Collier...a pleasure..."

Tekún intervened. "We were just going over some mission statements as well as working through the paperwork to obtain the legal 501 (c) (3), which all nonprofits function under in order to receive both state and private funding. Nothing very exciting, but necessary in order to build a strong financial foundation. Mayor Campbell, of course, doesn't have to deal with all that. He just wished to be present to lend his ear and his voice to the initial construction of my corporation. There will be a picture-taking session with the press in about an hour, if you'd like to stay for that." He looked at me with a smile of perfect gentlemanliness.

It was then that the mayor, a man in his early fifties who was known for his exuberance as well as his orderliness concerning the running of city government, directed his first words to me. "Young lady, I take it you're a policeman. Under what department do you work?"

I told him, homicide.

"Yes. I see. Just for your information, after this session with Mr. Murillo, I will be making a call to Lieutenant Patrick McCabe."

"Yessir." I looked down at the table and watched, as if in a vision, my home, my yard, and my job were plummeting down into that same giant toilet that had taken away the structure of my righteousness.

I walked out, excusing myself and apologizing profusely, my words falling into a jumble as I moved back to the door.

Jerry stayed at the door for a good minute afterward, also offering his apologies. "Mr. Mayor, please, I am very sorry. And Mr. Murillo, I do hope you will consider the circumstances and find it in your heart to forgive us this intrusion..." Tekún assured my partner that he would. Then Jerry followed behind me down the hallway.

We passed Pajarito and Miguel Martínez. The young Oaxacan grabbed his mop as if to hide behind it. He didn't have to worry. Any anger in me had been chased away by the relentless dog of shame. Then I heard Pajarito mutter in Spanish to Miguel, "I told her, not a good time, not a good time at all..."

Jerry opened the passenger door for me. He drove. We said nothing as he took me away from Tekún's old building and toward the homicide office.

CHAPTER SEVENTEEN

Murillo seems to have saved you from falling directly into your own boiling water."

I stood in front of Lieutenant McCabe's desk. He was sitting down. Jerry stood to my side. Jerry rubbed his nose a couple of times, as if almost ready to say something, yet not finding anything to say. I could not blame him for staying silent.

McCabe did not look at me as he explained. "I got the phone call from Mayor Campbell, all right. He said that at first he wanted your job. But looks like your pal Tekún talked with him for a while after you and Jerry left. Tekún asked for your pardon. So, because of him, you've still got a job. That's pretty amazing, considering you pretty much accused the mayor, a city councilman, and the state's attorney, of building a fake nonprofit company as a front for pushing drugs."

I felt a punch of tears. I breathed out a low, silent

breath, trying to control every muscle in my face so as not to cry. I would not cry.

"The mayor wants an apology from you to Mr. Rafael Murillo. In writing."

"Yessir."

"And I think it would be a good idea if you apologized also to the three city leaders. Especially the mayor. Damn, Romilia..." He shook his head. He turned to Jerry, who stood near the door. He didn't look so hot himself. He had been quiet ever since we had gone to Tekún's offices.

"Jerry, go out and get you some coffee. And close the door."

My partner obeyed our boss. McCabe and I were alone. He finally, after a good two minutes of avoiding my eyes, looked straight into them while leaning his elbows on his desk. Then he stood up and headed toward a file cabinet. "You know, Romilia, your reputation in Atlanta was a pretty good one."

I knew what was coming. I squinted my eyes.

"Great recommendations. Your trainers and your commanders in the Atlanta precinct had just about nothing but praise for you. Except for one thing."

He pulled my file. He cradled it in one palm and opened it. "How did he put it...oh, yes. Here. Your sergeant in the Atlanta precinct. This one phrase: 'Has difficulty controlling her anger, especially concerning the rights of victims.' When I first read that, I wasn't sure what your sergeant meant. So I called her. She was very nice, Sergeant Haggarty. But she also filled me in on a couple of incidents that you were involved in, concerning a boy who was beat up, and a young woman who was raped. I take it you remember those incidents."

"Yessir."

"The boy's case was not as clear, she said. You had to use some force in order to apprehend the suspect, and in doing so, you slammed his skull against a brick wall. He suffered a concussion. But the suspect on the rape case was a little different." McCabe stood right next to me, looking at my profile. "You were accused of pistol-whipping him."

"I didn't pistol-whip him."

"Excuse me?" His voice was angry.

"I didn't, sir ... he was struggling; I had to hold him down ... I hit him once with the butt of my gun."

For a moment he didn't say anything. He sat on the edge of his desk and looked at me. "You don't look like you could hurt anybody. I mean, I know you work out and all, that you're in good shape. That's on your record, too, how disciplined and rigorous you are with your physical training. Yet your everyday demeanor fooled me. You don't appear to be the violent type. But I guess you can be. And that's not good, Romilia. Not good at all."

He stood up and walked away from the desk, behind me, where I could not see him. Yet I did not dare turn and look at him. This may have well been the army, and I was in a respectful at-ease stance. But I was far from being at ease.

He talked from behind me. "I don't know where this is coming from, but I know you can get help for it. The department is connected with a couple of psychologists. I suggest you consider using one of them. You're still young, Romilia. That's in your favor. Whatever crap that's in your head, you've still got a chance to get it out." Then he came around and let me see his face. "But I'll tell you one thing. I don't want that shit you pulled in Atlanta transferred over to here. You have no idea who cut up Gato Negro. But on a hunch you attacked a very prestigious person who has become friends with Nashville's leaders. I like you, Romilia. I think you could do well here. But I won't hold you up if something like this happens again."

"Yessir."

A tear ran down my cheek. I quickly wiped it. He saw it, then moved toward his desk, ignoring it. "Now. What have you got for me on the Sáenz case?"

I told him about the information we found on the reporter's computer, including the word "kaibil." My words choked while I looked for a trench of objectivity in order to finish my verbal report.

"Kaibil? What the hell is that?" he asked.

"I don't know, sir. The file was blank. But I'll be doing some research on it."

"Why do you think it's so important?"

"Because he last opened the file the day before he was killed. His editor Stapleton told me that Sáenz was working on some big investigation right before he died."

"I see. Do you figure some sort of connection to Murillo?"

"I'm not sure, sir. But the word 'kaibil,' it almost sounds indigenous..."

"Excuse me?"

"It's just a hunch. But Murillo likes to use that Indian name, Tekún Umán. Maybe 'kaibil' is some Indian code word for him, and Sáenz was just about to learn something about the code."

"So you think Sáenz was onto something about Murillo, through this kaibil thing?"

"Yessir."

McCabe shook his head in slight understanding. "Keep going at it. If you can hang Murillo somehow, then maybe the mayor will forgive you. Just make sure you've got a real trail toward him. By the way, how's the kid?"

"He's in critical condition. Lacerated all over. Lost one eye."

McCabe shook his head. "That's horrible."

"Yes, it is."

He said nothing more, except to excuse me from his office. I walked out, passing Jerry's desk. Jerry did not try to stop me as I moved toward the bathroom. There I closed myself in one of the toilet booths and ripped a long piece of toilet paper from the roll and blew my nose and wiped my eyes, all the while whispering to my big sister, Catalina, "*Ay chingado*, Caty, *ese jodido me va a tumbar . . .*" Yet that *jodido*, Rafael Murillo, the Tekún Umán of the poor, could not crowd up my mind, not like the memories of my dead sister did.

CHAPTER EIGHTEEN

My mother can always tell when I have Catalina on my mind. It is the one time that Mamá and I switch roles. She becomes very stable and able to take on anything, including her surviving daughter's crumbling self-confidence. I let her do it. She could be strong, even during a time of transition, when she had no family or friends around her to keep her occupied from her own set of *demonios*, hatched and raised in the violence of another country.

The moment I walked through the door, she could see something was wrong. She asked, of course. I alluded to what had happened. She made the connections easily, remembering the other two times I lost it back in Atlanta, both incidents that had been written up in my permanent record. Up to this point, I thought that only she and my colleagues back in the Atlanta precinct knew about the one single yet major

flaw in my profession as a homicide detective. Now my
new boss and co-workers knew, or would know soon. I
felt blemished.

Mamá put her hand on my shoulder, though she
did not hug me. She looked me straight in the eye.
"You know what we could use? We should go out and
eat. I read in the paper recently that there's a good
taquería in town..."

I knew she was referring to Doña Marina's place
over on Nolensville. Diego Sáenz had written the
piece in the Spanish supplement. It had been printed
yesterday, in the morning edition of *The Cumberland
Journal*, the same morning that we had found Sáenz
dead on Market Street.

"Yes. I've been there."

"Really? *Hija*, you never told me. How about if we
take Sergio there for supper? I don't feel like cooking."

The sun was already setting as I drove my family
over to Nolensville Road. It was much busier here than
the last time I drove the street early yesterday morning. Black and white men and women and children
dotted the sidewalks, creating a lively atmosphere that
had not existed yesterday. The slightly warmer day allowed folks to walk about and talk with one another.
Watching the traffic go by, old men sat on a park
bench. Children played stickball dangerously close to
the curb.

This was also a chance for Mamá to see the condition of the houses in this area of town, the same houses
that she had hoped I would buy when we had first
moved to Nashville.

"You see, Mamá? None of them are in very good
shape."

Though she answered me, she seemed to be focusing

upon something else. "You are right, girl. They are a bit
broken down...look at that! Those boys over there, I bet
they're from somewhere in Mexico, maybe Guanajuato!"

I looked over at the small group of men walking
into a bar. They looked as if they had just gotten off
work. From the looks of their boots, they were either
in construction or landscaping. Then I thought landscaping, as I saw no splashed concrete on their clothes,
only grass stains.

I parked the car right in front of Doña Marina's
store. While we got out and I grabbed Sergio's hand,
half a dozen people walked in and out of the establish-
ment, most of them Latinos, though a few were white.

A huge, warm smile broke over my mother's face.
"*Ay, qué lindo,*" she said to herself.

I introduced Mamá to Doña Marina. "You
brought your mother over, just as you said you would!"
the old store owner exclaimed, smiling at me. I knew I
had won some points with her.

After a few moments of polite conversation, I
allowed the two women to get to know each other.
Sergio and I moved to another part of the store, he
pulling me toward the candy and sweet-bread section.
Though we had been in Nashville several weeks now,
he had not forgotten Atlanta nor the stores that we fre-
quented in our old neighborhood, ones that looked
and smelled very similar to this one. He made himself
right at home.

"Mamá, mamá, *por favor,* mami, may I have a *pan
dulce?*"

"Yes, child, just hang on, we have to buy it first..."

I looked out the window and up the street. There
was Gato Negro's house. When Mamá had proposed
the idea of coming over here to pick up some *tamales*

and tacos, I at first had hesitated. It had been a long day, and as upset as I had become over what had happened to that young man, I wanted to put this day behind me. A good night's sleep, I had hoped, would help to knock this melancholy and self-loathing out of me. I also had just wanted to go to the Y downtown and smack a few lead plates together. At the same time, I knew my mother's proposals usually were the correct ones. Getting out of the house and treating ourselves to someone else's food was probably the best thing for me.

No cars were parked outside Gato Negro's house. I figured that they were all over at Vanderbilt Hospital, standing around him, waiting for him to wake up from his drug-induced sleep in order to give him comfort as well as berate him for hanging out with the wrong crowd.

The shame snatched me again. Gato Negro would not be at Vandy Hospital had I been more careful. As angry as I was with Tekún Umán, I also despised myself for my stupidity. "Why did you even think of saying that?" I muttered to myself, remembering back to my conversation with Tekún in the bookstore coffee shop, how I had made a reference to a little cat telling me about Murillo. At the time I had thought little of it, believing that Tekún would have no idea whom I was referring to. But I also now knew that it had been my endeavor at coyness, a careful flirtation with the man, one meant to warm up to him as well as get him on something. It had been foolish, an act that did nothing but give away the identity of my new informant. Tekún had verified the name by adding the word "black" when we were walking around the Parthenon earlier today. I had fallen directly into a well-placed snare. The only three people who could possibly know about all this were Gato Negro, Tekún Umán, and me. That was more than enough. I realized that my blind rage against Tekún was in fact fueled by the hot shame that I held against myself.

Just then someone cut across the path of my vision. The man walked by the window then turned left into Doña Marina's store. It was Pajarito.

My heart slapped against my ribs. The shame kept it there. Pajarito saw me. He walked directly up to me. "Hello, Detective."

"Hello, Mr. Colibrí," I said.

"Please, call me Pajarito."

I said nothing to that.

"I regret what happened today," he said.

"No, I should be the one to apologize." But I wasn't sure what to say after that. It was true. I had to apologize; my boss had given me that order. But as far as I knew, Pajarito could have been innocent of whatever actions his boss was guilty of. Perhaps my apology toward him could be more sincere. "I didn't mean to yell at you today. I just thought that I had to, to talk with your boss."

"Ah. Yes. Well, Mr. Murillo also wishes to express his regrets over what happened today. He is sorry that, for whatever reasons you suspect him of certain behavior, those reasons now don't exist."

I was a bit confused by this wording. He saw this confusion.

"What I mean to say is that Mr. Murillo wishes to hold no ill feelings toward you. He would still like to be in contact with you in the future, if that could be possible."

My confused look turned into suspicion. "I see. Tell me, Pajarito, do you shop here often?"

"Shop? Oh, yes, the store. Yes, I come by from time to time."

"And did you come by tonight to buy groceries for your boss?"

"Actually, Mr. Murillo is a strict vegetarian. He eats little to no Mexican food." Pajarito leaned toward my ear, as if not to insult the proprietress standing one row away. "Much too greasy, you know. Bad for the heart. I, on the other hand, obviously love it!" He rubbed his round belly.

"So you're buying for yourself?" I smiled, then shot to the point. "Or are you here to deliver a message from your boss?"

He at first said nothing, then grinned embarrassingly. "Two birds with one stone."

"Very well." Then I leaned into Pajarito. "Then I'll kill a bird as well. Please tell Mr. Murillo that he will be receiving a written apology from me soon. But the letter will not be an invitation for him to call me."

"Oh. How unfortunate."

I half heard what Pajarito had to say to me after that, for I noticed that Doña Marina and my mother were moving to an aisle closer to us. I did not want my mother to know that I was talking with someone involved in my case. But I did hear Pajarito saying, "Very unfortunate, for Mr. Murillo seems to be taken with you. Oh, he doesn't tell me that directly. But I've worked long enough for him to know generally what he's feeling."

I turned my attention back to him, just as Doña Marina was showing Mamá a number of ceramic vases and bowls that had been produced in Mexico. Mamá was admiring the supposed indigenous drawings and reliefs on the sides of the vessels.

"So you're a longtime employee of Mr. Umán?"

"Oh, yes. We go back several years."

"Then perhaps you could give me some information. Do you know what the word 'kaibil' means?"

"What's that?" He looked slightly confused.

"'Kaibil.' I think it's an Indian word, much like the
name 'Tekún Umán.'"

"'Cable?' Oh, like *cabal*, isn't that Spanish for
'complete,' or something like that...?"

I shot out a breath, almost enough to make my
nostrils flare. "So you're telling me you've never heard
the word 'kaibil' before?"

"No, I don't think I've ever..." His slightly trembling voice was cut off by the loud, dry crash of a large
ceramic bowl that shattered over the wooden floor of
the store.

Everyone turned to my mother, who stood there,
her hands empty of the now broken vessel, her eyes
filled with a certain, specific horror that I had known
only vicariously through her. Doña Marina bent over
and started to pick up the larger pieces of the bowl,
muttering that the bowl was easier to break than she
realized, and that it cost about fifteen dollars, but perhaps for her new friend, she could lower the cost
slightly. My mother heard nothing. She just stared at
me, as if wondering where in the world I would learn
of a word that she now barely dared to mutter aloud.

"*Kaibil. Ay, Dios.*"

CHAPTER NINETEEN

I paid for the broken vase, giving Marina full price. Then I asked the proprietress to please quickly fill a bag with tacos, *enchiladas*, and a couple of boxes of beans and rice, along with an order of tortillas. She did. I paid for everything, thanked the older woman, and helped my mother walk out the front door. My son trailed behind. Pajarito stood to one side, looking confused. While Mamá climbed, trembling, into the car, I barely turned back and saw Doña Marina's face leaning out of the door, muttering *"Pobrecita, ¿qué le habría pasado?"* I would have liked to have been able to answer the woman's question, if only I had known what had happened to my mother.

"Mami, what's going on? Are you all right?"

"Yes, yes, I'm fine, fine..." But her breathing was off. She stared out at the stretch of Nolensville as I turned north to catch the interstate home. Her voice vibrated as words slipped from her lips. "Oh, god, Doña Marina will think I'm some *loca* ready for the asylum..."

"Don't worry about that, Mami. What happened? Why did you get so spooked?"

"Why are you talking about the *kaibiles?*" She turned and looked straight at me.

"The *kaibiles—kaibil*—what, they're a group? And Mami, how is it you know about..." I stopped myself, for an idea came to mind, and not a pleasant one. "Mami, does this have to do with my grandparents?"

For a long moment I thought she was ignoring me. But that was not the case. While she heard me, she also heard, and saw, the faces and voices of people from twenty-eight years ago, in a country and a world far from here.

It took three quarters of an hour and two shots of whiskey from a dust-gathering bottle before she would speak. During that time she just sat at the kitchen table. Sergio stood and stared at his grandmother while she rocked slightly back and forth in the immobile chair. I got him to bed, promising him that everything was fine, that his *abuela* would be all right. I kissed him and sang a very quick version of *Dormite niñito*, sounding like a record placed on the wrong rpm.

I returned to the kitchen. The moment I entered the room, she began.

"When your grandparents disappeared, it was during a time that the Salvadoran armed forces trained with the Guatemalan army. It was during that whole communist scare, when everybody was afraid of Cuba. Or at least, that's what they said they were afraid of. I don't think it had anything to do with Cuba. But that was their excuse, you know."

I had never really heard the story of my mother's parents, nor the full reason why Mamá and my father had decided to flee to the States. Perhaps there had been times when Mamá wanted to tell me. But either I was not ready to hear it, or she was not able to tell it.

"Both armies trained at a military base just on the outskirts of El Comienzo, our little town. We used to hear them at four in the morning as they ran in unison through the streets, yelling out their military slogans. There were two groups: the Atacatl, which were the Salvadoran Special Forces, and the Kaibil, which were the Guatemalan Special Forces. They trained for three months in our town, running through the woods, setting up tiny shelters next to our little plots of gardens. We would see them all the time, darting in and out of the forests. Then they'd have planes fly over, and the soldiers would fall out and open those big parachutes, and the whole town would look up, watching these men drop from the sky and float down. We had never seen anything like that before. Our town, mind you, was far in the mountains. No televisions, and very few radios. Any sort of event, such as the Kaibiles and the Atacatl coming to town, well, it was an occasion for sure. We were nervous at first. But after a while, we just got used to them. They almost became an amusement."

Mamá hesitated a long while after that. She breathed hard. The rocking began again. I touched her shoulder. She looked at me.

"None of us would walk by their camp, because everyone said it was bad luck. But I remember standing one time at the bus terminal, where the old Bluebird used to come in and take passengers once a week to the capital. I could see the opening of the camp. There was a huge skull painted upon a wooden sign, with two bones crossed under it. Its eyes were huge, like two entrances to caves. The skull wore the green beret of the Atacatl. Then another sign hung underneath the skull, which said 'Persígnate antes de entrar,' Cross yourself before entering. I remember, I smirked at that. Your father did not like that. 'Hija, don't laugh at them,' he said to me. 'They may hear you.' I said how could they hear me? They were far to the other side of the field from the bus stop. He said that they could hear, and see, everything.

"We had your sister with us. Catalina had a cold, I remember that. We were deciding whether or not to make the trip to the capital, due to her cough. But your father had a possible deal with a landowner there, someone who was willing to sell a couple of acres of land to us. It was an important trip, I remember. It was important then. So we went, leaving your grandparents for the weekend...It was the weekend of the Kaibil/Atacatl 'graduation,' or whatever they call it... That's when it all happened..."

She could not go on anymore. Her voice faltered, then shattered. I held her hand for a long while. She muttered scenes of her return, when she and my father saw what was left of her town. As I had never met my grandparents, I could only imagine an old couple whom I had seen in pictures, now dead underneath rubble and fire and the pile of other bodies strewn over a once active town.

I did manage to ask her, "Mami, the soldiers—were they kaibiles?"

She looked straight at me. Her brows almost frowned at my lack of understanding. "Kaibiles. Atacatl. There are no differences."

CHAPTER TWENTY

After the third ring, Jerry answered.

"Hey," I said. "Are you up?"

"No...yeah, I just fell asleep watching the news. What's up?"

"I've got something on *Kaibil*."

"Really? What?"

"*Kaibil* is the name of a death squad in Guatemala."

"What?" I thought I heard him laugh. "A death squad? I haven't heard that term in years. Where'd you pick up this little ditty of info?"

"My mother."

"Oh." He still sounded confused.

"I'll explain later. But listen: I've got my mother in bed. She's not feeling very well."

"What's the matter with her?"

I wanted to say what I knew it was, post-traumatic

stress syndrome. But instead I said, "Flu. I was wondering, do you have a computer at home?"

"Yeah. Why?"

"Do you have that Internet stuff?"

"Of course. I play with it a couple of hours more than I should every night. Such is the life of a divorcé."

"Great. Can I come over?"

His hesitation told me that he was just about to make a lewd statement, but then he decided not to. "Sure. But I warn you, I tried looking up 'kaibil' earlier today, and couldn't find anything. But then again, if you've got new information on it, maybe we can download some bigger files, and we'll find 'kaibil' on there somewhere..."

He started talking computer language, so I interjected. "I'll be over in ten minutes."

Jerry's apartment, though small, was very nice. The complex it was in stood ten minutes west from Nashville's central district. I'm sure its location jacked the rent up considerably. It was a good size for a bachelor—two rooms, a small kitchen, and a larger dining room/den that had a vaulted ceiling, giving the apartment the appearance of spaciousness. It looked as if he had just picked up while I was driving across town. A very large television and its accessories—video recorder, satellite system, along with an elegant CD stereo system—took up an entire wall.

His computer stood on a desk in the front bedroom. The only books I saw were ones related to computers. Not a novel in sight.

I tossed my coat over a chair. We got to work quickly. While looking through the Internet, I also got a crash course on using computers.

"Here. I think you should be the one to sit and run

the mouse, Romilia. My god, a young woman like
yourself living in the new millennium, and you can't
even turn on the screen."

"Hey, I've typed on a computer before. I just don't
care to use them for everything in my life."

"Fine, fine. Just stay societally primitive, while
the rest of us take the train into the twenty-first century..."

I ignored his sarcasm. Actually, I did not mind it.
Sarcastic statements and jokes were more hopeful than
a cold shoulder. I almost wanted to ask him how he was
doing in regard to the media questioning his Bitan collar. Then I decided against that, knowing the ice of our
relationship still had to thaw completely.

He showed me how to move the mouse to certain
little capsules and boxes, click the button on the
mouse, then watch the screen change. His enthusiasm
for computers was obvious. As he sat to my right, looking at the screen and verbally guiding me to move the
mouse certain directions in order to open more files, I
got this sense that he was trying to proselytize me. He
talked like a computer Moonie. That was fine. I was
actually getting used to moving the mouse around,
though I didn't always know what I was making the
computer do.

"What's that thing?" I pointed to a corner of the
screen.

"Oh. That's an advertisement for some chocolate
company. Don't open it. You're wasting your time if
you do."

"So I get the choice of whether or not I want com-
mercials?"

"Yep. And most of us choose not to look at them."

"I see. And that?" I moved the mouse over to the
far right corner.

"That's the date and time. See? It's almost midnight, November third. Oh, there it changed over. Now it's November fourth."

I rolled my eyes. "God. Already the fourth. Sáenz was killed on the second. I hate it when days pass on a case."

"I know what you mean. Time is mean and cold when you're working a killing."

"Yeah. Hey, maybe I could just click the mouse on the date and set the time back a day or so?" I chuckled at my own joke. "That'd make me feel like I've gotten some work done."

"Nope. To do that, you'd have to get into the guts of the computer. And as far as I've heard, computers aren't magical with time travel. We just got to keep working until we find our bad boy. Okay, now type in 'Central America.'"

I did. A long listing appeared before me.

"Okay, let's see. I don't see *Kaibil* anywhere. Let's try this one, 'Politics.'"

I clicked it. A whole other list displayed itself. Jerry leaned closer to the screen. "Try that one, 'Military Conflict.'"

Opening that one up, we saw some catchwords that looked hopeful. Guerrilla tactics. Guerrilla warfare. Sandinista/Contra War. FMLN, which I recognized to be the guerrilla group that once fought in El Salvador, but had become a political party there. FSLN was the defunct Sandinista regime. URNG, the Guatemalan guerrilla force. It too had become a political party, when the Guatemalan war was declared officially over.

"But not anything on Death Squads," I muttered.

"How about this one?" Jerry touched the screen at "Human Rights Abuses." I hit it. Much like the

Military Conflict list, it was broken down into each
country. "Open up at 'Guatemala,'" he said. I did. I saw
"Human Rights Violations: Military."

"That sounds juicy. Try it."

I did. A small list of military words appeared. And
in that list was the word "Kaibiles."

I clicked onto it. The screen opened wide with a
facsimile of a magazine article. There were even some
photos. I quickly scanned the screen. "Looks like the
Kaibiles made it into the *New York Times* back in 1991,"
I said. "Something about the murder of a U.S. citizen
in Guatemala. It looked like an obvious death-squad
attack, where the killers decapitated the man."

"God. That's gruesome."

"Yeah. It says here that the *Kaibiles* are one of
the Guatemalan Special Forces who are trained in specific military manuevers designed to combat guerrillas.
But there is a strong suspicion that they were death
squads, too."

Jerry put his hand over mine and moved the mouse
around. The touch of his hand surprised me; I'm sure
he felt me jerk slightly. He just kept moving the mouse,
as if to show that he meant to do nothing else. "Let's
see what else we can find here." He punched onto a
subtitle and drew up another file. "Here's a more recent article. 'What Happens to Death Squads after
Peace Talks?' Looks like it was written by some alter-
native paper."

I leaned over and read a couple of paragraphs from
the article.

Now that the peace negotiations have been
signed in Guatemala, the question for many is,
what will happen to the Death Squads that
have been so intrinsic to Guatemalan history

these past thirty years? The squads themselves, having been trained by the military to confront the guerrillas in the jungles and mountainsides of the country, are also trained to attack and kill specific people of the civilian population. While the army has been famous for burning and bombing entire villages of civilians, the death squads have done their work mostly at night, using some of the more insidious forms of violence to leave behind a wake of fear and oppression.

The targets of their aggression were not necessarily random. The death squads were trained to find out who were the "revolutionary instigators" that lived in the outlying villages, and terminate them. Though many of the purported instigators were individuals who supported in one way or another the guerrilla force, others were social workers, missionaries, community developers who worked for the betterment of the poor people's lives. It was not uncommon to find people who had worked in clinics or schools dead in the streets, their throats slit for their good deeds.

The question is, what happens to these trained killers in a country that is now striving to build peace? Some have said that they have no place in Guatemalan society. They should be arrested and forced to face trial for their crimes. Others in the military, knowing this to be a possibility, have fled the country rather than remain and stand trial. They have gone into Mexico, and some have moved into the United States. This also raises a number of questions regarding how such a group of people may live in our country. "I'll tell you one thing," one missionary living in the Guatemalan country-side said. "They'll give whatever gang up in Chicago or L.A. a run for their money."

As Jerry had me scroll down, I saw the photos that accompanied the article. I saw how the Internet displayed some things that were not necessarily for all eyes to see. I knew that I would never want my son on this, seeing such images as young dead bodies, lined up in a row, their brown faces fallen, their eyes either closed or half-closed with the look of passive death upon them. Their necks, opened by sharp blades, bullet wounds in their chests and abdomens. And there, upon the naked chest of a dead boy, perhaps no older than fourteen, was a word, *comunista*, cut into his skin by a very sharp blade.

Jerry scrolled more, but I could tell that the images were getting to him as well. He shook his head. "You want to see more?" he asked.

"No. I think that's enough. It tells us what we want to know."

CHAPTER TWENTY-ONE

ou think a Guatemalan death squad killed these people?" McCabe looked at us with little sense of confidence in our theory. His voice was laced with impatience.

"Maybe not a whole squad, Lieutenant," I answered. Though it was early morning, only seven hours after finding the Kaibil files on the Internet, McCabe's eyes looked as if he had already consumed too much coffee. I explained our theory: "More than likely it's one person. But this person is using death-squad tactics to murder local Nashvillians."

"But why? And who?" McCabe sat back in his chair. "And Nashvillians, for god's sake! We're three thousand miles away from Guatemala. Death squads are in Latin-American countries. We don't have much of a Latino population here. And the victims aren't Latino, except for Sáenz. What are the connections?

And why kill a doctor, a nurse, and a reporter? You two
have got a lot of holes to fill."

"That's not necessarily true, about the Latino population," said Jerry. He talked carefully, though clearly.
"As you know, the Latinos are coming more into this
area. Like the article on the computer said, some of
the soldiers from the *Kaibiles* disbanded and fled into
Mexico, and some came into the U.S. Could be that
one of them made it here to Nashville. And it's hard for
him to get rid of old habits."

"Yeah, but why the doctor, for god's sake? Why the
nurse? What's his motive?"

"According to the article," Jerry continued, "doctors and health technicians and anybody who worked
for community needs were targets. A lot of innocent
people were murdered in Guatemala. Dr. Hatcher and
Pamela Kim were medical experts who also devoted a
lot of their time to helping poor people. Hatcher
opened that clinic out in Shelbyville. Kim worked in a
soup kitchen in town."

McCabe still shook his head back and forth.
"What about Sáenz? What did he do, multiply the
loaves and fishes?"

"That's where we're not sure yet," I said hesitantly.
"As far as we know, he wasn't involved in any community work, except for some ESL teaching. Well, he also
wrote those articles about the Hispanic community.
But he wasn't as involved in community work as were
the first two victims."

"This is really hard to swallow, folks," said
McCabe. "You're trying to sell me the idea that a
death-squad soldier from Central America is now
creating havoc here. That he's got a thing against do-
gooders. Why? Is he nuts? Has he gone from becoming a political murderer to a serial killer?"

I finally answered, "Those are the things we don't know. Motive is still a little bit cloudy for us."

"Cloudy. I see. So give me an angle on the little pyramids." He waved his hand around in the air, which I suppose was a way to pantomime a pyramid.

I looked down at his desk. I hadn't thought about that much. Jerry, however, had. "Last night while I was cruising on the web, looking for *Kaibiles*, before Romilia showed up, I looked up pyramids and jade. That got me on a track about the Mayans. The Mayan pyramids in Guatemala and Mexico. And the jade. They're both things that are part of Guatemala. Have you ever heard of the famous Mayan pyramids of Tikal?" I could see in McCabe's face that he had never heard of them. Not a time to dwell upon the boss's ignorance of geography and culture, Jerry, I wanted to say. Jerry kept explaining. "They're these huge temples in the jungle...and jade, it's a mineral that is indigenous to Guatemala."

"So?"

"Maybe this *Kaibil*, if he exists, is leaving this as a symbol of who he is."

McCabe looked straight at Jerry, then at me. He crossed his arms. He said with no emotion, "That sounds like a sicko to me."

"I wouldn't rule that out," I said.

"And what about your little Murillo lead, Romilia?"

"I'm not sure whether or not to comment on that, sir."

"Why not?"

"I thought I was told not to."

"By whom?"

At first I paused, then said, "Well, by the mayor. And you said..."

"I said that if you're going to bring him in, make damn sure you've got some evidence against him. I don't know if the man's a snake or a saint. If you find out he's a snake, bring me the scales off his back to prove it to me."

Jerry jumped in, as if trying to rescue me. I did not mind. "But on the Internet, sir, one of the MOs of the *Kaibiles* is to, to carve words into people's bodies. That's what happened to the boy, Gato Negro. And like Romilia said, Murillo had asked her about a 'black cat' ratting on him."

Though I knew everyone in the room knew about this incident, it still burned me with shame to hear the words out in the air. Jerry didn't seem to know about my mistake. Maybe he did, but didn't want to embarrass me. Still, would I get the reputation as the one cop in the department who released the names of her informants to the informants' enemies? That could ruin me on the street. The two men before me did not seem concerned about it.

Jerry kept explaining to our boss the possible connections. "Murillo is Guatemalan. He likes using that Indian name Tekún Umán. And *Kaibil* is an Indian name. Maybe he's hired an old *Kaibil* graduate to do his dirty work for him."

"You still got big holes to fill, Jerry. Maybe Murillo had that kid carved up. But he didn't kill him. And the three murder victims had no carvings on their bodies."

"But they did have slit throats," said Jerry.

"Two of them did. But that's still not a carved word in a stomach. If you can connect them, great. But I don't see it yet."

Jerry sighed. It was a breath of momentary defeat, for both of us.

A thought came to me. "How about Murillo's

bodyguard? I think his name is Raimundo. He looks like he could do some heavy damage to someone. He could easily have been the one who roughed up Gato Negro."

"Then check out the bodyguard. Connect some dots. Maybe they'll lead you to Murillo. Until you do, don't touch him. I don't want any more trouble with the mayor."

I was still ruminating. "But why would Tekún have someone on his payroll from a death squad? That seems too ludicrous, too risky for a businessman, especially if he's involved in drugs."

"Not really," said Jerry. "The drug world is not exactly made up of a group of nuns, you know. Maybe Tekún's got family connections in the old country, and they decided to send him some of their very best in military enforcement."

"That's another thing, children," said McCabe. Strange word for him to use on us, I thought. "While you're connecting the dots, make sure that they spell out clearly 'drug cartel' before you start pinning that to Murillo. If he's a trafficker, great, we'll book him. Leave him alone until you know. But I'm telling you, if Atlanta's narcotics squad hasn't been able to touch him, what chances do you two have?"

CHAPTER TWENTY-TWO

Wilson and I were heading out the door from McCabe's office to go visit Gato Negro in the hospital, when my phone rang.

"Hang on a second," I said, not wanting to miss a call that could have something to do with the case. Jerry went to the bathroom as I answered it. At first I was glad I did. It was Tony Stapleton from the paper. Considering he had helped us yesterday with Sáenz's computer, I almost started seeing him as a voluntary assistant to our case. My first error of the day.

"Hey, Romilia, listen. I just wanted to pass something by you. I was looking up that word *kaibil*, for a long time, and couldn't find anything on it. You had said it sounded like an Indian term of some sort, so I had one of my people go down to the library, try to find something on it. Nothing. They even tried the Internet, and zippo."

I was smiling at this point. It was better, I thought, that the newspaperman did not know what we possibly knew. No need to send the city into a panic before we got more facts on the case.

Stapleton continued, "So I stayed here late last night, thinking about this word. I tried putting some thoughts together, you know, trying to fit the word in with the crime somehow. I looked into Pamela Kim's files that we have on hand here, and there was nothing much. Then I turned to Hatcher's file. I had interviewed Dr. Hatcher myself about a year ago. We did a feature on him in the Sunday paper, and I wanted to be the one to meet the guy. I was interested in his work, especially his overseas volunteer work through the years. The guy had been to Bosnia, the refugee camps around Rwanda, Guatemala, Nicaragua, Chile. He was also very interested in the environment, and had traveled down the Amazon River with some nonprofit group from Memphis. He started telling me stories about those places, especially Central America. His heart was there, you know, among the struggling poor..."

I wondered how long this was going to go on. He seemed like he was moving toward a certain point, and the closer he meandered toward it, the more fidgety I got. My foot started bouncing up and down, like an idling motor.

"... and he also told me about the violence that the people live under. Especially in Guatemala and El Salvador, where there's been a history of death-squad activities for decades."

Uh-oh.

"I was thinking of those conversations with him. He told me how each death squad had a name, which I thought was very strange. He threw off a few of the names to me, and I, of course, didn't remember any of them, they sounded so foreign to my ear. But then I thought, well, the word 'kaibil' is a strange word. And then I started thinking about how Dr. Hatcher and Pamela Kim were murdered. I started looking up some specific stuff on the Internet regarding Central America and death squads and such..."

Damn. I listened as he told me how he had pulled up some interesting files. According to the information he gave me, they were more than likely the same files that Wilson and I had read at midnight.

"So, Detective," he said, now aiming a barrel of questions right at my ear, "would you have anything to say on the possibility that the three victims were all killed in a death-squad fashion?"

"Not really."

"You're not denying nor confirming?"

"I'm not commenting."

"I see. So you haven't found any information on the word 'kaibil'?"

"No comment."

"Ah. Interesting, Detective Chacón."

I said nothing.

"Perhaps I should give a call to your boss, Lieutenant McCabe."

"Fine. Go right ahead. But I have a feeling you'll get the same from him."

"Right. Now, off the record: This is a juicy story, but it's also a scary one, Romilia." He spoke to me as if we were sudden friends. Considering our history the past forty-eight hours, I'm not sure where we were in a relationship. He had been very helpful to the case; at the same time he wanted to know everything we knew. His newspaperman's blood was always pumping hot. He continued, "You know, I think I'm going to have to print what I've got. If you've got anything that can perhaps shed some logical light on this piece, I'd be glad to hear it."

I let go a sigh, not ready to play this game. "I can't tell you much, Mr. Stapleton. We're working the case, and we hope to find new information relatively soon."

He thanked me and hung up.

I grabbed my coat and threw it over my shoulders. Jerry came out of the bathroom. "Come on," I said to my partner. "Let's get the hell out of here."

Traffic was thick around construction on the interstate, which held us up a good twenty minutes. Wilson was noticeably quiet.

"What is it?" I asked.

He glanced at me, then turned his eyes away and looked down the road at the construction. His right index finger went automatically to his teeth, where he chewed on a fingernail. "Benny," he finally said.

I nodded my head affirmatively, slowly, and said nothing, giving him the entire space of the car to talk.

"I think he was just a few years older than me. Let's see, I'm thirty-one. I think he was around thirty-seven, thirty-eight. But god, he looked like he was way over fifty. Drank too much, you know. You could see that in his face. His damn nose looked like Rudolph's, all knotted up with broken veins. His hair, it was thinning, and it just slapped up against his skull like an old rug. He was a sight to see. He could hardly get a correct sentence out of his mouth. The smell of old liquor, Jesus, it reeked from his whole body. You could smell that whiskey even on Pamela Kim's body after we had taken Bitan in.

"I don't understand. I mean, he seemed like he was giving a confession, you know? He talked like he was guilty, like he hated the fact that she was dead, but that it was true, she was dead..."

I waited a good long moment before asking, "Are you considering maybe he was innocent?"

Wilson turned to me. I thought it was a look of aggression, maybe of defense. But it quickly melted. "Considering what the prison guard told me...I guess that's what I'm saying."

His fist shot out and slammed against the dashboard. I know I jumped, from both the fist blow and his almost growling curse. "I'm sorry," he said, "but goddamnit, he's dead now. He's dead, and it looks like there was no reason for it."

"Look, Wilson. Wait a minute." I was about to say that it was not Wilson's fault that Benny Bitan committed suicide, but I didn't know if it would have come out sounding sincere. Considering his attitude yesterday morning, when we left the prison and Bitan's swollen face of blood, I was not yet ready to let go of the possibility that Benny Bitan did have Jerry Wilson on his mind when he jumped off the bed with a knotted sheet wrapped around his neck. But I could take this conversation another way, and perhaps use it to the advantage of the case. "If Benny knew he was innocent, you think he would have killed himself? It seems to me he would have tried to fight for his rights, prove to the world his innocence. But instead, he hanged himself."

"So you're saying maybe he was guilty?"

"No, that's not what I'm saying...I have no idea at this point. But it could be that he killed himself because of other reasons, ones that we have no clue about. Maybe he was depressed, or was having a nervous breakdown. You know, being homeless, having nowhere to go, drinking too much, sleeping under bridges. Maybe it just got to him, so he killed himself."

"Yeah. Maybe being arrested was the last straw for him." Again he looked out the window.

"Hey. Look. You can't think that way, Jerry. You did what you had to do. You found him with Pamela Kim's body. He had her blood on him. He was sleeping with her mutilated body, for god's sake! You had to bring him in. You had no other choice."

The traffic started to move again. The flag woman moved us on down the one lane of the interstate.

"I guess so," he muttered to himself. "Maybe." Then he adjusted himself in his seat. I thought he was going to thank me for listening to him, which would have been surprising, having something that gushy coming from this guy. But he didn't thank me. He actually gave me something better. "Either way, I suppose we don't have much choice except to open the Hatcher and Kim cases again."

The sigh that left me was a thankful one. "Yeah, I guess we should," I said, relieved that I would not need to walk on any more eggshells around his dubious success of clearing those cases. Yet to make sure, I went ahead and carefully asked, "If that's the case, does that make you the primary for them?"

He stared forward, and with even more humility. "No. I'm sure McCabe would say that, since you're on the Sáenz case, and since it looks like the killer may still be out there, you should be the primary for all three cases. And I would have to agree with him. You point the direction, Detective Chacón." He turned toward me. "I'll be right behind you."

We left it at that. Except for a "Thank you" from me, we said nothing more. The construction opened. We picked up speed.

CHAPTER TWENTY-THREE

I really couldn't say that Gato Negro looked better than he did yesterday. Only his bandages looked new, clean, and his bedsheet had been changed. He had been moved into a semi-private room. One other person was his roommate, a middle-aged gentleman whom we could not see due to the pulled curtain between us.

Gato could see us with his one eye. There was no other eye behind that white bandage that wrapped his skull at an angle, holding down a round, thick gauze that kept the hollowed-out socket from dripping. His skin was healthy, young, brown. But there was little of it to see, considering all the gauze and bandages that wrapped his entire body, his neck, shoulders, arms, hands, the tips of his fingers where the numerous barbs of the fence had made shredded contact with him. His good eye seemed lost in its socket. Sometimes it would avoid me; other times it made an orbit and swung around to hold me in its single stare.

I asked the inevitable, ridiculous question: "How are you feeling?"

"Fine," he said. Nothing more.

I ventured on. "Those are some nice flowers someone sent you there. A girlfriend, perhaps?"

"My sister, from Texas."

"Oh. I see. Have you had a lot of family around, Gato?"

"Yeah. They been around. My mamá's out in the hallway now."

"Yes, we saw her. She's looking hopeful, considering the situation."

Again, he remained quiet.

Jerry tried. "Look, son, we don't mean to bother you. We know you've been through hell and back. We just need to ask you some questions and find out who it was who did this to you."

"I don't know."

"Now come on, Nelson," Jerry kept going. I knew he couldn't remember the boy's Spanish nickname, so he had peeked at the clipboard at the base of the bed. "Didn't you get a chance to see the guy?"

"How could I? I lost an eye, man!"

His yelp shut down the room.

I sat down on the bed. He did not welcome that, but didn't kick me off it either. He was too weak to do that. "Listen, Gato. Whoever did this needs to pay for it. They need to be brought to the courts. You don't have to be afraid of them anymore. If you're worried about being involved, you don't have to be. As far as I can see, your record's clean. And don't worry about reprisals. I promise you, you're safe now..."

"Yeah, right, I'm safe. I thought I was safe, talking

to you, thinking you were all right, a cop, but a Latina cop. But look what happens to me the moment I open my mouth to you!"

"So are you saying Tekún Umán did this?"

"I ain't saying nothing, man! I'm not saying a word about nobody. Especially to you."

He looked straight at me with his one eye. Then the eye orbited away to stare at the void of space before him, while a tear thickened and rolled out of its corner and over the edge. It trickled about an inch before meeting a bandage on his cheek. I wondered if the other tear duct functioned, if it too let go a tear, one that would be absorbed immediately by the stained patch over his socket.

I was surprised that he continued speaking. It was a mutter, one released with the tear, perhaps a way of riding the emotion out through a trickle of words. "Just like that reporter said, man. No one's safe from this. You can get killed just being with the wrong people at the wrong time."

"Reporter?" I asked. "What reporter?"

At first he said nothing, as if deciding whether or not to explain. Then he spoke, figuring that what he had to say had no bearing on his own self-protection. "The guy from the paper. He came by. Nice guy. He was worried about me, said he wanted to make sure I was all right. Said that there's the possibility of some type of group, some gang or something, wandering the streets of the city."

"Death squad?" Jerry offered. His eyes were big, waiting for an answer.

"Yeah. That's it. That's the word he used. I said I didn't know nothing about that, but I did know that gangs were starting to get pretty rowdy. But this wasn't no gang who did this to me, I said to him, and showed him my stomach. He asked me who did this, but I didn't tell him."

"What else did he ask you?" Jerry questioned.

"Not much else. Just said he wanted to know if I was too concerned for my own well-being to talk about it. I said yeah, that's about right. And that's about all I had to say. Which is all I got to say to you two."

We left the room. Jerry ducked into a bathroom. I paced the hall. When he came out, he smiled at me. His eyes were bright. I took it he was trying to cheer me up. It didn't work.

I knew I would not get out of this without his asking me about it. He did so in the car. "What was that all about?"

It was my turn to confess. I think I was just waiting for the moment to tell him. "I think Gato Negro believes that I snitched to Tekún about him."

"Oh." Jerry looked around, then straight at me. "Did you?"

"I think...yeah. I think I did." I tried to explain what had happened. But the more I tried to tell it, the worse it seemed. The only thing I could offer as a reasonable explanation was, "I just can't believe that Tekún would have known who I was talking about."

"Unless Tekún had had direct contact with this kid," he said as he pointed up to the hospital. "Maybe what's his name...Gato? Yeah, Gato. Maybe he was selling on the street for Tekún."

"That's possible. But Gato told me, when I first met him, that he was clean."

Jerry chuckled. "What else is he going to tell you, Romilia?"

That hurt, because what he said was true. And his

allusion was that only a rookie would believe otherwise.

"Well, let's move on," he said, pulling away from
my shame without having to appease it. "Gato seems
like a dead end for us. What do we do next?"

I pulled out a small notebook from my coat pocket
and opened it up. I had drawn some diagrams in it. "I
was trying to piece together who knew whom. As far as
we know, the three victims did not know one another.
Hatcher and Kim were both medical professionals,
but Hatcher had his own practice in Bellevue, while
Kim worked . . . hey, she worked here, in the Vanderbilt
Hospital."

"That's right," said Wilson. "So?"

"The only people who may have had any connection were Benny Bitan and Pamela Kim."

"How do you figure?"

"She worked with the homeless at a soup kitchen
in town. And he was homeless."

"Oh. So you think maybe they met in the shelter,
while she was working there?"

"Exactly."

Jerry rubbed his nose with a finger, then nodded
his head. "Sounds logical to me. So where's the homeless shelter?"

"I don't know. But maybe one of her co-workers
does." I got out of the car. Jerry followed. We re-
entered the hospital and walked to the nearest nurses'
station.

The head nurse on call directed us to an African-
American man named James who worked a number of
shifts with Pamela Kim. Young, about my size, with a
ready smile and eyes that looked casually sleepy, James
parked an empty wheelchair to one side and talked
with us. He told us he knew only the name of the

shelter, "The Manger." "I think it's with one of the Catholic churches in the area," he said.

"Thanks. By the way, did you know Pamela Kim very well?" I asked.

"Oh, yeah, we were pretty friendly." His handsome smile revealed some sadness, as did the way he cocked his head slightly. "Actually, I wish it had been more than a friendship. I asked her out a couple of times, but she didn't seem too interested. To tell you the truth, I think she loved those guys down at the homeless shelter more than she did anybody else."

CHAPTER TWENTY-FOUR

The Manger was in the basement of St. Augustine's, a large Catholic church in the middle of downtown. It stood on Broadway, about a block down from the original Grand Old Opry. I figured that we were less than a mile west of the area where Diego Sáenz's body had been found, and about two miles east of Tekún Umán's offices. I had no idea if this geographic mapping had any relevance in the case, but I did keep it in mind.

Though a large, ornate building, I could tell that St. Augustine's was not a rich people's church. A cornerstone next to the door's outside marked its construction in 1923. The business world of Nashville had grown tall and shadowy around it. Just a few blocks down, you could see the window shops where dozens of guitars hung from hooks, along with a few flutes, drums and keyboards sold secondhand. A legion of people walked about down there, shopping and selling,

making deals with retailers. Others, wearing suits, ties,
dresses, and expensive shoes, left their office buildings
to find a place for lunch. Here, in front of the church,
there was less movement, except for the traffic that
passed us by, making its way in and out of the downtown district.

Inside the church a few individuals were on their
knees. Others, sitting, either thumbed rosaries or books,
or just sat there, silent, not moving, even as we passed
by. To the right of the altar a sign displayed an arrow
pointing downward. Three men wandered toward the
sign and disappeared around a corner. All three, with
their thick hats and scarfs and old gloves, with some of
their fingers sticking out of the gloves, looked like they
knew where they were going.

Jerry and I walked in that direction. At the altar my
knee automatically gave out from under me. I went
into a half-genuflection, then stopped myself, realizing
my partner's presence. I don't know exactly why I hesitated, except that it seemed hypocritical. Why should I
make a religious move, something that I did only twice
a year? Besides, given my recent behavior regarding
Gato Negro, and how my smart little mouth had gotten him into a hospital bed, I didn't feel I had the right
to refer to my thin religious roots.

"You Catholic?" Jerry asked as I pulled out of the
quick kneel.

"Uh, yeah. A little."

"I was raised Methodist myself. But it's been a long
time."

"Yeah. Me, too." I didn't feel comfortable dis-
cussing religion with him. I moved quickly to the sign,
which said "Manger" with its arrow pointing down to
some stairs.

The stairs took us to a basement. Though simple,

with cinder-block walls painted a cream color and a cement floor painted dark gray, the room was cheery
enough. The long fluorescent bulbs hanging from the
beams in the ceiling offered light over every line of
tables throughout the room. A large radio with double speakers played a country station. Garth Brooks
crooned a love song. White-and-red-checkered plastic
tablecloths covered all the tables. Five people worked
behind the cafeteria line, handing out food. This was
more than just a soup kitchen. Though soup was offered, so was ham, broiled chicken, mashed potatoes,
rice, gravy, biscuits, fish, rolls and cornbread, colas,
coffee, juices, and milk. A second table of food featured
a variety of cakes and pies. A small ice-cream freezer
stood next to the dessert display.

"Wow," said Jerry. "This looks great."

"Help yourself," said a young man on the other
side. He was probably about my age, white, with blond
hair and blue eyes. He wore thin, wire-rimmed glasses.
The circumference of the rim itself was just barely
larger than the roundness of his eyes. He was thin, as if
he had worked among poor people much of his adult
life. Dressed in jeans and a T-shirt, he also wore a full
apron that covered his entire abdomen.

"Oh, no, I really shouldn't," said Jerry, putting his
hands up.

"Why not?" said the worker. "There's plenty for
everybody."

"Really?" Jerry smiled.

The worker gave Jerry a plate and a tray. "Make
yourself at home." Then he gave one to me.

"This is nice of you," I said, smiling. "But you see,
we're not, well, you know . . . homeless."

He nodded his head, closing his eyes slightly in an

"It's obvious, Detective" manner. I felt I didn't need to introduce myself.

"This looks delicious!" said Jerry. "You really put out a spread, don't you?"

"We like to think we're serving dignity as well as food."

As we filled our plates, the worker introduced himself. "I'm Robert. Is there anyone I can help you find?"

"You seem to know we're looking for someone," I said, grinning. "Yes, as a matter of fact. We're detectives, working on the recent murders."

He nodded his head again, understandingly. Always so understanding. I felt like I was dealing with a church worker.

"So we're looking for anybody who would have known Pamela Kim. Or Benny Bitan."

"Yeah, we heard about Benny," said Robert. "That was sad. Though not surprising."

"Really?" said Jerry. "Why's that?"

"Benny was manic-depressive. He used to take medication for it, but he wasn't very disciplined with the dosage. Then he'd go on a Jim Beam binge for a week and end up half dead somewhere. I always wondered if he was actually trying to drink himself to death."

Jerry moved his head in understanding. I knew that a certain relief and vindication hid somewhere underneath the gesture.

"Did you know Pamela Kim?" I asked.

"Oh, yeah. Wonderful worker. Lovely person, inside and out." He smiled. "She had been volunteering here for a long time, I think from the time she came to Nashville. I'm a northern transplant myself, and I started working here after she was already volunteering. She'd come in twice a week, sometimes three. We also do evening meals. The nice thing about her was, when she finished serving up here, she'd get her own plate and sit down with the guys and eat with them. Not all the volunteers do that. They want to volunteer, but they may be a little afraid to mingle."

"Naturally," said a man standing right next to me, serving himself a piece of fish, "you know how we homeless folks are. We'll slit your throat when you're not looking."

Robert raised his eyebrows to the man, more in a sense of understanding and empathy. "The news calls it hard, doesn't it, Jack?"

"Precisely," said Jack. "When all else fails, blame the poor." Jack turned and looked down at me, then smiled. He was a tall, thick man, white, with a rolling moustache and a two-day-old shadow of beard on him. His brown hair stuck out from under his ski cap. A flat gray scarf was wrapped around his neck. Over what seemed like two sweaters, he wore an old sports jacket that looked newly acquired. The tag was still on its sleeve, Ralph Lauren. It must have been given to him from some clothing store. No doubt it had a tear or an uneven seam in it, something that would not allow it to be sold. So old Jack ended up with a five-hundred-dollar coat for free.

Jack walked away. I said to Robert, "I take it Jack there knew Benny Bitan."

Robert just nodded.

I grabbed some coffee and carried my plate over to Jack. He was sitting with some other people, mostly men, except for one woman at the end of the table.

I suddenly felt what Robert had referred to: the disconcerting sense of sitting with those who relied on this place on a regular basis. Jerry walked by my side, his plate filled with chicken and ham, along with the side dishes. We both moved toward where Jack sat.

They had been talking. They all stopped talking the moment we sat down.

I introduced Jerry and myself. I was about to go into our investigation when Jack put out his half-gloved hand to me. "Pleased to meet you. Jack Fardle."

We shook hands. Then Jack had us shake hands with everybody else there. I could not tell if it was sincere, or a quiet joke played on us.

"How can we help you now, in your investigation?" he asked. His voice was clipped and articulate. It sounded educated.

"Did you know Pamela Kim?"

"Oh, yes. Wonderful young woman. Really kind. Nun material." As he said this, a couple of guys next to him mumbled their agreement. But they did not seem ready to speak about anything. Jack did all the talking.

I asked, "Did Pamela know Benny Bitan?"

No one said anything.

Jack pulled a case from his breast pocket. He pulled out some old wire glasses and put them on, as if needing them to see his food better. He looked like a disheveled professor once he placed them on his nose. He spoke while placing the case back in his pocket. "Of course, Benny and Pamela knew each other. They were good friends. Now that poor Benny's dead, there is no real harm in manifesting that little piece of information." He stabbed his fork into the fish.

"Yeah, but Pam was friends with a lot of folks," said the woman at the end of the table. She looked up at us, then straight at me. Her brown eyes did not move as her ebony face kept its hold on me. "Pam was good people. There wasn't any need for one of us to do her in. If you'd come down and asked us about it beforehand, we could have told you that. Then maybe Benny wouldn't have been found hanging from the prison rafters."

"Now, Yolanda, you know that's not completely fair," said Jack, holding one hand up while delicately holding a biscuit in the other. "Benny was a bit of a romantic, we all know that."

"That's true, that's true," said Yolanda.

"And he had trouble with the balancing of his hormonal flows, you could say," continued Jack. "He never kept on his medicine, which made his mood swings a real sight to behold sometimes, especially when he was drinking. Benny could have ended up doing himself in anywhere. But I guess being put in jail was just too much for him." Jack told this in a matter-of-fact way. He did not seem to recognize Jerry as the man who had arrested Benny. Jerry, however, looked down at his plate, leaving the questions to me.

I searched out one. "What do you mean, Jack, that he was a romantic?"

"Oh, he was hopeless," answered Jack, smiling. "Especially when it came to Pamela."

"How's that?"

"He was in love with her! Oh, all of us were in love with her. Even you, right, Yolanda?" The men laughed at that. "But Benny, he truly did love her. He even said this to her. She just laughed goodheartedly and said that she cared for him, but she couldn't love him in the same way. That she already had someone in her life."

"Really?" asked Jerry. "Who was that?"

"Benny didn't know," said Jack. "Some highfalutin guy with money, I suppose. Anyway, Benny was all torn up about it. If you ask me, it was her lover who did her in. I bet Benny was following them both. The lover killed her and left her there. Benny found her, and then lay down with her, you know, mourning her."

"So you don't think Bitan killed her?" I asked.

Jack waved a hand in the air again. "I have no idea. Maybe he did. Maybe he didn't. The only problem, Detective, is that most people are very willing to blame somebody like Benny before looking other ways. As I said earlier, it's easy and, in most people's minds, legitimate to blame the poor."

Obviously, this guy had an attitude about him. He also had an articulate way of expressing it.

"And this lover of Pamela's, you have no idea who that was?"

"No. He never came down here, that's for sure."

Yolanda spoke up. "I think Benny said that Pamela met the guy in some meeting down in Memphis, what was it...some sort of gathering about the environment, clean water, save the jungles, something like that."

"No doubt about that," said Jack. "Just like Pamela to want to save the world."

After a few scant moments of staring into the air between me and these homeless people, I picked up my plate. "Come on, Jerry. Time to go."

"What? I still got some ham here to get down me."

"Get a doggie bag."

We walked away from the table, thanking them for their help. As I moved toward the cleanup line, I heard Jack's voice, "*Au revoir, le policier!*" in what sounded, to me, like perfect French.

"Man. That guy's an anomaly," I muttered.

"What's going on?" Jerry asked.

"A hunch. You still got Kim's belongings under Evidence wraps?"

"Of course. Bitan hadn't yet gone to court. All

evidence needs to be held until long after a prosecu-
tion or an acquittal."

"You think she carried a purse?"

He thought a moment. "Yes. There was a purse on
her."

"Let's go."

At Evidence they handed me a plastic bag with her
purse in it. Then they gave me a dozen other bags that
held all the purse's contents. I looked at each item: lipstick, car and house keys, a billfold, checkbook, three
packages of condoms still joined together by the seams
(this did not get by my sight), a hairbrush, a small
makeup compact separate from the lipstick, a telephone and address notebook, a small, expired can of
mace, a half-used pack of gum, and a paperback book.

I took the telephone/address book. After I wrote
my initials and the date down on the index card clipped
to the bag, I extracted the little book and flipped
through it.

"Will you tell me what you're looking for? Whose
name?"

"But if she had a lover, maybe she put him down
in here."

"Great. So you're going to call everyone in her
book and ask them if they were Kim's lover? Why
don't you also check with each one and see if they
whacked her?"

"Quiet," I said, turning directly to the "H"s.

There were only three numbers under H. Han and
Harrison were both in California, Pamela's home state.
But the number that had no name before it began with
a local Nashville three-digit code before the following
four numbers. Another three-digit extension number
followed, 319.

I looked for a phone in the evidence department and rang the number. A secretary answered. "Whole Health Physicians," she said cheerily.

"Yes, extension 319, please."

She hesitated, then said, "I'm sorry, that extension is not in service anymore. Dr. Hatcher, he passed away last month. Is there any other doctor whom you would like to speak with?"

CHAPTER TWENTY-FIVE

So you think Hatcher and Pamela Kim were lovers. Just on a hunch that they attended the same Greenpeace meeting in Memphis. What does that tell us?" Jerry asked me.

We were heading to our car again. The afternoon promised us a turn in the investigation. The possible adultery meant a possible motive. This, of course, meant a need to make a visit to the good doctor's widow. I knew this was bound to happen sooner or later, the moment we reopened the Hatcher and Kim cases. The anonymous phone number in Kim's notebook made it sooner.

"It clears the air on one thing," I said. "It tells me that this was not some random serial killing. Serial killers' victims usually have no relationship with one another, except for some patterned trait that the killer uses as his barometer. Like elderly women being victims. Or male prostitutes. Or thin little girls. But there are no relational connections. Here, there is. Love. A lot of people kill for love."

"Yeah, but we're not completely sure they were lovers. I mean, he may have been her doctor for all we know. And maybe Ms. Kim made a habit out of just writing phone numbers down without the names. Who knows?"

"I flipped through her entire phone book. Pamela Kim was a meticulous woman. Nice, clean handwriting, and each number had a name beside it. All except that one."

"Okay. Fine. I see. But why did she feel the need to keep it such a secret? Adulterous affairs aren't exactly anything new."

"I don't know. Maybe it wasn't she who needed to keep it secret, but the good doctor. He was a well-known public figure in this town. He had a big reputation, something that perhaps he didn't want to get tarnished."

Jerry didn't say anything to that. In his silence, he seemed to be agreeing. Then he said, "Jeez, I hate having to take information like this to a widow. Then again, if the widow's possibly guilty, it won't be news to her. But I can't imagine Mrs. Hatcher being behind these types of killings. She's not a weak, petite wife in any stretch of the imagination." He whistled, then laughed. "Actually, she's one good-looking, refined lady. I had to tell her about her husband's death. She broke down all right, though there was a part of her that wanted to control her shock. But the response seemed real enough." He looked out the window. "I hate giving information like this. Do you realize how much power we have over people, just with the information that we discover?"

"What about the power over us," I pondered, "if they already knew the information?"

"What do you mean?"

"Just like you said. If Mrs. Hatcher is guilty of these crimes, then she already knew about the affair. What she's doing is playing a poker face on us, lying to us with her fabricated emotions. It's up to us to judge whether or not she's crying the truth, or just faking the tears. So she's got some power as well."

"You're not exactly consistent, are you, Romilia? First, you believe whatever a young kid from the streets tells you—like Gato Negro—then you're ready to turn around and nail a little middle-aged widow to the wall."

I wasn't sure what to make of that. "You're the one who told me not to believe everything someone tells me."

"True."

"There are still too many pieces missing, though," I said. "If she killed them, then did she kill Sáenz, and why? Or did she have someone do the killings for her? Also, where is this whole *Kaibil* angle coming into the picture, if she's the perp?"

Jerry looked straight out the windshield as if trying to swallow all that. "Maybe she hired Tekún Umán to do the killings. And he had them done in the ways of his Guatemalan ancestry. But that's crazy. Why in the world would she have a connection with him?"

I shook my head back and forth, slowly. Not in disagreement. Just in confusion.

He finally asked, "Do you believe there's a death-squad soldier walking around this town?"

"I have no idea. But if there is, I still say what I said—it's not a serial killer. Somebody's got a clear motive to want to see these people dead."

We didn't talk for a while. I didn't even have the radio on. For the moment I needed some silence. This, to my mind, had been a loud case. The din of others' voices—which were, in fact, not really that loud—slammed up and against the insides of my skull. My boss's voice, reprimanding me for my performance at Tekún Umán's office. The mayor's voice and his razor eyes, who told me, in so many curt words, that he would have my head on a plate that same evening, served up with new potatoes and salmon and whatever other food mayors eat. Even my new partner's voice sometimes pricked away at me, though less than before. His threat, when we first got together, about me staying out of his way. That was now gone, thank god. I was a little unsure why it was gone, except for his more recent efforts at humility and ability to listen. There was also Tony Stapleton's clipped, professional voice that was ready to break news over Nashville like a gang of tornadoes. I wanted—no, needed—to beat him to the killer before he beat me to the morning-paper deadline.

Then, of course, there was my mother. But that was not a loud voice. That was the one voice I wanted to hear, the scolding, doting words that kept her daughter and grandson *mimados*, spoiled and pampered. That voice had shut itself down. I knew that, while I was out scrounging the city for a killer, she was home, walking in hallways that were still not her own, looking through windows at a strange city, waiting for an undefined enemy to approach the house and tear it down and reach for her. Sergio would sense the fear in her, that of a little girl who has seen too much, a young adult who has lost everything. In his young life he had seen her act this way only a couple of times. I didn't want him to see it at all. I wanted to be the barrier

between her violent past and his quiet childhood. I
didn't always succeed.

The car and the silence between us was a balm.
Now, without the radio on, and with our taking a few
minutes to sit in the car as if we were alone with ourselves, I could try to take those voices and pick them up
like tiny mice and drop them into a mason jar in my
head and screw the lid on tight. I learned this little
trick from some writer who said it was a good way to
help strip guilt out of you, or whatever negative emotion you happen to be feeling at the time. Just take all
those rat-like voices and seal them up.

As I did that, an inevitable question came to mind:
What did Diego Sáenz have to do with Hatcher and
Kim? Was there a love triangle going on? Perhaps he
and Kim were lovers. Or he wanted her as his lover.
This led to the idea that he was the one who killed
them both—leaving me with no idea who killed him.

Either Jerry was reading my mind, or his own
thoughts were following a similar track. "Maybe Sáenz
knew something about Hatcher and Kim's love affair."

"Yeah?" I asked, waiting for more.

"I don't know, I'm just trying to flesh this out.
Maybe Diego knew about their affair, and he wanted
to expose it. But nah, that doesn't sound like it'd hold
water . . ."

"Don't forget the death-squad angle," I said.

"Oh, yeah. Right. The death-squad angle," and he
rolled his eyes. "You wouldn't know if there were
lovers'-quarrel death squads back in Central America,
would you? One named 'Killers for Cupid,' perhaps?"

I ignored him.

Wilma Hatcher's presence could make a person
wonder why in the world her husband would go out

and have an affair. Then again, no one has ever explained to me well enough how men think, except for
the adage that the little head in the pants has more vote
than the big head on the shoulders. Mrs. Hatcher was
lovely, in her late forties or early fifties, trim, an obvious woman of exercise. Her blond hair wisped over her
head as if God's winds had put them in exact place. Her
blue eyes were crystal-like, though not necessarily
threatening. She ushered us in with a tight, formal
smile, yet it seemed sincere enough. "I was wondering
when I would be seeing you again, considering the
news about that young reporter," she said matter-of-
factly as we walked through the door. She wore brown
slacks, a light cream top that showed her well-hewn
figure, and two gold bracelets on her left wrist that set
well with the colors of her clothes. Her house slippers,
which padded lightly upon the floor, could compete
with some of my better dress shoes.

Hatcher's home was opulent enough. "Doctor's
house," I thought. Though not overdone, it was way
beyond what I could ever dream of buying. The foyer
itself looked about the size of my son's room. A long,
rounded stairwell made its way upstairs. The floor tile
clicked as I walked over it, my heels and its expensive
ceramic base making for a nice musical instrument.
There were no noises, only the melodic rhythm of a
classical piece coming from a distant radio. I believed
it was Albinoni, an adagio for the organ. Fitting, I
thought, for a widow still in mourning. The only smell
in the house was a fresh pot of coffee, as if she had
known we were coming to visit. She offered us a cup.
We both said yes. "I'm really addicted to caffeine," said
Jerry. Mrs. Hatcher just looked at him, offering no
chuckle, something, I think, he was looking for.

I automatically opened up my notebook as I sat

down upon the leather-upholstered chair. She did not seem to take issue with this as she poured our coffee from a thin, tall decanter. "I understand that the questions regarding my husband's death could be wide open again," she said. "The little piece of jewelry they found on Mr. Sáenz, it was the same type found on Larry?"

"Yes," said Jerry, "a jade pyramid."

"I see." She poured carefully. "The killer leaves an interesting mark. So I take it that Mr. Bitan was not guilty?"

"We're, we're not sure about that, Mrs. Hatcher," Jerry said, his voice trying to dissuade shame. "We still have a bit of ground to cover before making such presumptions to make sure it's not a copycat crime."

"This must be difficult for you," she said to him, straightaway. "You were in the news a great deal recently. Now, all that you investigated is put to question."

I could not tell if this were meant to be insulting or just factual. Neither could Jerry. I could see he was just as uncomfortable, if not more, with the question as was I.

"I read this morning in *The Banner* an editorial that mentioned you, Detective Wilson. It was making the point that perhaps you had tried to close the investigations of my husband's and that young woman's murders too quickly. That for your own sake, or your reputation's sake, you put the blame upon that homeless fellow. What do you think of that?"

Jerry took in a deep breath. It was not in preparation for a sigh. I believed it to be a way of collecting enough oxygen to blow out flames, like an angered dragon. "The only thing I think is I'm out here again because I want to make sure that the investigation is complete, Mrs. Hatcher." Whatever lascivious thoughts he had about her while in the car, they were burned away now with his own anger. He did not hesitate to cut straight to the bone. "Tell me, Mrs. Hatcher, did you ever suspect your husband of having an affair with someone?"

It did cut. It caught her off guard, or at least, she led us to believe that. She shifted left in her chair. Her eyes dropped down to the floor for a moment, only to float up again and lock onto Jerry's sight. "No, I did not. Do you believe I had reason to?"

Not wanting this to become a stare contest between the two, I interjected, "We found your husband's private office number—his extension number—in Pamela Kim's personal phone book. Your husband's name was not next to it."

Her tongue rolled inside her left cheek. Then it disappeared. "My husband did not give his extension out to anybody."

Neither Jerry nor I said anything.

Again, she shifted, this time to the right. Her head dropped slightly. I could see a glisten over her eyes. "No," she said, "no, I knew nothing of an affair, Detectives. Are you sure of this information?"

I responded, "All we know is that his number was in her book. So we're now trying to confirm a connection between your husband and Ms. Kim."

"Which means, of course," she replied, "that these were not random killings. They were targeted killings. And now you're looking for a motive, and one strong motive would be if I knew something about an affair. I see. Then why would I kill the newspaperman?" As she asked, a quick, thin smile pulled over her lips. She looked back and forth at us.

"We're not accusing you of anything, Mrs.

Hatcher," I said. "We're just following out an investigation. But you are right. This possible affair means that these were more than just random killings. There could be a connection. Would you have any idea who would want to kill your husband?"

"I already told you the last time you were here," she said, looking at Jerry, her voice curt and almost growling low. "I have no inkling of an idea why someone would kill Larry. He did nothing but good for this city; he gave his time away, too much of it, damnit..."

This passed right into my notebook. She's bitter over his charity work.

"Larry was always thinking about other people. He was always feeling guilty about our, our wealth, like we're filthy rich people. I tell you, everything we own we worked for. Larry broke his back getting us to this position. Then he gets in his mid-forties and starts feeling guilty about it. Most men have a mid-life crisis, but Larry, he had to have a conscience crisis. He wanted to save the world, feed the poor, help the homeless, save the jungle, stop wars overseas. Shit."

That final word sounded foreign, coming out of her well-kept mouth. Then I thought, perhaps, when we are all gone, when no one is in this opulent home but she, such words were hurled easily from one room to the next.

"Even our daughters were wondering what was going on with him. Now you come in and give me this new tidbit, that Larry had a lover on the side, and it may have been this Korean woman. There, now my life is damned complete!"

She cried. I thought at first this would soften Jerry's demeanor toward her for what she had said about his failed investigation. It did not. He kept his arms crossed. He cocked his head to one side and just kept staring at her, waiting for her tears to stop. Finally, he asked her, "Did your husband have any problems with his work? Was there anyone in his office who had a grudge against him, or maybe that free clinic out in Shelbyville—did he have any difficulties in getting it going?"

She struggled quietly to stop her tears and dabbed her eyes with a tiny paper napkin. "I don't know. The same problems that any office has in running a business. He rarely spoke to me about his charity projects anymore. We had some...falling-out with that, as you can tell. I was tired of him spending so much time away, working on projects, trying to get that damned clinic off the ground. Then he started 'borrowing' from our own investments to pay for the clinic's cost. Now I find out that he was doing more than just saving the poor whenever he wasn't here, at home...The clinic, yes, it was on his mind a lot before he died. Something about money problems, not having enough to finish the project. I'm not sure." She shook her head, confused and angry.

"But the clinic is finished," I said. "At least, that's what I read in the paper."

"Yes, it's finished, it's finished. It's supposedly running fine. Larry had someone help him out in the end, or that's what he told me. After I bitched enough about him taking our hard-earned money. He did some sort of business negotiation with some bigwig from somewhere, I don't know...Atlanta, I think he told me. But he never told me much, Detective," she looked at me. Then she added wearily, "Larry and I spoke little in those last days."

CHAPTER TWENTY-SIX

The Free Health Clinic that Dr. Hatcher had set up in Shelbyville was right on the edge of the small town, next to the corner of a horse ranch. As we drove by, I noticed the long stretches of black fences, with horses standing out in the fields and men walking about or driving small tractors that hauled hay to different feeding areas. Medium-sized barns dotted the landscape. Many of the men who walked about were obviously Mexican. One middle-aged Latino man rode a horse that looked a little jumpy, but the man seemed to have full control over the animal's still unharnessed energy.

The clinic itself was nothing spectacular. It was well kept and relatively clean, with walls of paneling and cheap carpet on the floors. Chairs that looked as if they had been bought used lined the walls. Small end tables sat in the corners. One quick glance over the tables showed Spanish copies of *Reader's Digest*, *La Biblia*,

Hispanic Magazine, Time, Newsweek, and other magazines in both languages.

Most of the chairs were filled. Young mothers with
children sitting on their laps or running around their
feet sat still, waiting their turns. They whispered to
each other in Spanish, asking, "What are you here
for? Yes, my boy has another ear infection, can you believe it?"

I motioned to a cluster of them. "*¿Qué tal?*" I asked
them, and they all answered "*Bien, gracias.*" Though all
Latinas, these women who may have crossed the Río
Grande on foot while carrying the same babies in their
arms were a world away from my U.S. Latino upbring-
ing. They could spot me in a Latino crowd in a New
York second, seeing me for what I was not: one of
them. I had still to create a callus thick enough on my
soul not to be bothered by this.

A few people of other ethnicities were also present.
A couple of African-American women sat together,
chatting quietly. Three white women and one white
man were salted through the room. None of them
spoke to anyone. Most everybody had that weary look
of having someone in their family sick and having to
spend a day in the clinic in order to get a bottle of
antibiotics or a prescription of strong cough medicine.

The receptionist, a young white southern woman
who didn't look like she knew a lick of Spanish, smiled
and surprised me: "*¿Sí? ¿Cómo podría servirle?*" It was
pretty chopped up in a southern accent, but it was clear
enough.

Still, I answered in English, introducing myself
and Jerry, and explaining why we were there. "We
were wondering, could we bother you to let us in to
Dr. Hatcher's office?"

"Sure, yes, I suppose that's fine. Did you not find

what you were looking for the last time you were here?"

Jerry was standing back behind me, looking around and making googly eyes at a couple of kids, keeping them laughing. "No, I guess not," I said. I promised we would not be long.

She ushered us into the back room. "We haven't done anything in there yet, you know, clean up or anything. It may be a little musty; it's been closed up since his death. I think most of us just don't want to go in, you know?" Her voice was low and sad.

She opened the door, then left us to return to her responsibilities at the reception desk.

"So," Jerry asked, "what are we looking for?"

"Well, you were here last. Maybe you can tell me what you found."

"What? Me? I wasn't ever here."

I looked at him. "The receptionist said you had been here. I supposed it was you, since it was your case."

He shook his head negatively. "We checked out his private clinic in Nashville, the Whole Health Physicians place, where you called with Kim's notebook. But we didn't come out here. At the time it wasn't relevant."

"Funny, she said that we were just out here last week."

"Maybe they were the bill collectors or something. We all look alike, you know." He pulled at his lapel, referring to our ways of dress.

"Speak for yourself," I retorted kindly, referring to my preference for red, and how it was not necessarily a color used by tax people or detectives. "Anyway, we may have to be looking through some files on financial matters. Mrs. Hatcher said he was having money problems, and that he got help from someone in Atlanta. And Tekún Umán's from Atlanta."

"Right. If not love, why not money?"

We meandered about, taking our time at first. I lifted up papers from the desk and read them off in a whisper. Most were tax files, nonprofit reports, fund-raising reports, newsletters, a donor list of people's names and addresses, budgets, and financial reports. Though boring stuff to me, I knew I should give them a fairly clean study. "Looks like he left his last day here without finishing up his work. Or maybe he was getting ready for some meeting..." Then I saw the man's date book. I looked through it. "Hey, Jerry, what was the date when Hatcher was killed?"

"October seventh."

I looked for that date on the man's appointment book. It was a filled calendar, lots of meetings with local bigwigs, city councilmen, other doctors, lawyers. He wrote out all their names in each block for each day and time, all except for the appointment at eight o'clock in the evening of October sixth, with FC.

My mind rattled through the names I knew in this case. Sometimes I got a little confused, considering the nicknames, such as Gato Negro for Nelson Garcia, Tekún Umán for Rafael Murillo.

Jerry interrupted my train of thought. He had his hands inside an open file cabinet. "Nothing much here but paperwork on the clinic. Sounds like some of the same stuff that's on the desk: budgets, financial reports, newsletters, boring, boring, boring." He closed the file cabinet.

"Look at this," I said, holding a financial report in my hand. "This is all broken down into line items. Here's an income item for an 'Anonymous Donor.' Seventy-five thousand dollars. Can you believe that?

That's an incredible donation for a small operation like this clinic."

"Nice donor," said Jerry, looking at some pictures of Hatcher's family that sat on an end table. "I wouldn't mind making his acquaintance."

"Maybe that fellow's name is in the file. I can see someone making a big donation for a thousand dollars, or maybe five thousand. But what guy can give away seventy-five grand?"

I turned to the cabinet that Jerry had just closed. Flipping through the files, I found the one marked "Financial Statements." But I found no names. The only thing I found were more copies of the same statement that I had found on the desk. There was only one difference: though supposedly the same financial statement for the same quarter, the numbers under "Income" were not the same.

I jerked one of the copies out of the file and brought it to the desk. "Wait a minute. This one on the desk says that an anonymous donor gave seventy-five grand, and that it had a miscellaneous income of ten thousand dollars. But the one from the file says that there's eighty-five thousand dollars in miscellaneous income, and there's no mention of an anonymous donor."

"Let me see that," muttered Jerry. He stared at both copies of the same statement. He chuckled. "Well, I'll be. Looks like the good doctor was cooking the books, doesn't it?"

"Exactly," I said. "I don't know a whole lot about budgets. But if I remember something from my accounting classes back in college, you should never have a very big miscellaneous on a budget or a financial statement. It always looks a wee bit suspicious."

"Yeah. Makes people wonder where you're getting

so much 'miscellaneous' money. Now the question is, which one of these statements is telling the truth?"

I pondered, then offered, "Like you said, 'miscellaneous' on any budget should be small. But here," I pointed to the eighty-five thousand, "it's big. Very big. The one on the desk makes it a lot smaller, only ten thousand. But he had to account for the seventy-five somewhere, so he made up a new line item: 'Anonymous donor.' I bet he was planning to go to some board meeting, where he had to show the numbers to the committee members. He made them look more legitimate by referring to an anonymous donor."

"So. Which rich person in Nashville should we suspect?" Jerry looked down at me. "There's quite a few, you know. The music industry by itself has millionaires by the dozens."

"I don't think music has anything to do with this one."

"So, you, I take it, are thinking of Mr. Tekún Umán."

"Mrs. Hatcher mentioned the bigwig from Atlanta. Who else?" Then I looked over to behind the desk and barely saw, in the shadow of the seat, a cigarette butt. The room itself did not smell like cigarettes. I would have guessed that Dr. Hatcher had not been a smoker in life. His daily morning runs also attested to that guess.

I leaned down to get a better look without touching the butt. It had been crushed onto the thick plastic sheet where the wheeled desk chair could roll over without hurting the rug.

"Jerry, you got a plastic on you?"

"No, but I could go get one. Why?"

"I got something here we should lift."

He went out to the car and brought me a plastic

bag with a tag. I picked up the brown butt with the bag over my fingers, then brought it up to the light.

"What've you got?" he asked.

I stared at the brown butt. I at first smiled, knowing how this would help me with McCabe. But then I frowned. Something wasn't right. "Evidence. I think."

We walked out of the office and into the main lobby. The receptionist called out to us, "I hope you found what you needed, Officers."

"Oh, yes, thanks very much, ma'am." I was about to leave, but then turned and asked her, "By the way, what did you mean when you said about the last time we were here? We've never been here before." Jerry also stopped, curious as to what she would say.

"Oh, I didn't mean you. But another person from your department."

"Really?" asked Jerry. "Who was it?"

"I don't remember the young man's name. But he said he was with the police force. He showed me a badge and everything."

"You mean this kind of badge?" I showed her mine.

"Oh, no. Nothing like that. His was gold, and shaped like a big star, you know? And I think the word 'Deputy' or something like that was inscribed on it."

I thought about my boy, Sergio; he had a little gold-colored toy badge with "Deputy" written in bold letters over it.

"He was kind of a good-looking young man, in his early twenties. Had black hair, spoke Spanish, but spoke excellent English as well, like a northerner speaks it..."

I turned and looked at my partner. His mouth dropped slightly at what he heard.

Then I whispered the obvious: "Sáenz."

CHAPTER TWENTY-SEVEN

We drove through Nashville right as the evening traffic was getting heavy. It had been a long day that had begun early, had in fact started at midnight, when Jerry and I had sat at his home computer to look up the information on Guatemalan death squads. All day long we had visited a lot of places and had spoken to a number of people. I was tired. Though frenetic over our findings, and wanting to follow up on them immediately, I was ready for a few minutes of relaxation at home, even if it meant only a meal with my mother and son before spending part of the evening trying to follow up on our leads by phone.

As I pulled onto Broadway, I saw a newspaper truck stop and drop two loads of bundled papers in front of a newsstand. The newsstand proprietor waved at the driver as he walked out and cut the ties from the bundles with a pocketknife.

"So," said Jerry, "you think this is Tekún's cigarette butt?"

"No. It's his bodyguard's. The guy had the audacity to smoke in the Daniel Childs Bookery, up in the coffee shop. He scared the shit out of the waiter who asked him to put it out. He must be a real smoker, to have lit up in that clinic office..."

"Yeah, but how are you going to pin Tekún with rifling through Hatcher's office? Lots of people could smoke that brand."

"True. I wouldn't use this butt in court. But it's something to show our boss, who'll then let us sniff around Tekún some more."

"Ah." Then he looked out the window, as if something else pulled at his interest more than our conversation. He finally told me what it was. "You hungry?"

I thought about it. "Yes, as a matter of fact, I am."

"Want to stop and get a sandwich?"

The idea sounded good. But I hadn't seen much of my family. "Thanks, but I better get home. My boy's going to get on my ass if I don't see him soon." This was my tough detective rhetoric for I'm missing my son.

"You got just one boy?"

"Yeah. Sergio's his name. Three years old."

"That's nice. And your husband, is he at home?" Jerry hesitated slightly in asking, perhaps not wanting to pry into privacy.

"I'm not married."

"Oh. Sorry."

"That's fine, no need to be. I'm happy with the arrangement."

"I'm divorced myself," he said. "Some people think divorce is a god-awful thing. But I don't know. My two kids are happier now than when my wife and I were together. We just weren't made for each other, I suppose, though we thought we were. This job was hard on her."

"I've heard that's pretty common," I said. "So you got kids?"

"Yeah. Two boys. They're eight and six now. Great kids."

"You see them much?"

"No." He looked down at his lap. "They live in Seattle now with their mother. But we keep in touch. You know, through e-mail, phone calls, child-support checks."

"Right."

I pulled us into the precinct's parking lot. We walked in, two people worn out from a long day. Jerry was already pulling down his tie as we took the elevator up to the third floor. I was ready to pull my shoes off, tie them together, and fling them over my shoulder to take the rest of the evening barefoot. That wasn't about to happen.

We looked through the door of homicide and heard the racket of phones ringing off their cradles and detectives picking up and explaining away something they could not explain. Then there was our boss, also on the phone, who saw us and stared daggers straight through the crowd, beckoning us toward his office.

He closed the door behind us. "You two look like you haven't read the paper today." He threw the evening copy of *The Cumberland Journal* at us.

TRIPLE MURDERS CONNECTED TO POSSIBLE DEATH-SQUAD THEORY

"Death Squad" is not a term we Nashvillians are accustomed to using. Indeed, death squads are more known in countries like El Salvador or Colombia, where drug cartels and oligarchies use such terrorist groups to keep the population in check. Yet that is the term that may be the link among the Lawrence Hatcher, Pamela Kim, and Diego Sáenz murders this past month.

The Homicide Division of the Nashville Police Department has not confirmed nor denied the existence of such squads here. However, Detectives Romilia Chacon and Jerry Wilson found a file recently upon Diego Sáenz's computer in the offices of *The Cumberland Journal*, which could indicate death-squad involvement in these murders.

The file, marked "Kaibil," was opened by Sáenz on November 1, one day before he was killed. Sáenz, an investigative reporter, was apparently researching this word before he became another victim.

"Kaibil" is an indigenous word from Guatemala which means "warrior." The Guatemalan army used the term for one of its specialized forces thought to have functioned as a death squad. In Guatemala, the Kaibil are squads known to dress as civilians at night, hunt specific individuals down, and kill them in manners to inspire terror.

The article theorized every which way it could without getting caught in libel. Then again, I could not think of who would sue the paper for this. There was no mention of Tekún Umán, though it quoted Gato Negro saying that he could not remember who had attacked him. Gato Negro's doctor was quoted as saying that the boy was in too much trauma to remember. The paper made the obvious connection between the Guatemalan Kaibiles' manner of slicing words into their victims' bodies and the way Gato's attacker slit "snitch" into his stomach. It also pointed out that Guatemalan death squads were known for slitting their victims' throats, as had happened to Hatcher and Kim. Finally, it allowed the reader to draw some conclusions regarding the jewelry. "Guatemala, a country known for both its jade and its Mayan temple pyramids, is a land of both violence and poverty..." Shit, I thought. No Nashvillian was going to come out of this thinking highly of Central America, or its people.

The article did not leave Jerry alone. It pointed out that the once lone detective who found Benny Bitan with Pamela Kim's body, now worked with a partner. "When asked if it was due to the mistaken arrest of Bitan, Lieutenant Patrick McCabe, chief of homicide, replied, 'Our detectives have followed all possible leads.'"

"Damn. First, you're in their spotlight, then they eat you alive, Jesus Christ..." Jerry threw the paper down. He walked away from McCabe and me, left the boss's office, and headed out into the open homicide room. On his way, his left arm bolted out and slammed his fist against a file cabinet. The receptionist, a young woman who sat next to the cabinet, jumped in her seat. She stared as Jerry disappeared behind the bathroom door.

I couldn't worry about Jerry's wounded esteem right now. "My god," I said, looking down at the paper, "this could make the city go down in a panic."

"It *could?*" McCabe's eyes looked like orbs, landing upon my face. "Romilia, you hear those phones ringing? It already has! I got everybody from the mayor to the janitor downstairs calling us, demanding that we

get our butts in gear and catch these Kaibiles! I've gotten at least ten phone calls from people ordering me to
get a hold of immigration, so that they'll come in and
cart away every Hispanic they see."

That made the hairs on the back of my neck bristle
up. "Great. Now there's going to be a backlash on all
the Latinos...shit..."

"There wouldn't have to be if you all clear up this
case. And do it before Stapleton calls me again. That
jerk rides my ass every chance he can, the son of a
bitch."

Obviously, my boss had an attitude toward Stapleton.
Then I remembered when I first met the editor, when
he snarled out the facetious statement regarding how
the department was trying to "diversify." I guessed that
Stapleton and McCabe had had their tiffs long before I
came to Nashville.

"So. You got anything at all?" McCabe barked.

I glanced out the open door, hoping Jerry would
be back soon. He just then left the bathroom. He
swung around to the receptionist, smiled a huge smile
at her, and gestured as if he were apologizing for his
sudden burst of anger. Then he tipped an invisible hat
at her, which seemed to win her over. As he walked
back into McCabe's office, Jerry grinned at the both of
us. "Sorry. Nature called. Where are we?"

I quickly, and tremulously, told McCabe what we
had discovered thus far. My voice trembled all the way
through, as if somehow I were guilty for the din of
phone calls just outside McCabe's office.

After I finished, McCabe just leaned over on his
desk while still standing, and stared at us. "So you're
saying you want to check out your friend Tekún
again?"

"Yes."

"Because of a cigarette butt?"

"Well, no, not just that. Something else that I found in Hatcher's office." Jerry also looked at me. In the bustle of everything, I had not told him about the doctor's appointment the day before he was murdered. Since then my mind, as it had been rattled around with different pieces of information, had finally been able to decode "FC."

"I think Dr. Hatcher had an appointment with Pajarito the day before he was killed. I saw in his calendar the initials FC. I think they may stand for Francisco Colibrí."

McCabe just lowered his head and looked down at his desk. I figured he was staring vacuously, but then again I couldn't see his eyes.

"Just get out of here," he said.

I took that as permission to form a stakeout.

CHAPTER TWENTY-EIGHT

Jerry and I stopped at a local barbecue grill that stood about two blocks from where Sáenz was murdered. There were a number of people in the place. Just about every one of them was talking about the newest "finding" of *The Cumberland Journal*.

"Honey, ain't no way I'm staying out late anymore. Not until they find that killer."

"You mean 'killers.' Supposedly, there could be a whole bunch of them. What'd they call it, a 'squad'? That's some scary shit, man. Sounds worse than a gang."

"My wife used to help out at the church rummage sales. But I won't let her do that anymore. The paper said that those Hispanic death squads go after do-gooders."

I rubbed my face with my left hand. In one upper corner of the small restaurant a television was on. As the news came on, everyone shut up. The local announcer went through the same theoretical statements that we all had read about in the *Journal*.

Then they brought on a professional, some professor from a university whom they had interviewed earlier that day. His specialty was Latin-American Studies. "If this is a death-squad activity, then we've got something to worry about. It's not like a serial killer who kills people for supposedly no reason, or has to kill in order to appease some inner sexual guilt. Death squads are trained military personnel who know how and where to terminate someone in a horrible, violent manner. They're usually indoctrinated in a certain political perspective, one that we would call fascistic."

"What about the jade pyramids found in the victims' mouths, Professor?" the interviewer asked.

The specialist raised an eyebrow. "Death squads like to leave their mark in order to frighten the rest of the population. You kill one person in a village and leave some sort of symbol of who you are, and you'll keep the whole village in a state of panic. No one else will want to get involved with whatever the victim was involved in. It's a way of controlling, through fear, the entire population."

When asked if he believed that there was a death squad somewhere in Nashville, he hesitated, then said, "I have no idea. But I do know that the war in Guatemala is officially over. What does a country do with their numerous trained killers? Maybe they want to get rid of them. Maybe they shipped them out of the country and some of them traveled here, through Mexico. If so, just because they've changed their location doesn't mean they've changed their ways."

"That's it," said a fellow sitting three people down

from me on the bar. He stood up. "I'm going home
and loading the rifle."

"I tell you," said another, "I knew something bad
was going to happen someday, with all them wetbacks
coming into the area. They're coming in by the truck-
loads! You're bound to have some nutcase in one of
those trucks, saying he wants to pick tomatoes but
what he really wants is to slit a few throats. That immigration needs to come in here and clean up!"

He was a white guy. A black man sitting right next
to him agreed. Terrific, I thought: white and black
against brown. And the worst of it was, I had something to do with all this. I was the one who found
"Kaibil" on Sáenz's computer. Though the waning
voice of logic in my head tried to talk me out of it, saying that all I was doing was my job, other voices, many
of them in Spanish, spoke to me of other concerns, especially my relationship to my own people in the dark
light of doing my job.

I pushed my plate away, leaving half the barbecue
on it. "Let's go," I said.

Jerry looked at me with a mouthful of barbecue.
Then he rolled his eyes. "Damn, woman. I'm surprised
your mother didn't raise you better. You're making me
eat so fast I'm gonna get heartburn."

I asked Jerry to pull over into a gas station. "I need
to make a quick call home." He didn't say anything,
just waited in the car.

"*Hola*, Mamá," I said, putting a finger in my other
ear to tap it closed from the traffic on Broadway. "How
are you and Sergio? Everything all right?"

Though I tried to sound cheery, her response
would have none of it. "*Hija*, please come home."

It was a plea, one that had been soaking all afternoon

in tears. "Mamá, are you all right? Listen, is Sergio okay?"

"Yes, yes, he's fine. Fine. But all these news about *los escuadrones*. Even *Univisión* has picked up on it. They even called us, can you believe that?" Her voice actually lifted up slightly with that. "That good-looking Cuban anchorman who does the news, I actually talked with him! He wanted to fly into Nashville and talk with you about the Kaibiles." The mere utterance of that word threw her into the original, thick fear. "Romi, please come home now."

I wanted to grab her through the phone line, hold her and reassure her. Yet I was sure of nothing myself. "Mamá, I think you and Sergio are fine. Just keep the doors locked. I'll call the precinct and ask if they can make sure one of the uniform officers circle the neighborhood every hour, okay? You don't have anything to worry about."

"I've got you. You're out there, looking for them, aren't you? Romilia, these are *Kaibiles! Por favor...*"

For the first time, her fear pierced through my ignorance and bit me. I thought of Hatcher and Kim, their throats open on both sides, from the jawbone under the ear to the collarbone, like two bloody gills. I thought of Sáenz's hollowed-out head. I thought of jade-like pyramids placed upon the tongues of the victims. Then I thought of my grandparents and a whole village back in an old country that I did not know. For the first time I felt my mother's fear. I could not so easily blame those people in the barbecue restaurant for their callous, trembling statements.

But the fear also bit into my anger. "Mamá, listen. I will be home. I promise. I just need to bring this son of a bitch down."

Her breath scoffed at my remark, as if to say "You

don't know who you're dealing with." But she didn't
say that. All she did was repeat, "*Por favor, hija, veníte a
la casa.*" Come home, child. Please come home.

It was five-thirty by the time we made it over to
Tekún Umán's office building. I thought we would
have been too late, that he and his employees would
have closed the door and gone home for the evening. I
was partly right. Tekún's emerald green Jaguar was
nowhere to be seen, nor was the Lexus that his bodyguard drove behind him. The light in his presidential-
like office was off. The only light on was that of the
receptionist's office. Pajarito walked by the window a
couple of times, his corpulent body tossing a large,
squatty shadow to the outside. I could not see the janitor, Miguel Martínez.

"Looks like our boy has gone home for the day,"
said Jerry, noticing the absent luxury cars and the dark
office. He looked back down to his notepad that rested
on his lap. Scrunched down in the chair, his legs were
pushed up slightly higher, forming an angled table for
his doodling. It seemed all he had in the notebook
were doodles. At first I couldn't see what he was drawing, as his left hand—the one he used to draw with—
blocked my vision. Then the hand dipped down in a
number of brisk strokes as he filled in a shadow area. I
looked at the drawing. "That looks amazingly like
Mrs. Hatcher," I said, surprised at his talent. "But you
make her look a little meaner than in real life."

"You really think so?" He smiled a mean smile. "I
thought it was a perfect representation, myself."

I complimented him on his artistic skills. "Very
nice. But you seem to have certain feelings about the
dear widow."

"Yes. The poor, dear, helpless widow. Helpless like a panther."

I chuckled, then looked back out at Tekún's building. "Let me ask you something," I said. "If Tekún's this highfalutin drug lord that Atlanta thinks he is, then where's his army of protectors?"

"What army?" Jerry kept doodling.

"You know, his gang of men who surround him, take care of him, do his dirty work."

Jerry shrugged his shoulders as an answer.

"The only people I've seen around him are his gorilla bodyguard and Pajarito. Nobody else, except that janitor."

Jerry finally responded, "You said he's kind of new in town, didn't you? Maybe he's got his retinue back home. He'll call them over once he gets set up here."

"Maybe. But it seems he would have sent people over first to check the place out. You know, get a pulse on Nashville's drug trade before he moved in."

"He could have done that." Jerry looked up from his drawing. "Just because we don't see them doesn't mean they're not here. And think about it: Tekún has this philanthropic reputation to keep clean. He doesn't want to stain that with the presence of a bunch of hit men around him. Or maybe his army is the Kaibiles. And if they're so well trained as we think they are, then they know how to keep hidden."

"True. That's very true." I stared, not really seeing the building very much. "And maybe Tekún did case Nashville before he moved here. Maybe he had something to do with that other drug dealer, Two-Bits, going down in a bust."

"Could be," muttered Jerry. I could hear his pencil working over the paper. It worked almost too hard, as if wanting to fill the sheet with graphite. The stakeout

blues must be boring him, getting under his skin. He
said, "The fact remains: if he's a Kaibil, or the boss of a
bunch of Kaibiles, he is one dangerous *hombre*." His
southern accent pushed through the Spanish word.

Twenty minutes passed. Within those twenty minutes, three different men had walked into the building.
All of them, as far as I could see, were of Latin descent.
It was dark, so I could not be sure. "Doesn't that seem
strange, to have people come in at this hour?"

"Why's it strange?" he said. His voice sounded
jumpy with boredom.

"It's after business hours. And even during the day,
Tekún never has this type of traffic. His nonprofit
company hasn't even started yet."

Jerry looked up and through the windshield.
"Maybe they're friends of that guy's, what's his name,
Pajarito?"

"Yeah. But why visit him here? If they're friends,
they shouldn't be doing their visiting at work. And
these guys have all left rather quickly, as if they just
came in to pick some stuff up."

"Like what, drugs?" he asked.

"Wouldn't that be a nice find? Look."

Just then two men walked through the shadows of
the de-leafed, spidery-branched oak trees that grew in
the front yard of the building. One chunky fellow wore
a fairly large cowboy hat. The other was hatless. His
tall figure loomed over his squattier companion. Once
they both passed underneath a streetlight, I could see
that they wore jeans, jean shirts, and cowboy boots,
one a brown pair, the other black. They appeared to be
Mexican. They walked like day laborers. They almost
kicked their legs out in front of them, walking from the
sockets of their hips, in no real hurry, unlike some
businessmen who would be rushing to a meeting.

They walked inside. Lucky for us, they stood right in front of the large window, where Pajarito manned the office. They seemed to talk amiably to Pajarito, but Pajarito did not necessarily offer them the same bright smile that he had given me when I had first met him. He stood back slightly from them as they entered, barely giving them his hand in greeting. They stood for a moment before saying anything. Finally, the squattier one with the hat spoke. Pajarito put his hands up slightly in an "It's not my fault" fashion. The hatted man stuck his hands in his pockets, then pulled them out, crossing his arms over his chest. Then the thinner fellow without the hat pulled out his wallet and began slapping bills of money upon the counter. At that, Pajarito pulled down the shades.

"Hey. That's a hell of a lot of money passing between hands to be a nonprofit company," said Jerry.

"Damn, he closed the window . . ."

"What do you think?"

"I don't know, but I wish I had a wire in there, to hear what they're saying."

Five minutes later the two men left. "What do we do now?" Jerry asked.

"I think we follow them." I started my engine.

They had not been able to park their large pickup truck in Tekún's parking lot, because it had been chained closed for the evening. The two Mexicans had parked about three blocks away from the building, near Centennial Park. There was an empty space right behind their vehicle.

I parked. Jerry and I both jumped out before they got in the pickup. I heard one of them say to the other, *"Ese cabrón nos va chingando, creo. Quiere demasiado . . ."* So I said, in Spanish, excuse me, but we'd like to talk to you. Then I flashed my badge.

They bolted. The thin one stumbled over a fire hydrant before he could get a good kick into running speed. He picked himself up and took off. "Stop! Police!" yelled Jerry. It did not faze them, but perhaps made them run even harder, verifying their very fears. I pocketed my shield and ran after the fat one with the hat.

He may have been overweight, but he wasn't slow. He cut between two parked cars, jumped over the sidewalk, and cut across the large lawn of Centennial Park. The thinner guy also went the same way. In the right corner of my eye I saw Jerry trying to catch up to him.

"¡Deténganse!" I yelled. It did no good. They ran across the grass where Tekún and I had talked yesterday. Both men headed straight for the Parthenon.

Once I got to one of the huge columns of the Greek building, I stopped and squatted down to pull my gun from my ankle holster. Jerry had made it to the other corner. He was close enough that I could talk with him. "You think we need backup?" I asked.

"I don't think these guys are armed," he said. "They ran too fast, instead of turning on us."

"Maybe."

"Then again, I could be wrong." He looked at me, a quick, uneven smile over his face. He pulled his gun from his breast holster and held it in his right hand, his left steadying him against the pillar.

At the same time we both pulled around our pillars, our guns held up ahead of us. Though I kept my eyes mostly in front of me, following the line that my two hands and my barrel created, I also darted my vision left and right, seeking them out. Jerry walked parallel with me, his one right arm in front of him, his left to one side. Then he disappeared around the inner corner of the Parthenon. I pushed myself against the

wall and looked out at the row of thick, huge columns
that held the roof of the cement patio up above me.
Through the columns I could see the large, deserted
lawn of the park where the Vanderbilt students had
played Frisbee yesterday. The area was now almost
completely dark. The streetlights and headlights and
distant stores up and down West End Avenue offered a
glowing background.

Then a figure cut across the scene from the left,
running between each column, like a kid running on
the other side of a giant fence.

I ran, deciding not to yell out until I got close
enough. He cut to the right, heading back into the
shadows of the Parthenon, then disappeared into
them. At this point I was more angry than nervous. I
ran right into the shadow with him.

We could not see each other. I did have one advantage: he was overweight, and the weight was getting to
his breathing. Then he coughed. No doubt a cigarette
smoker, too.

I held my nine-millimeter up into the shadows and
clicked back the hammer. "*Ya, basta,*" I said.

"*Ya, ya.*" He coughed again.

My eyes became accustomed to the night. He fell
out from the shadow of one of the columns and leaned
over into the light of the streetlights behind us. Carefully I came up behind, pulled a bracelet from the back
tuck of my pants, and started slapping them on him. I
asked him, "*Y ¿por qué corriste?*" Why did you run?

"*Porque es usted la migra, pues...*"

La Migra. I was about to tell him that I wasn't immigration. Then I decided to leave such information
for the box.

One minute later I walked my catch from the
shadows of the Parthenon and into the blue light of

night. Jerry was there already, catching his breath, with his collar next to him. The young, thin man's hands were also behind him in cuffs.

Between breaths Jerry asked, "You ever been here before?" He was pointing to the Parthenon.

"Yes," I said. "Yesterday, with Tekún."

"Oh, that's right . . . You should see the inside," he said, still panting and coughing slightly. Obviously, he had had to run farther than I did. "When they open the Parthenon up, you can see all sorts of shit: statues, Greek goddesses, stuff like that. Really neat." His little tour-guide talk ended in a short breath. He turned and gently slapped the young Mexican fellow on the back. "Okay. *Vamoose*, amigo."

CHAPTER TWENTY-NINE

As it was after the day shift, McCabe was not in his office. He had left the mess of panicky phone calls from civilians and curious calls from the media to the night shift. Now he was probably at home with a Manhattan or scotch in hand. I'd bet that he'd have more than one tonight.

The night beat was coming on just as we walked through the door. No one was in the interrogation box.

We only had one box. It was a small room, with tile that covered all the walls, one window to the outside where the rest of the detectives could see us, and a small mirror that allowed people to see inside without being seen, something that just about everyone knew, even these two guys whom we had just brought in. We decided to put the thin guy in McCabe's office for the moment, where one of the other night cops could watch him while we questioned the hatted fellow.

This was my first time in the box here in Nashville. I had had the opportunity to question people in Atlanta, and had done pretty well. I had received high scores from my superiors there. Now, here, with a new partner, I felt like I was starting all over. First off, I didn't know how Jerry worked in the box, if he was a hard-core cop who wouldn't hesitate to use a phone directory up against a suspect's head, or if he preferred the soft touch, getting into their skin comfortably, asking them questions as if he actually gave a damn about their well-being, only to open them up enough for them to give freely the information we desired. Perhaps he did both, weaving them, keeping the suspect off guard, confused, comfortable one minute, squirming the next. But I had other questions. For instance, how did Jerry do with a partner, and a woman partner at that? I was about to find out.

Then again, I had another advantage. These guys spoke no English. I had to give them Miranda in Spanish, something that I had translated years ago when I had first become a cop: "*Usted tiene el derecho de no hablar; tiene el derecho de emplear a un abogado ...*"

Jerry seemed to be understanding of this. He even said at one point, "Good thing you're on this; otherwise, we wouldn't get anywhere with these guys." This, actually, was the original reason why I was hired—my ability, and the rest of the department's lack of ability, to speak Spanish, to question in that language, to gaze in and see if the suspect from the other culture was lying or being truthful.

Our suspect, named Chamba Rodríguez, took off his hat and placed it on the table. He was nervous, pulling at his small goatee with his thumb and forefinger, not daring to look up at me. I sat in front of him and stared him straight in the face and asked, in Spanish, "Why did you run?"

"I thought you were *La Migra*."

"You want to tell me why you're so scared of *La Migra?*"

At first he looked away, then looked back up at me. "You know why by now. I don't have my papers."

I cocked my head back, then sucked a tooth. I translated this to Jerry, then went ahead questioning, "So what's the deal with Pajarito? Why were you visiting him and handing him so much money?"

With that, the man turned angry and started using every word that my mother told me to never use. "*Hijo de la gran chingada, que le haga a su madre, ese pendejo que sólo roba a la gente.*"

I didn't translate all that to Jerry. Instead, I snatched at that last piece, "What do you mean he robs all the people?"

"Charging too much for his damned services. Then it takes two years to get your green card, when he told us at the beginning that it would only be six months. I've paid that bastard three thousand dollars for my papers, and he still hasn't gotten them to me yet!"

Again, I translated for my partner. "So this doesn't have anything to do with drugs?" Jerry asked me. I asked that to Chamba.

"What drugs, miss? I don't do drugs. I got a family waiting for me in Mexico. I send all my money to them. Hey, wait a minute, you think I'm dealing in some marijuana or something? No, no way, I'm not into that, neither is my friend over there!"

He sounded fairly legitimate about this. "Then what were you giving Pajarito all that money for today?"

"My papers! He said he would have them, but then he raised the price on them right there! So I got mad and threw all my bills at him, telling him that's the amount we agreed upon. Daniel did the same. I think he got a little nervous, because he was about to give us the papers. Then he said he didn't have them here, but that they were at his house. He told us to go there tonight and pick them up. I think we made him a little scared."

"I see. And what time were you supposed to meet him, Chamba?"

"Nine o'clock tonight. He said the papers would be ready."

Great, thought I. And so would we.

The only time we brought the two men together was when we started wiring them. They were more than happy to cut the deal, especially when we kept alluding to the possibility that they were involved in a drug operation. In order to show their innocence of this, they were very willing to raise up their arms and let me tape and clip the microphones to their chests.

"Excuse me," I said as I tucked the transmitter/tape recorder into his back pocket. I explained, "That is the transmitter. It sends your voice through the air and into our car, where we'll be listening. But it also has a tiny tape recorder on it. We'll be taping you in the car. This is a backup recorder, in case we get cut off."

"It feels funny back there," said Chamba. "It sticks into my cheeks."

"Don't worry," I said. "Just don't sit down on it, or you'll break it or shove it up your butt."

He looked at me, confused perhaps that a woman could make such jokes. I probably dropped down a few notches from his vision of what a Latina *dama* should be. Then he cocked his head back, as if to silently say, What else to expect from a cop?

Afterwards we separated them again. Jerry made a trip to the bathroom. I couldn't help but comment when he came back out, "Coffee runs through, doesn't it?"

I think I embarrassed him. He turned slightly red. But he grinned at me. "You ready?" he said, excited over this bust, more than what I thought he would be.

"Yeah, but I've got an idea."

"What's that?"

"You know how the press has been so diligent about keeping their noses up our butts? This may not be exactly about the Kaibiles, but how about we give them a bone to chew on, with just a little meat on it? This could also be a way to shake Tekún Umán from his tree."

Jerry just smiled.

CHAPTER THIRTY

ajarito's apartment was right above Doña Marina Osegueda's *taquería*, on the second floor of the same building. Doña Marina owned the entire building and rented the upstairs rooms to individuals. Obviously, she had various avenues of income.

We watched from our Taurus as Chamba and Daniel made their way up the outside stairs and to the second floor. Two streetlights provided us enough light to watch their actions in the night. Once they disappeared behind the door, Jerry asked me, "You sure they won't try to sprint, or maybe tip Pajarito off?"

"I really don't think so. They know they're wired. That means we can hear everything they say. And they're sufficiently scared to keep put."

"So let's see. Once we do the bust, I'll take our two friends here and load them in my car," he said, glancing over his shoulder to another Taurus that we had parked around the corner of Doña Marina's building. "You all right with bringing Pajarito in by yourself?"

"Sure. He's not a lot to deal with. But it's better to keep them separated, considering Daniel and Chamba are part of our little sting party here."

"Great. I think it's better that I take them anyway."

"Really? Why?" I was baiting him, knowing what he was going to say, that the two men would perhaps be too much for me to handle.

He was very diplomatic, seeing in my smile the fact that I was ready to pounce upon any hint of sexism. "Just helping to protect the well-being of my partner."

"I see. Hey, did you call for backup?"

"They should be here any second."

"Good."

He changed the subject. "You know, I was thinking, we could get in trouble for this."

"Why?" Looking at the door as it closed, I kept my eyes through the upper portion of the windshield. The headphones slipped off my ears slightly. I had to readjust them as I craned my neck.

"Because this is out of our jurisdiction. U.S. Immigration should be the ones making this bust, since it deals with false immigration papers."

I thought about that for a scant moment. "As far as I'm concerned, we're following up on a possible drug operation that is connected to our murder investigation. All the data we received from Atlanta pointed to the possibility that Tekún Umán is a drug dealer. Pajarito is one of his workers. I know nothing about immigration papers."

He grinned at me. "To be so young, you've got a sly little mind." He looked up the stairs. "But our two friends here have lost just about everything. No papers, they've just gotten caught in our crosshairs, and now, after we finish using them here, we'll hand them over to immigration."

"Better than going down for a drug rap."

"But that's not really the case," he said. "There are no drugs involved."

"Look, I can't be bothered with their life stories, Jerry." I looked over at him. His talking was keeping me from hearing them through the earphones. Even though they were just walking down the hall, I wanted to hear everything, even their heavy, nervous breathing. "They got caught. That's their problem. They'll be okay. Immigration will ship them home, and they'll be back here again in about two weeks."

Again, I could feel his gaze upon me. In his eyes, I suppose I was also cold-blooded, along with being sly. Perhaps my being Latina meant I had to think a certain way, specifically regarding undocumented foreigners. Right now all I wanted to think about was nailing Pajarito, and ultimately his boss.

Three backup cars pulled up around us as I heard, through the earphones, one of the boys knocking on the door upstairs. I could hear their knuckles against the door. Jerry got out and directed the cops. I listened to my earphones. The door opened. Pajarito's voice greeted them. "*Entren, muchachos.*" They said their hellos and nothing more. Pajarito's door closed. He sounded conciliatory, saying that he was sorry he couldn't find the papers in his office downtown, but that he had left them here, in his apartment. I wished he had specifically said whose office it was; it would have put more pressure on Tekún later. But I had to take what I could get.

"*Aquí están,*" Pajarito said, handing them papers. I could hear them being rifled through their fingers. He said that everything was taken care of, the stamps had been put upon their cards, everything was made to look perfectly legit, and in fact, looks were everything. So, as far as he and the rest of the world were concerned, they were legit. Then he asked about his payment, *por favor,* what they had originally agreed upon. Wallets were pulled out, money extracted, counted, placed in his hand. "*Gracias, jóvenes,*" said Pajarito.

"That's our cue." I ripped the earphones off my head and pushed the door open.

Jerry and I made our way up the stairs. Two officers followed behind. The others circled behind the building. I was afraid that, with the distance between our car and the second-floor apartment, we were going to lose them somehow. That became a realistic concern the moment I looked down the hall and saw that there were six doors, three on each side. "Damn," whispered Jerry, "which one did they go in?"

I played back in my head how many steps they had taken. They had appeared to have gone the distance of the hallway, from what I remembered of their breathing and the wordless walk. I walked to the end of the hall, stopped, and listened. Spanish came from the left door. I leaned in. "They're in here," I said to Jerry.

He kicked the door in. We shoved our weapons in the air and pointed them at the men. Pajarito's eyes looked ready to leave his body. He meant to leap out of the closed window behind him. His eyes glanced from me to Jerry. He looked as if he wanted to say something. He stumbled back toward a filing cabinet that stood in one corner, a Mexican serape covering its top in order to make it an end table. I knew he meant to close it. "Don't you dare, Pajarito!" I shouted, knowing that, once closed, I'd have to ask for a search warrant to get it open again. He raised his hands up high. I walked to his side. Jerry was busy shuffling the other two men out the door and toward our car. Pajarito stared hard at the three as they left.

With my gun on Pajarito, I moved next to the filing cabinet and looked down. He was a very organized crook, I had to give him that. All the files were in neat arrangement, with their little tags sticking out, telling me, like tiny captured legal documents, what each of them were. "Goodness, Pajarito, what an interesting file cabinet. You look like your own local satellite office of the United States Immigration and Naturalization Service. Biographical Information, Temporary Residence, Legal Resident, Birth Certificates, Marriage Certificates, Death Certificates—you've just got a slew of blank documents here, ready to be filled in for a price." I kept my gun in my right hand and used my left to flip through a few of the files. "Looks like you've gotten really good at making false green cards, even false American citizen documents! That's very impressive, Pajarito. How much is it to become an American citizen overnight?"

He didn't say anything. He kept his hands up. His eyes whirled around me, avoiding me every chance he could.

"I need to read you your rights, Pajarito. How would you like them, English or Spanish?"

Jerry had already packed away Daniel and Chamba in the other Taurus. He was gone. I moved the cuffed Pajarito down the hallway and ordered the backup police to secure the scene. They rolled out the yellow tapes. In a few minutes no one would be able to touch the file cabinet of evidence.

People had heard our movements. A woman peeked out of her door, the crack of the door only as open as the chain allowed. A man stuck his head up

against the window as we stepped onto the stairs outside. I'm sure he watched us all the way down. About
five people stood at the window of Doña Marina's
store, including Marina, staring at me as I led Pajarito
away.

Across the street stood a white man wearing a
large parka. His hood was down, showing his long hair
and a large earring in his left ear. He held up a camera
and was shooting away.

As I placed Pajarito in the back seat of my car, the
photographer waved at me. "I already got some of
Detective Wilson with the other two guys. Thanks."

"Fine. No problem." But I wanted him to stop
talking to me.

He didn't feel my wish. "By the way, Mr. Stapleton
wants to know when he can interview you about this."

"He can call me at the office in about an hour."

"Great. He really appreciates your help on this,
Detective."

"Fine. Fine." I slammed the door on Pajarito, then
walked around the car. The backup police cars flashed
blue over my face. I could feel every single eye that
pushed themselves against the windows of Marina's
building, watching me, someone of familiar skin, doing something so very foreign to one of our own.

CHAPTER THIRTY-ONE

PHILANTHROPIST'S EMPLOYEE
ARRESTED IN IMMIGRATION SCAM

I just smiled at the headline.

Tony Stapleton's article was very thorough. He had not only talked with me, but he had called U.S. Immigration in Memphis to ask if Pajarito was an employee of theirs, to which they said wholeheartedly, clearly, and without a doubt, no. He was not. They were also very interested in knowing how Pajarito had gotten hold of such documentation, considering that most of those found in his apartment were documents printed only by and for immigration. "This is a federal case now," said the head of immigration in Memphis. "Mr. Colibrí will no longer be in the hands of the Nashville police. He will need to contend with us." There was anger in the words, felt even on the printed page.

Then Stapleton made sure to call Mr. Rafael Murillo to ask if the well-known philanthropist had known anything about, or was even involved with, Mr. Colibrí's false paper scam. "Absolutely not," said Tekún, "and I am shaken by this news." When asked if it were true that Mr. Colibrí had worked for Mr. Murillo for several years, and if so, how was it such a shrewd, philanthropic businessman as himself could be so blind to his employee's actions, Tekún replied that sometimes even the wisest can be fooled.

Jerry walked into the office. "Good morning," he said, his smile only exacerbating his cheeriness. "You take a good picture, partner."

"As do you." I flipped again to the front page to stare once more at the two photos, me with Pajarito, Jerry carrying the other two men to the car, the police blues in the background. "It also looks like you're back in the news, Jerry."

"Yeah, well..." He said little more, but his grin gave his feelings away. This bust put a warmer public light back on him. The way he moved back and forth in front of my desk, I thought he was ready to do a jig. "I just love catching bad guys!" he exclaimed in an enthusiastic, southern falsetto.

A uniform cop approached my desk. It was Beaver, the young officer whom I had first met at the Sáenz murder scene. He looked at me with much more respect and perhaps some admiration. I allowed for this. Also, his eyes didn't fall down from my face and try to outline my body. "What's up, Officer Beaver?"

"That fellow you brought in last night. We've still got him in custody downstairs until the Feds come to cart him away. He says he wants to talk to you."

Just as he said that, my phone rang. Jerry quickly

stood up and offered to go downstairs. I thanked him, then turned to my phone. "Homicide, Chacón."

"I'm sure you're pleased with yourself this morning."

Tekún Umán. I smiled, but a muscle leapt out of my chest and up into my throat. "Good morning, Mr. Murillo."

"Not really. Not at all. You see, this is a very bad morning, *mi amor*. Very bad."

"Why should it be bad? Are you having guilty pangs about something?"

He forced a chuckle. "I have no guilt, Detective. But I am angry. I like you, Romilia. I like you a great deal. But I don't like having my name dragged through the muck, just so you can feel better about trying to bring me down."

"Mr. Murillo, if you're presuming I have some personal vendetta against you, you're mistaken. I just did my job, which last night meant collaring one of your employees. Now if you're involved in any way in Pajarito's immigration scam, then of course we would need to deal with you through the law."

"Stop that shit right now, Romi," he said. It sounded like a father reprimanding a child. My body reacted like a daughter's. "You know damn well that I have nothing to do with Pajarito's dirty-paper business. He was caught at home, you remember, not in my office. What my employees do with their private time is of no concern to me."

"Then you should be more careful who you empl..."

"You, *hija*, should be more careful where you step."

My voice froze and locked into my throat.

"I know what you want, Romilia. You want to

connect those murders to me. You're hoping that Pajarito is another link between me and Sáenz, Hatcher, and that woman, Kim. You probably even feel like you're getting closer to some truth, don't you? As if you're closing in on a catch." His voice lowered. It almost seemed warm, as if I could feel its heat through the wire. "*¡Púchica, mujer!* You have no idea what you're digging into."

I cocked an eyebrow up. The shiver that was working through me stopped momentarily.

"I suggest that you start looking elsewhere, *mi amor.*"

His continual reference to me as "his love" was getting under my skin. "I will look wherever I need to, Tekún."

"I see. Recalcitrant little lady, aren't you? Fine. Just remember, as you continue thinking that you're closing in on something, be careful that that something doesn't feel too cornered. It's liable to leap from the darkness. You should warn that new partner of yours to watch his step as well." He let that sink in, then ended with, "Always be sure whom you're dealing with. Black cats may have nine lives. But you, my dear, have one." He hung up.

The shiver turned into a clutching sensation around my windpipe. Just then Jerry walked back into the office.

"Well?" I asked, my voice obviously shaky. I decided to say nothing of the phone call until I could control the leaping muscle in my throat. "What did Pajarito want?"

Jerry shrugged his shoulders. "I go all the way downstairs just for Pajarito to tell me that Tekún Umán knew nothing about his illegal paper operation, and that he knows nothing about Umán's business deals."

Jerry picked up the paper to look again at the article. He sat down with all his weight into the chair by my desk. "He's making sure to lawyer up. I guess we won't get anything out of him about Tekún's possible drug business. Or his possible connection to the killings."

I looked down at the desk. I swallowed. My breathing fell shallow. "No," I almost whispered. "I guess we won't."

CHAPTER THIRTY-TWO

I called home and asked my mother what "*Púchica*" meant.

She laughed over the phone. It was the first time I had heard her laugh in two days. She was just happy that I had made it home last night, after busting Pajarito. Now, in the daylight, she felt less fear. "*Púchica*, it means, well, it really doesn't mean anything."

"But it's got to mean something, Mamá. You've never heard of it before?"

"Of course I have. Especially when we left El Salvador. We had to spend a month in Guatemala before crossing into Mexico. Your father had gotten robbed, so we had to work in order to get back some of our savings. He worked in construction in Guatemala City for a while. I used to tease him how he would come back home and sound like a Chapín."

So the word was Guatemalan. "Then why do they say it?"

"It's an exclamation, like the gringos say 'wow!' Like '*Púchica*, look at that good-looking man!' or '*Púchica*, can you believe the price of this chicken?' That's how they use it."

Which was exactly how Tekún Umán had used it. And Tekún was Guatemalan.

"Thanks, Mamá," I said, ready to hang up the phone.

"Wait a minute. When will you be home tonight?"

"The same time as usual, I hope."

"Just like last night, when you were out playing heroine, arresting that bird man. I see." The cheeriness was stripped from her voice. The moment she thought about night, she also thought about the Kaibiles. I had yet to catch the killer. She had yet to completely re-bury a past that had been so recently and dramatically dug up. I could almost feel her shaking her head as she hung up.

Jerry had taken a lunch break when I had called Mamá. I thought about waiting for him to come back before following up on this, but I wasn't sure when he would return. Besides, this *púchica* business was eating at me.

I drove back out to Tekún's offices and sat in my car. "This really is a long shot, girl," I muttered to myself. Or perhaps not. Either way, I sat and waited, watching the only person who moved around in the building.

Miguel Martínez pushed his mop over the front hallway floor of the old, abandoned school. I stared at him for a long while. He could not see me in the distance, not with the shade of the trees keeping my windshield dark. Clouds hung over Nashville like thick, gray metal, not allowing very much sunlight in at all. That depressed me. Then again, I was not sure what made me feel this way, the day's weather or the question that I had in my mind about this boy who now pushed the huge dust mop out the door and let the dust and debris billow away from the building's interior. He walked outside and sat down a moment to drink a cola while leaving the mop handle to rest on the cement and brick steps just outside. Though it was cool, he did not wear a jacket. He had also rolled up the sleeves of his shirt. I could see the sinewy muscles under his brown skin. He was small, but obviously strong, svelte, with not a bit of fat lining his body. He lit a cigarette and smoked it casually. Obviously, the boss was not around today. I could not tell, with Pajarito absent, if Miguel was feeling lonely. After finishing it, he dropped the butt to the ground without grinding it out. A tiny wisp of smoke left its end.

He tossed the cola can into a nearby garbage receptacle and walked back inside. I waited until I could see that he had taken a flight of stairs in order to sweep the second floor.

I left my car and walked quickly across the street and toward the steps where he had been sitting. The butt was not brown, but white. "So you and the bodyguard, Raimundo, smoke different brands," I muttered aloud. I thought back to the butt that we found in Hatcher's office. Were they both involved in something together? Yet I had no proof connecting the bodyguard to this janitor. That, for the moment, was not important. What I wanted was in the garbage bin.

I lifted the cola can carefully, wrapping it in a plastic bag and tagging it. Then I left. I almost pulled out too quickly from my parking space and barely missed the front end of a passing Toyota. He beeped at me. I ignored him.

The rest of the afternoon moved too quickly. I met with Nel Schmidt at the Fingerprints Office. Nel was a little guy, six inches shorter than I. He had little brown hairs that he tried to sweep over his white, balding skull. He took the can and leisurely dusted it, his eyes never showing anything but a sense of calmness, almost as if bored. Two pieces of toilet paper were stuck to his cheeks from a poor shave. He tossed dragon's dust onto the can, took a tiny brush made of fine fiberglass, dusted the print, took tape to it, lifted it and placed the tape onto an index card. Then he flipped through one of the legions of index files he kept organized in his office. As he pulled the one file from a box, I could see my own handwriting on it, "Sáenz Crime Scene, 2 November, cigarette wrapper, approx. twenty feet from the body."

Nel put the two index cards together and stared at them, as if trying to test his mere human sight. He smiled. Then he placed the two cards underneath a black magnifier that was equipped with a bright light and two peepholes. He stared through the lenses for a very short time. Then he raised his head up and spoke without even looking at me.

"It's a match."

Jerry seemed angry. I thought he was pissed because I had taken off without him and had made my fingerprint discovery. It probably roused the competitive spirit in him, afraid that I would make it into the papers again, but this time, ahead of him.

"So it's a match. You think this little Mexican runt is our perp, then?"

"That's the thing. He's not Mexican." Again, I

explained to him what had led me to think about Miguel Martínez: how Miguel had used that word *púchica* when I had first met him in Tekún's office three days ago, and then how Tekún himself had used the word on the phone today. "Miguel must be Guatemalan, too."

"Then why did he say he was Mexican?"

I thought this was obvious enough, but still I explained. "He's probably hiding out as a Mexican, because a Guatemalans would be more suspect of being a Kaibil."

"I thought all you people spoke the same language," he muttered. The grumble sounded acidic. "What's with this thing about different words in different countries?"

This ticked off something in me, especially his phrase "you people." "It's just like here, Jerry. Southerners say 'you all,' northerners say 'you guys.'"

He didn't seem to hear the anger in my voice, so caught up was he with this new find. "And you think Miguel is the Kaibil?"

"What do you think? His print was found at the murder scene. We've verified that. Who else could that point to?" Then I thought about the boy, how he looked, his body. "He's small, but he's in good shape. He looks capable enough of doing something to someone."

"If that's the case, then we better be careful with him," said Jerry. "I mean, if he's a Kaibil, then he's been well trained. Backup would be wise."

I thought back to Sáenz's body and its doughnut-formed head. Then I thought back to the slit throats I had read about on the other two victims. My mind drifted back to the photographs Jerry and I had seen on the Internet, ones that depicted the work of death squads back in Guatemala, how they carved up people before killing them off. I thought of Gato Negro's stomach with its carved word, then Tekún Umán's threat to me this morning, of black cats having nine lives, my having only one. As the pieces fell into place, they did so quickly. Up to this point I had been concerned about the bulky, muscular, threatening presence of Tekún's bodyguard, Raimundo. But if the reports on the Kaibiles were true, Raimundo was not the one to be frightened of. Now, with Tekún's words still whispering in my ear about my own life, I thought about that boy Miguel, and wondered if he had already talked with his boss and had already been given new instructions—about me.

"Yes. Backup would be very wise," I said.

We returned to Tekún's office. All the lights were off. Miguel was just leaving the building.

Jerry and I got out of our car. To my far left I saw two more detectives leave their vehicle, as did two more to my far right. The three sets of us closed in on him. The building was behind him. It would take a strong sprint for him to get between any of us. Then I thought, Kaibiles no doubt were trained in fast running, as well as endurance. He could run. Could he also attack? I kept my nine-millimeter behind me, held tucked in my lower back. Jerry did the same with his pistol. All the other men in our backup crew were armed. We had put on vests under our coats. Six of us against him. Those were good odds. Just as long as his training was not better.

He looked down at the sidewalk, shook his head, then turned back to the building. Shoving the key into the door, he opened it and walked back in. "Shit," I said aloud. "You think he saw us coming?"

"I don't know," said Jerry. "Maybe he just forgot something. But he did go in pretty quickly."

Jerry and I arrived first at the door. I took the knob and opened it wide, walked in, holding my pistol before me, my body tight from my ankles to my forehead. Outside wind pushed around the door and tousled my loose hair over my eyes. I cursed, wishing I had tied my hair back today, hoping it would not get in my way right now, in a time when getting in the way could mean too much.

The entire building was dark. Miguel had not turned on a light, as if knowing the building too well to need lights. Though it appeared that he had forgotten something, that could have been a ruse, as he was now inside and nowhere to be seen. I climbed a small set of stairs that stretched the entire width of the foyer, then walked around a corner of the hallway toward the main office. The light there was not on. But the door was open.

I nudged up to the door and moved my nose around it to look inside. Nothing. I flashed around, my gun ahead of me, pointing at the four corners of the room. Jerry came up from behind. I could hear his rapid breath. The door to the long hall that led to Tekún's opulent office was open. I moved toward it and edged myself down the hallway to the other open door that, now with my eyes accustomed to the darkness, I could see was open. From that opening I heard a noise. Objects moved about. Something hard dropped against the floor. "*Ay Dios*," said the voice to itself. If something had dropped, that meant he was probably squatting down to pick it up, which would be my chance. I took it. I stepped through the open door, held my gun to the darkness, and yelled "*¡Deténgase!*"

His mouth let out a yelp. He was bent over, as I

had predicted. As he stood back up, I saw the flash of
metal in his hand, long and sharp, barely reflecting the
streetlight just outside the window. "*¡Suéltelo!*" I yelled,
telling him to drop it. He either did not hear me, or he
froze. Jerry came from behind and yelled, "Drop it,
you son of a bitch!" and he cocked back his gun. I
thought he was about to fire. Perhaps Miguel thought
the same, as he dropped both objects, the metal letter
opener and the can of cola. Both hit the floor. The can
rolled slightly. Then Miguel hit the floor himself. He
yelped. He said in Spanish, "Don't hurt me, please. I
did nothing wrong, nothing wrong." No one, of
course, but I could understand. The rest of the crew
walked in, their pistols drawn. Yet I drew down, sensing that my aim was not necesssary now, not with this
boy sniveling and shaking on the floor.

CHAPTER THIRTY-THREE

Miguel sat in the box. For half an hour we watched through the one-way mirror.

"I don't know," said Jerry. "He doesn't act much like my picture of a Kaibil."

Though I said nothing, I had to agree. From the moment we had brought him in, Miguel Martínez was, for lack of better word, a sniveling, cowardly, sorrowful wretch of a suspect. He offered no resistance, even when we carefully had approached him in Tekún's office and had told him to get away from the large letter opener that he had picked up off the floor.

It seemed obvious now that the only reason he had returned to the office was to retrieve an empty cola can that he had left on Tekún's table while cleaning. The guy was a carbonated beverage addict. Even now, as he sat there, the only thing that he had asked for was a cola. We watched him as he drank the whole thing down, while he barely turned his head right and left to look around at the small room, darting his eyes to the only door, waiting for one of us to walk through it. Jerry had given it to him half an hour ago. "It's got caffeine in it. He'll need to take a piss. That'll keep him antsy."

"He does seem too spindly to be a murderer, doesn't he?" I said. "Not the violent killer that a Kaibil has been trained to be."

"Yeah, well, this may be all an act, you know?" hypothesized Jerry. He pushed his fingers through his blond hair. His matt of hair seemed to have taken on an even more disheveled look in the past couple of days. He also had forgotten to shave this morning. "Maybe he's just putting this show on for us. Maybe," and his voice turned with the lilt of a developing theory, "just maybe, he's a psychopath. A serial killer. You know, he was traumatized as a child, hit in the head one too many times, which damaged his brain. The psychology of a serial killer is planted in him. Then he gets this training from his own army, and he's a true fighting machine. He's later hired by Tekún, who's a Guatemalan. Maybe this kid only takes orders from fellow Guatemalans."

I shrugged my shoulders. "If that's the case, he's a good actor. Look at him. The true essence of a spineless man."

Jerry put his hands in his pockets. "Why don't you let me lean on him?"

He seemed to be asking for my permission. "What's your thinking?"

"Well, if he's playing a game with us, maybe I can shock him out of it."

I only saw one obstacle. "He only speaks Spanish."

"Fine. You translate. I'll ask the questions. He may

feel even more frightened, seeing me through the language barrier."

I wasn't at first sure what he meant by that, but I agreed. I had interrogated the two men yesterday. Even though I was ready to take on Miguel, I also knew how important it was to keep peace with my partner. I let him have his turn. Besides, he had a point: maybe a good jolt of hard interrogation would crack the boy.

Jerry headed to the box. He grinned at me, showing me all his teeth. "You ready?" he asked. I walked ahead of him.

Miguel jumped the moment I opened the door. He stared at me, then turned away, then stared at me again. I said to him, in Spanish, that I was going to translate the questions that my partner had for him. Then I said this to Jerry in English.

"Good," said Jerry. He smiled at me. "Ready?"

"Ready."

"Fine. Miguel, is that your real name?"

I translated. Miguel said yes.

"Then what's the deal about you saying you're Mexican when it's so obvious that you're Guatemalan?"

It had been a while since I had last translated orally. It was difficult, in the split second, to find something appropriate for "what's the deal" in Spanish. Still, I leaned the translation hard on Miguel, "*y por qué demonios la mentira,*" and continued.

Miguel asked how was it that they knew he was Guatemalan? I said this to Jerry.

"You're not the one asking the questions, boy! You just answer mine!" Jerry walked around the sitting Miguel as I kept up with the words. "You're Miguel Martínez, you're Guatemalan, but you say you're

Mexican. What's the matter, you ashamed of your heritage or something? Is it embarrassing to be Guatemalan?"

Miguel said that he was not embarrassed to be Guatemalan. His voice shook. I kept mine deadpan, stripped of either man's emotion.

"Then there must be something wrong about Guatemala for you to not claim it. Did you do something wrong back there? Are there people back there who would like to find you? Or maybe you had affiliations with some people that you'd like to tell us about. Such as the Kaibiles. You've heard of the Kaibiles, haven't you, Miguel?"

Miguel said that he had.

"Then tell me about them. What kind of people are they? They're soldiers, right? But a special kind of soldier, I believe... what was it you and I had read about the Kaibiles, Detective Chacón... ah, yes, that their motto is 'We are killing machines.' Isn't that what we read? Come on, Miguel, tell us what you know about them."

At first he said nothing. Then Jerry's open hand popped the back of the boy's head. I jerked in my chair. But I said nothing.

"You know about the Kaibiles, Miguel. Tell me about them."

I thought he was going to cry. But he did not. Miguel sucked in a thick breath, then muttered something: *Son diablos.* I translated, They are devils.

"That sounds like an apt description, I'd say. Devils. Bloodthirsty. Killing machines." Jerry then walked about one more time and leaned over, as if to whisper into Miguel's ear. "You've probably heard there's a possibility that one or two Kaibiles are visiting our beloved capital city of Nashville, haven't you? Anything

you could tell us about that, Miguel? Tell me, why
would trained death-squad soldiers ever want to come
to Nashville, Tennessee? What is it, the climate? It's
pretty cold now, not much like Guatemala. Or maybe
they were brought here. Maybe they were hired by
someone to do certain types of work in the area. What
do you think?"

Miguel's voice quivered, saying he knew nothing
of this.

"You know what, Miguel? I think you're a goddamn liar." Jerry smiled when he said this. Though I
fidgeted slightly in my chair, I had to admit that I was
fascinated by his cruelty. This was cruel; yet perhaps
Miguel's own possible malice deserved such a grilling.

"I think you're lying, Miguel, because there are
three Nashvillians dead and gone, all three very good
citizens. One a doctor, the other a nurse, the third a reporter. All dead either from gunshots or from their
necks getting slit open. You heard about them, I'm
sure. Dr. Lawrence Hatcher. Ms. Pamela Kim. Mr.
Diego Sáenz. All very mysterious killings, indeed."

Just as he said this, a tear formed in Miguel's left
eye. I'm sure the other would follow suit. His face
squinted tight, his lips pulled toward each cheek. Jerry
kept going. I kept translating. "Mysterious, except for
one thing. A cigarette wrapper, with blood on it, with
a perfectly formed fingerprint on it. Found nearby
Sáenz's dead body. And you know what? It fits your fingerprint to a T."

Miguel broke. His tears burst from his face. His
mouth opened wide. Yet his caught breath would not
allow a scream to come out, like a child who has been
hurt on the playground, held in that one moment of
silent pain before an inevitable bellow could burst

forth. Finally, words did come forth, through the chokes of a cry: "I didn't kill him, I didn't kill Diego."

The moment I translated this, Jerry stood up again, looking straight down at Miguel's crown. "Diego? So you knew him?"

Miguel nodded his head up and down. "Yes, yes, I did."

It was then that a story came out. He choked it out, fighting with the contortions of his own throat and lungs to tell us. I translated the entire thing, keeping it a direct translation, saying "I" instead of "he says that," as if Miguel's voice were mine. Only mine was stripped of the emotion, the obvious chaos.

"We were good friends. Diego and I. He hung out a lot in the neighborhood with us. He and I would go to movies together, even though I didn't understand any of the words. We'd go shopping together. He once took me up to his newspaper place, where he works. I liked him a lot. He was the only one I trusted about me being Guatemalan, though I didn't tell him that I had gotten my fake Mexican papers from Pajarito... You see, Guatemalans, we can't get residency here, unless we have a lot of money. But Pajarito did not charge me. His boss, Mr. Umán, told him not to let me pay."

I wanted to get that down on paper, and follow up with some questions. He had just confessed that Tekún Umán knew something about Pajarito's immigration paper scam. But I was translator. My job was to be the conduit, keeping the translation as pure as possible. I could stop for nothing.

"Mr. Umán took to me, I suppose, because he's Guatemalan, too, by blood. I like Mr. Umán. But then Diego started asking me questions about him. He said he thought that Mr. Umán was involved in drugs somehow, and asked if I knew anything. I told him I

didn't. I hated hearing that about Mr. Umán, because
he had been good to me. Then those two people got
killed, the nurse and the doctor. Diego said he knew
about the killings, that he had learned even more about
them—the doctor was involved in some drug operation. He was selling drugs, like cocaine, to his patients.
I'm not sure about it all, but it was something like that.
Then he said that even Pajarito was involved. I didn't
want to believe that..."

Though Jerry did not interrupt him, he leaned
over the table. His eyebrows formed a bridge over his
eyes, a place to allow a hot anger to rest upon. Where
this anger was coming from, I was not exactly sure. His
unkempt hair and two-day shadow on his strong jaw
lent to the rage. Perhaps the anger was the frustration
of closing in on a killer, only to have the suspect try to
talk his way out of suspicion. Any detective will tell you
that the longer a case drags out, the more it works on
your nerves. This case was now three days old. Jerry's
eyebrows almost contorted, as if forming an image of
nerves themselves.

Miguel dared not look up. He kept telling the tale,
as if to speak were his salvation. "A few days later,
Diego said that he was onto something big. He believed that the doctor and the nurse were murdered by
a paid killer, or something like that..."

I couldn't help it. I broke my translation and asked
him, "*Y ¿no dijo nada de los kaibiles?*" for which I translated quickly to Jerry, "And he didn't tell you anything
about the Kaibiles?" Jerry snapped his angry eyes at
me. I was not sure if it was just a continuation of his
growing rage, or perhaps he was miffed at me for in-
terrupting my own translation.

"No," said Miguel, "he never said anything about
them." This sounded resolute. Being Guatemalan,

Miguel surely would have remembered something about that. This also seemed strange: Sáenz told Miguel so much, yet said nothing about a death squad.

"When was the last time you saw Diego?" Jerry barked.

"The night he was murdered," I translated, listening to Miguel's every word. "He came to my apartment after work. I invited him in for a beer, but he didn't want to drink anything. He was really, really scared. He said he had a tip on the killer. I asked him what he meant, because the killer had been caught by the police. No, said Diego, he had not been caught. He was still out there. Diego said that he and a *compañero* of his were going to go down to the river that night, that the *compa* had some information on the killer showing up there. He said that the meeting would nail the final proof on the fact that Tekún Umán was guilty of the killings. I told him he was crazy, that he shouldn't get near any killer like that. But as nervous as he was, he was also excited. He was a reporter, you know. That sort of thing was important to him. He said he was going to go after midnight."

I had not translated *compañero* to Jerry, nor its diminutive form, *compa*, as it was one of those solid Spanish words that loses meaning in the translation.

"What's that word mean?" Jerry asked, his own voice shaking.

"It's like 'companion,' or 'partner,' only stronger." I was about to ask Miguel who the *compañero* was. But he kept telling the story.

"I couldn't even sleep that night. I was pleading with Diego not to go down there. What business did he have tracking down a killer, something that would put him in danger? But he insisted on going. He said he would take some protection with him, that he could get hold of a gun. Then he left. I couldn't sleep. I tossed in my bed all night. I mean, I didn't want to believe that Tekún Umán was guilty of the killings. But I didn't want my friend to get hurt. Then, sometime after midnight, I left my apartment and started walking."

Miguel's voice vibrated with the continuation of the tale. I was afraid that his voice would rattle away before he ended it. "I knew the place Diego was talking about, because he and I had gone down there with some kids from the neighborhood for a picnic one day. It was a long walk. I think I ran most of the way. I was exhausted when I got there. I walked into the trees and looked over and could barely see Diego's red car. It was really dark, and the only streetlight was way in the back, so all I could see were shadows. But I could tell it was Diego by his shape. He had just stepped out of the car. He held something in his hand. I figured it was a pistol. Then he pointed it at me while he fished around in his coat for his phone. He was dialing it and aiming the gun right at me. I figured he had seen me. But I was in the shadows, so he couldn't see me completely. Then I heard a car pull up nearby. I was just about to yell out to him, you know, 'Hey, Diego, it's me, Miguel!' so he wouldn't shoot me, but just then someone came up from behind Diego. Diego swung around with the pistol in his hand. I thought he was going to shoot the other person. But he didn't. He first laughed, then almost greeted the other man. Then he started talking really fast in English, and I thought he was about ready to point at me, when it happened."

Miguel choked. A bellow came out. I waited. My brain was both tired and excited, like an exhausted animal being touched with a cattle prod. Then Miguel worked through the next part.

"The other person's arm lashed out. His hand

grabbed Diego's hand, the one with the gun in it. At first I didn't know what was happening, until the man jerked Diego's hand up to Diego's face, and then it looked like he grabbed Diego by the waist to hold him. I don't think Diego had a chance to react, because then, that was when the gunshot...Oh, god... Oh, god."

Jerry's patience, if he had any left over, disintegrated. "Come on, Miguel, spit it out, what happened? Did you see the guy? What did he look like?" Jerry leaned in on him.

"I don't know...he wore strange clothes. He had a hat on, one that covered his ears and the sides of his face. And his coat, I guess it was a coat, it was huge, almost like a tent or something. It reflected the light of the streetlamp."

Plastic, I thought. The killer wore plastic, like a poncho. If any of this was true.

"Then the man lowered Diego to the ground. I couldn't see what he was doing then, because his big shadow was in my way. I was scared. I hid there, doing nothing, hoping that my friend was alive, hoping this killer would go away so I could help Diego. Then the killer turned to me. I think he must have heard me, but then I hid deeper in the trees. Then he took off. I heard a car start. Then I ran up to Diego.

"Blood was everywhere. I stopped about five feet away from him, and looked down. I could tell he was dead. He was dead. But I dropped down on my knees and tried to help him. I touched his face, behind his head, to help him up, but I felt his hair, it was all wet. I got up, and I ran. I ran back to the trees, I think I fell a couple of times. The only thing there was a wall, and I jumped over it, and before I knew it, I had fallen into freezing cold water. I thought I was going to drown. I fought for what seemed like forever, then made it back to the bank."

Jerry just stared at him for a long time. It took him almost a full minute to formulate his following words.

"You mean to tell me that you just happened to be in the area when Sáenz was murdered? That you hid out and saw the whole thing?"

I translated. Miguel shook his head up and down.

At first Jerry said, almost casually, with a grin, "Well, I must say, some fish stories are meant to be entertaining." Then his fist flew through the air between Miguel and me and cracked against the table. I jumped back, scooting my chair two inches. Miguel also jumped, with a cry leaping from his throat. "So you're just damned innocent of killing Diego Sáenz, right?" Though startled by the blow, I resumed the translation. "You say you knew Sáenz, but you didn't kill him. You mean to tell me that some mystery man came up from behind Sáenz and grabbed Sáenz's own hand and forced it up against his head, not you. You didn't kill Sáenz, just like you didn't kill Hatcher or Kim. You didn't stick a jade pyramid down into Sáenz's brains after blowing his head off, did you? You're just as innocent as Jesus Christ himself!"

Though I was flowing again, my translation nipped at itself, like an old phonograph record whose needle has jumped. My brain rattled about, looking for the line of the words, trying to catch up to what my partner was saying. Yet my brain also crackled, as if other thoughts wished to break through the translation. It was weariness, no doubt, a crack in the conduit of interpretation.

Jerry finished his rant. I caught up with it. Then Miguel just whispered, "I didn't do it. I didn't kill him." He broke down into a mournful weeping.

Jerry leaned over him. "Okay, little man. Let me tell you something. You're saying that Mr. Sáenz suspected Tekún Umán about possible drug selling. And that the good Doctor Hatcher was a drug dealer, too. If this is the case, and if your story's true, then you ought to be willing to prove it."

Both Miguel and I looked up at my partner. I, too, was wondering which way Jerry was going.

"As far as I'm concerned, Miguel, you're guilty," he continued. "That fingerprint we found at the crime scene, the one dipped in Sáenz's blood, tells me the whole story. And the story is much different from yours. You killed Sáenz." All through this Miguel was moaning over and over again, "No, I didn't, I did not." But Jerry kept on. "You're toast, Miguel. You're toast. Unless you can bring us to Tekún Umán. Prove to us your innocence by showing us his guilt."

After I translated this, Miguel looked up at Jerry for the first time, staring him straight in the eye.

CHAPTER THIRTY-FOUR

I leaned up against the wall next to the water dispenser and waited for my brain to drain out of my ear. Simultaneous oral translation always has that effect on me afterwards, the feeling that a giant pile of tied logs has washed through my skull, pounding my gray-celled sponge into a lumpy mush. I barely glanced over through the interrogation box window to see Jerry wiring up Miguel. The young man raised his arms up so that my partner could get the microphone properly installed, with the transmitter/recorder tucked back into his pants.

"Great job, Romilia," Jerry said as he rushed by me. "Your translating skills are incredible. I've never heard such a flow. I felt like I was in a U.N. meeting."

"Is that so? I felt like we were in the ring with Mike Tyson, with two ears already hanging from his teeth."

"Oh, it wasn't so bad, was it? I just had to lean on

him a little bit. Sometimes that's necessary. But don't worry. I'm not that way with every suspect."

I rubbed my forehead. "So, do you believe his story?"

"I don't know. Maybe. I'm hoping that the shadowy stranger who he saw shoot Sáenz was Mr. Umán, of course."

"But what we know of Tekún, he's not going to do the dirty work himself. One of his hired guns is more likely to do it."

"Oh, his hands are dirty, all right. I can feel it. We'll pin him."

I wanted to argue, as I saw Tekún Umán as a veritable Teflon President, someone who keeps his own workers far enough away not to let guilty blood splash on his lapels. But Jerry was too ready to get this sting operation going to talk about such obstacles.

The sting would happen that same night. Before finishing the interrogation, we got some practical information out of Miguel. He said that, as it was Thursday, Tekún Umán would return to his office and work on his financial records. "That's why I went back into his office," he had told us. "I had left a cola can on one of his tables. He would have been upset finding it along with all his antique pieces." It was Tekún's habit to take one night a week to get through the paperwork that only he could do. Miguel also told us that tonight was the one night his bodyguard had off. "Raimundo won't be with him," he had said, "because on Thursdays he always likes to go to mass." Though I smirked at this, it also ticked me. If this boy, Miguel, was not guilty of any of the crimes that had recently occurred, the first person that came to mind was the large, crude bodyguard. What did the guy do, confess

his sins about taking young boys and throwing them
up against barbed-wire fences?

The bodyguard's absence excited Jerry. "It'll make
our job easier." He ushered Miguel out of the interrogation box, actually treating the boy nicer than before.
You wouldn't know this was the same guy who had
slammed his fist against the table, almost cracking it
in two.

Jerry checked into the locker room to suit up. I
drank more water and rested while my mind tried to
land upon the earth of one language, after having spent
the past hour flying about in the hurricane winds
of two.

Miguel made the call to Tekún Umán, verifying
that the man was in his office. He asked his boss for an
appointment to speak about a personal matter. Tekún
agreed. I was listening in on another line. Miguel did
not give too much away, though his voice trembled
slightly. Tekún asked no questions.

We drove back to Tekún's building. The light was
on in the oval office, as was the one in the receptionist
area. But the curtains were drawn.

Jerry ordered Miguel out of the car. "You think I
should tail behind him?" he asked me.

I thought about it. As shaky as Miguel was, he
could easily choose to sprint. "Could be a good idea.
But I need to stay with the earphones. I'm sure they'll
speak in Spanish. Just keep back, make sure Miguel
gets in, then out, without Tekún seeing you. Then
usher our friend here back to the car."

"Right." Jerry shut the door. He nudged Miguel
ahead, then started walking about ten paces behind the
boy. They moved in and out of the shadows of the oak
trees, making it difficult for me to see them.

I watched them disappear into the shadows, then turned up the sound on the earphones. "You just take it easy, son," Jerry's voice came clearly through the microphone. Two pats also came through. I envisioned Jerry's hand on Miguel's shoulder. "Now go on in. I'll be right here at the door. Go on." Miguel probably didn't understand the words, though he said *"Vaya pues,"* and walked on. I heard his steps down the hallway. A door opened and did not close. Then the low sound of metal runners, like those of a file cabinet, pulled through the frequency. Miguel's steps continued.

I hoped he was ready for this. We had coached Miguel on some questions and statements to make, regarding his "fear" of the Kaibiles, as he was Guatemalan and was afraid that maybe they would come after him. He could also ask about Pajarito, as if concerned over his friend's fate with the Feds, perhaps getting Tekún to speak about his own relationship with the falsifier of immigration documents. But the more I thought about it, the more I believed that Miguel would probably walk out of there with nothing after a long, winding, and exhausting conversation. Why would a high-stakes drug boss share information with a peon janitor?

Then again, I was surprised that Tekún consented to see the man this evening. Perhaps there was a bond between them that I did not know about. Tekún had ordered Pajarito not to charge Miguel for falsifying his Mexican papers. That action in itself said a great deal. And Miguel did not want to believe anything bad of his boss. Perhaps, through this *confianza*, we could walk away with something solid.

I would never find out. It happened before I even had a chance to tense myself up in the car seat. Miguel

knocked on a door. I could hear his nervous knuckles
rap five times. "*Pase adelante*," said Tekún on the other
side, his voice muffled by the wooden door. The door
opened. I could imagine Tekún looking up from his
desk, writing on a pad of paper or signing his name to
a document, barely glancing up to say "*Ey, Miguelito,
¿qué tal, vos?*" Tekún's words sounded friendly, a ben-
evolent boss speaking to an employee. Then it all
changed, with Tekún's growling voice saying, "What
the hell . . . ?"

Shots burst through the earphones, two of them,
one immediately after the other. Two more shots blew
from a different gun. I could tell this by the sound of
the caliber. But the four shots rang in my head like
sharp, piercing gongs. Then came my partner's voice,
swift, loud, running into the room, "Stop! Police! No,
Miguel, don't!" But there was a fifth shot. My partner
screamed.

"Jesus Christ!" I ripped the headphones off and
called for backup on the car radio. I screamed at the
dispatcher to send blues out to Tekún's office, along
with paramedics, for an officer was possibly down. I
jumped from the car and ran to the building, hearing
through the night air and the building's muffling
walls two more shots. "Oh, god, Oh, god, *¿qué te pasa,
Jerry?*"

The door ricocheted off my palms and slammed
against the wall. I stumbled through the dark halls
and into the receptionist room, then headed toward
the long hallway that led to Tekún's oval office. I ran.
Something smacked against my thigh and knocked a
curse out of my mouth. It was an open file cabinet. I
dodged around it and ran again, then fell to my feet
and snatched my gun from the ankle holster. I approached Tekún's door. There was no other shot. I

heard groaning. It was Jerry. This made me push through the door faster than procedure would have demanded. But he was my partner. I was too young to lose my first partner.

The low, subtle light of Tekún's office showed everything. To the left of the door squatted Jerry, his right hand covering a bloody stain on his left coat sleeve. There, in front of me, a little to my right, upon the dragon's belly of the expensive carpet, lay Miguel. His white shirt bloomed a crimson stain over his chest. Dangling in his right fingers was a fairly large pistol, what I thought was a forty-five. And there, on the opposite side of the office's round circumference, at his desk, sat Tekún Umán. He too had stains on his chest and lower abdomen, though they were smaller.

Jerry looked up at me as if a ghost ran across his face. I thought he was going to pass out. "Shit," he muttered, "god almighty..."

He had been hit in the upper arm. It looked like the bullet had passed completely through, ripping through a shallow part, plowing just underneath the skin. It looked bad. I helped him get his coat off to look at the wound, then tore at his sleeve, exposing his sinewy, wounded arm.

"... can't believe it, I just damned can't believe it," he kept saying. His voice shuddered.

"Just take it easy, Jerry. We'll get you taken care of." I took the ripped sleeve and used it as a bandage, pressing it hard against the entrance and exit wounds.

"Where the hell'd he get a gun?" Jerry asked, the first complete sentence since getting shot.

"God knows," I said, dabbing his forehead with another piece of the sleeve. "What happened?"

"I just watched Miguel walk in and down the hallway. Then a few seconds later I heard gunshots. So I ran down and saw Miguel there, a pistol in his hand, shooting away at Tekún. But then there was Tekún, with a gun himself, Jesus, and he starts shooting it out with Miguel. I guess, with his bodyguard off for the night, he packs a pistol. I yelled 'Police,' then saw that Miguel was turning around on me. I yelled at him, but he shot at me. I got two shots off before I realized that he had hit me."

He started to look faint. I yelled at the room, "Come on, damnit, where is the ambulance?" Just then the sirens began. They sounded like mechanical angels swooping down. The backup police arrived at the same time.

"You know," I said, "when I first ran down the hall, I slammed into an open file cabinet."

"Yeah, so did I. What about it?"

I turned and looked toward the door. "You okay?" I asked. He nodded his head. "I'll be right back." I ran down the hall, flipped on a light and looked at the file cabinet. There, in the back part of the cabinet, was an open box half filled with forty-five-caliber bullets. A number of the bullets had rolled around the bottom of the cabinet, no doubt from where both Jerry and I had hit it while running inside.

"Check it out," I said. I showed him the box of bullets.

"Damn," muttered Jerry, "the bastard had the gun hidden ... but why? Why did he want to kill Tekún?"

I just shook my head. "I have no idea. Unless he went off the deep end, thinking that Tekún had killed his friend Diego."

Jerry said nothing, but he shook his head in half understanding.

The ambulance pulled up through the front yard. Within a few minutes the paramedics worked around

Jerry, making sure he was not hit anywhere else. I stepped back, knowing that I was worthless now.

I turned to the scene to freeze it up in my head. Miguel lay faceup, his dead eyes staring themselves into that final relaxation. He had fallen right where he had been standing after shooting at Jerry. There, behind the desk, sat Tekún. One of the paramedics squatted over Miguel, checking his eyes and his pulse. Another walked over to the desk, looked down at Tekún, then jerked his head back to me and his two partners. "We got a live one here!"

Jerry looked up. So did I. We stared at Tekún, whose stunned look had momentarily fooled me for death. Yet he did not move. His body had slipped into shock. The paramedics swarmed around him, hooking drips into him, ripping his shirt off to get to the entrance wounds. Another paramedic took Jerry by his good arm and helped him toward the door. He hit a light switch on the way out to give the other paramedics more light to work with. The light helped me see two tiny holes in the perfectly formed, smooth white finish of Tekún's round office walls. It was no wonder that Tekún had missed Miguel, as Miguel had already hit him twice in the chest. I stared at the two holes for barely ten seconds, measuring them about a foot to the right of the door. Then I stared at Jerry's back as the paramedic took him down the hall.

"My jacket," he said, barely pointing back with his face, "please get my jacket."

"Don't worry, Detective," said the paramedic, "we'll get you a blanket in the ambulance. No way we're going to let you get chilled."

He still asked for his jacket. I picked it up from where I had placed it on one of Tekún's chairs. "Don't worry, Jerry," I said, smiling at him as he moved down the hall. "I'll hold it for you." I held the jacket up for him to see.

The other workers had Tekún strapped to a stretcher. They had an oxygen mask strapped to his head, a bottle of glucose drip and its thin tube impaling his arm. They talked brusquely to one another, almost yelling orders out about calling Vanderbilt Hospital to prepare the ER for a possible shock victim with two bullet wounds to the chest, one just below the thorax, the other in the left pulmonary tract. I stepped out of their way. Then I stared at Tekún's closed eyes.

"Don't die," I whispered.

The paramedics almost ran Tekún through the door. The ambulance's siren once again pierced the cool November night air. Its red lights slapped up against the window of this office. Other paramedics worked more slowly with Miguel's dead body. Then they were gone. The backup boys worked to secure the area, cordoning off the doors with yellow ribbon. I stayed behind and looked once more at the scene of the crime, always returning to those two bullet holes in the white wall.

CHAPTER THIRTY-FIVE

As a college student, I had taken a class in simultaneous, oral translation. It was one of the more demanding classes of my college career. Though I spoke both my languages fluently, I realized that to take others' words and interpret them, placing them into correct, intelligible sequence in the other language, taxed me in a way that no other brain exercise did. Not algebra. Nor memory games. Not even mind puzzles. The teacher stated our goal was to translate ninety-eight percent of the words being said. Our skulls were a living, pulsing beaker where the alchemy took place. Phrases in one language became coherent statements in the other. Sayings, such as "Getting caught between a rock and a hard place" would make no sense in Spanish, so we had to train ourselves to find, as quickly as possible, the most appropriate saying in the other language (in this case, *entre la espada y la pared,* or "standing between the sword and the wall"). All this had to be done within seconds. Our translation, the professor challenged us, should stay about one half-phrase behind the original speaker.

He also warned us that our position within an oral simultaneous interpretation was to be neutral. We could not participate in the conversation itself for it to be a true translation. In being neutral, we were to embody the voices of the speakers, talking in the first person, just as they did. "Usually you will come out of these sessions remembering little to nothing of what was said," he told us. "This is a good sign. It means you were being pure in your work. But if you do remember something from the conversation, your translation was, no doubt, at that point faltering." He also suggested to us that we drink no alcohol nor coffee afterward, as either could throw us into a mucky cauldron of melancholy or a stirred-up, frenetic, electrified fury of nerves. "I suggest chamomile tea and a mystery book in order to calm down."

He was full of such suggestions and advice. As the years passed, I began to see how he was right in almost all of them. The moment of remembering, for instance: I could see where I had failed, had faltered, within the translation between Jerry Wilson and Miguel Martínez, for I remembered pieces of the conversation. Pieces that would not let me go.

I sat in a small office on the first floor of the precinct. It was quiet down here. It was eleven p.m. Even though there were few people on the homicide floor at the time, I wanted to be able to hear nothing but the tape recorder. Other cops and detectives had used this room for a variety of reasons, everything from listening to tapes to getting away from ringing phones and demanding lieutenants for just a few minutes with a cup of coffee. They all called it the Ghost Room, as it was so desolate, with no furniture except for the desk and its chair.

There was a lone phone in the abandoned office. I called Doc Callahan. He was not there. I left a message on his machine, asking him to call me back as soon as possible, and if he could, please have in hand the Sáenz autopsy report. Then I gave him the number to the Ghost Room.

I turned to the tiny tape recorder/transmitter that had been tucked into Miguel's pants. I had taken the apparatus from his dead body, unhooking it from the microphone and extracting it from his pants pocket. "McCabe will have my ass for this," I thought. Then again, maybe McCabe would do absolutely nothing.

The transmitter held two miniature cassettes. I took out the one that was partly filled with the recording of the shooting. Then I put the transmitter with the second mini-cassette into my purse. I had the illusion of sneaking it back onto Miguel's body right after this.

I had brought down a larger, hand-sized tape recorder from the office. I plugged the cassette into it and listened, with no need for earphones. The little speaker tried to fill the Ghost Room.

"Ey, *Miguelito, ¿qué tal, vos?* . . . What the hell . . . ?"

I listened to each and every gunshot, two high-sounding shots from a forty-five, two distant shots from Tekún's thirty-eight, Wilson's frightened, harsh voice, "Stop! Police! No, Miguel, don't . . . !" cut by the fifth shot that had made Wilson scream and had made me drop the earphones and run in. Then I heard clearly what I had heard through the muffling walls of Tekún's building, a sixth shot, a long pause of perhaps forty seconds, and a seventh shot. Then came the groans from my downed partner.

I rewound the tape and played it again, this time paying more attention to each shot, distinguishing them one from the other.

The first two shots, a forty-five.

The immediate second two, a thirty-eight.

Jerry's yelled orders of "Stop! Police!"

The fifth, a nine-millimeter parabellum. Jerry's scream.

Pause.

The sixth, a nine-millimeter parabellum.

Pause.

The seventh, the forty-five.

"Oh, Jesus Christ..."

The phone rang. It was Doc. "What's up, Romi?" He was cheerful. I could not afford to be.

"Doc. Tell me, where do you think the jade pyramid was on Sáenz's body?"

"What? You found it on the ground, Romi. Between the bricks."

"I know, I know. But it fell out of his body. I'm thinking it fell out of the top hole in his skull."

"That's funny. I thought it would have been in Sáenz's mouth, just like the other two victims." He flipped through a file. I could hear the pages. "Let's see ... I don't see it written down here anywhere. Since you found it outside of the body, it wouldn't really be part of the autopsy."

"Yeah, but what about the pyramid itself? Didn't you give me the stats on it the other day? When you told me about the blood on it, that it matched Sáenz's?"

"Okay, okay, let me see. Are you all right? You sound like you're hyperventilating."

"I'm fine. I just need to clear something up."

"Here it is. Yes. I remember, my assistant did the work-up on it, while you and I were at the prison, cutting down Benny. Here." He started mumbling through some technical forensic phrases that I didn't understand. But then he read something that I did. "Traces of brain tissue found, along with blood verified as A negative. It also says that some tiny slivers of bone fragments from the parietal were stuck on the pyramid's base. That's the bone on top of the skull. So. I guess it was placed in Sáenz's head, and not in his mouth. How did you know that, Romilia? Romilia?"

"I didn't know that. Not until tonight." My hand moved by itself to hang up the phone. I heard him yelp "Wait a minute!" But I had to make a final call, one that would answer rampaging questions.

"*The Cumberland Journal*," the voice of a woman reporter answered.

I explained who I was. Then I asked the reporter to do me a favor. "Please get to Mr. Sáenz's computer and turn it on."

"Sure, Detective. But I can't go any farther than that. I don't know what his password was."

"It was *pendejo*." Then I spelled it for her, all the while my heart threatening to explode and blow right out of my throat.

"Okay. I'm in. But I think I better call Mr. Stapleton before I go any farther, Detective Chacón. You know, for permission to open these files."

"You don't need to open any of them, ma'am," I said, "just look for a file named 'Kaibil' and tell me the last time it was opened."

She did. "Let's see. November first."

"You're sure?"

"Sure I'm sure. The date's right after the name of the file. November first."

I drew short breaths, knowing that we had opened that empty file on November third. "Tell me, ma'am, what's the date up in the corner of the screen?"

"Well, it should be November fifth, that's today's date... No, wait a minute. This computer's wrong. It's dated November third. Looks like Mr. Sáenz was working on a computer that was two days behind the rest of us."

I wanted to correct her that no, not at all, Sáenz never worked on a late-running computer. When he had worked on it, it had been dated most correctly.

"Is there anything else I can do for you, Detective?" asked the reporter. I was about to thank her and say no, just turn off the computer, when I heard the click of a nine-millimeter parabellum. It was not mine.

I did not turn around, knowing that would not be wise. All I said was, "I suppose you've come to get your jacket."

"Hang up the phone."

I obeyed. He said nothing more for a moment. I filled the space, "Looks like Vandy let you go home early from the hospital."

"Miguel only gave me a flesh wound."

"You mean you only gave yourself the wound."

"Shut up. Just shut up." Jerry's voice growled. It also trembled. He sniffled, as if a cold was coming on. But it was no cold. All those trips of his to the bathroom finally made sense.

He spoke again. "You don't know how goddamned tired I am of all this. It just keeps going on and on. But now it stops. Finally. Don't move." He lowered behind me, pulled up my right pants leg, unstrapped my gun, then pulled it out of my holster. "Now, come on." He got right behind me and pushed me toward the door.

"Where are we going?"

"I said shut up. Don't talk until we get to your car." I opened the door, keeping my hands to my sides. I guess his hatred was so big in him that it made him mumble, "We're just going to pay a little hospital visit to Mr. Tekún Umán."

CHAPTER THIRTY-SIX

Jerry's anger now dominated his actions. In the parking lot I fished around in my purse for a few seconds longer than he wanted. He screamed, "Hurry up with the goddamn keys!"

He had me drive so he could keep the gun pointed at my rib cage. It was past midnight now, early Friday morning. Little traffic was on the highway.

"How did you find out?" he asked. His voice trembled with rage.

At first I didn't want to speak. But I could feel that nine-millimeter's barrel six inches from me. "Something you said to Miguel while you were interrogating him. That the jade pyramid had been pushed down into Sáenz's brains. When I translated it, it didn't sound right. All of us, Doc, me, and McCabe, all believed the pyramid had fallen out of his mouth, not his brains. But you were the only person on the investigation who knew exactly where it was. Only the killer could have known that."

He rattled his head back and forth. "The bastard's jaw was clamped shut. His whole body was frozen. Damnedest thing I've ever seen...I had to stick the jewel somewhere..."

Cadaveric spasm, I thought. So Doc had been right.

"You're a pretty smart girl," he said. "Why did you want my coat?"

"When I saw the bullet holes in the wall, I knew something was wrong. Those holes were right above your head, where you had been standing. They were nowhere near Miguel's position in the room. That's what Tekún meant when he said 'What the hell.' He wasn't talking to Miguel. He was talking to you. You were already in the room. He was shooting at you, because you were shooting at him."

"The son of a bitch packed a pistol. I didn't expect that. But I guess it took the place of his bodyguard..." He talked as if he would have another chance to do it again, and this time get it right.

"You knew Dr. Hatcher. What was it, you bought coke from him?"

"Why do you say that?" He looked at me.

"You've been making too many trips to the bathroom. You've been getting more edgy the closer you got to framing Tekún Umán. But why?"

"WHY?" He pushed the barrel into my temple. "Because Murillo is one mean goddamn son of a bitch, that's why!" Then he lowered the gun and started pulling at his clothes. I thought he was going to strip. He just pulled up his shirt. "Because he gave me this, that's why!"

We passed underneath a streetlight. It showed

me the scar over his abdomen, in the form of a well-written word: *Ladrón*. The accent was there, just like on Gato Negro's stomach.

I was both disgusted and confused. Jerry's shallow breathing filled the interior of the car. "You see now?" he screamed.

"What, you were ripping off Tekún? That's why he wrote 'thief' on your stomach?"

He grunted a laugh. "Hardly. Just a little off the top. But I thought I was taking it from that goddamn Pajarito. I never knew Pajarito worked for Tekún Umán until recently, before Hatcher died. Pajarito had approached me six months ago. Being on the take's nothing new, Romilia. You'll like the idea in a few years, after getting paid shit for picking up cadavers. I collected revenues for Tekún. It's good money. And Tekún Umán deals with everybody. I mean everybody. He sells cheap shit on the streets, but he also sells good smack and Colombian gold to some of the more notable people of Atlanta, and now, to our wealthier Nashvillians. One of his avenues was through Dr. Hatcher."

"So Dr. Hatcher sold drugs..." I mumbled.

"Oh, but for noble reasons. He sold only good stuff, and to his own patients. He wanted to get that free clinic going. But he wasn't getting all the money he needed to build it. Somehow Tekún Umán got hold of him and cut him a deal. Sell drugs to the rich shits in town, and keep some of the profits. So the good doctor did. He sold to housewives, lawyers, preachers, teachers, anyone who walked into his private clinic and showed interest. They knew it was illegal. But hell, a doctor was selling it, so it had to be good shit. He made Tekún a lot of money. And I was the one to collect.

"But then Tekún started leaning on me, just

because I was skimming a little from the collection plate. Hell, it wasn't hurting anybody, only a thousand more here and there. Pocket change for somebody like Tekún Umán. But he didn't like that, once Pajarito told him about the loss." Jerry's voice rattled. "That gorilla bodyguard of his forced me into a shed on the edge of town. Tekún was sitting there. He did this to me." Jerry pointed at his stomach. Then he started to cry. "Goddamn, that was torture. His fucking gorilla sat on top of me while Tekún just took that razor of his, and wrote..." Jerry could barely control his voice. "I was screaming my head off, and all he said was, 'I learned this from some of my relatives back in the old country. Just a little reminder of who you're dealing with.' Then he says, 'Just remember, Detective Wilson, I own you now.' Goddamn him!"

Jerry slumped down into the seat. But the gun did not go down. He tried to compose himself. He talked as if I were his captive confessor.

"Then all hell broke loose with Hatcher. It was too much for the good doctor's conscience. He started thinking about mending his ways, which is not a good thing to do when you get into this business, let me tell you. One day he starts going on and on about how wrong it all was, and that he was going to confess, even if it meant him going to jail. I tried to persuade him not to do that. But he wouldn't listen. He was going to the cops. He had already confessed everything to his girlfriend. I said, 'Girlfriend? What girlfriend?' He was afraid of me. But I found out who she was. Hatcher and I argued. I told him to keep his stupid mouth shut. He wouldn't listen. He said the following day that he was going to turn himself in. So I got to him before he did that. Then I found Pamela Kim."

"You killed them both," I said.

He looked at me, as if I had suddenly turned stupid. "Right," he said.

I pushed my purse toward him and kept asking specific questions. "But why the whole Kaibil thing?"

His nervous, weary voice suddenly flipped, becoming almost festive. He relaxed the gun on his lap. "Now don't you have to agree that was a work of genius? And it all came from that bastard Tekún, when he told me about his relatives back in 'the old country.' I started doing research on his old country. I plugged into Guatemala on the Internet, and found what I had shown you the other day, all those gory pictures of gutted civilians with slit throats and gunshot wounds. Then the whole jade pyramid deal I created to use like a symbolic arrow. I thought, well, if I want to make this look like somebody else besides me did it, why not make the trail lead back to Tekún Umán? Why not make it look like Hatcher and Kim were murdered by a militaristic, trained killer from Guatemala, hired by Tekún? All I had to do was connect enough dots back to Tekún. By the time Tekún figured out what was going on, the heat would have been on him for dealing drugs.

"But then Benny Bitan messed me up. He followed me and Kim out to the bridge; then after I pop her, he goes and lays down with her. At first I thought, 'Damn, what a mess-up.' But it went to my favor. I was a hero. But Tekún was still on my back.

"Then Sáenz got into the picture. That young punk was just too smart for his own good. He started calling me, asking me, 'How was it you happened to be in the area when Benny Bitan was killing Pamela Kim?' Then he went down to Benny's homeless shelter and found out that Kim was having an affair with Dr. Hatcher. Sáenz investigates on his own and learns about the connection between Hatcher and Pajarito. So he calls me about it.

"I figured I could make Sáenz the one to connect the dots back to Tekún Umán. I was going to give this kid a great story. I was going to tell him about the Kaibiles, then have him go out and do the research on them. He would have figured out that Tekún was the death-squad man. It would have launched his reporting career. But before I could do that, he goes and interviews Pajarito! He mentions my name to Pajarito, saying that I'm an investigator who was working various angles on the two murders. Pajarito just turns to him and smiles and says something like, 'Maybe you should find out how Detective Wilson spends his recreational time.' That little Mexican bastard. He just wanted to put the heat on me. Sáenz started asking about my personal life, the little shit. So I set him up, all right. I told him that no, Benny was not the real killer, but that I had a lead on who the killer really was, and if he wanted to be a part of the collaring, he should meet me down by the river. So he did. But Diego brought a gun with him. I guess it was like Miguel said, he was nervous.

"Since he was armed, I had to take him differently. I grabbed the gun and turned it on him. I couldn't point it at his heart, so I pushed it up into his throat. After I had him shoot himself, I tried to open his mouth to put the gem in there, but it was clamped shut. So I stuck the gem in his skull. Then I heard someone nearby. Miguel. So I lifted Sáenz's notebook and left."

Though he spoke as if the plan were one that he had worked on for a while, I could tell that, the more killings he did, the sloppier he had become.

"It would have all worked out perfectly, if it wasn't

for people getting in the way. Some things went right. Pajarito is in jail. But that son of a bitch called me down into his cell just to tell me that, if the cops didn't get me, Tekún would. Lousy threatening scumbag..."

He got quiet. I was pulling into the Vanderbilt Hospital parking lot. He turned and looked straight at me. "Then you. I thought you were going to be a help in all this, too. Through your investigation I could get to Sáenz's computer, and at least make it look like he was doing research on Kaibiles. I was able to play you along for quite a while. You actually thought I was angry with you when you found the pyramid near Sáenz. You don't know how elated I was! Doc Callahan had knocked it out of Diego's head, but you found it. I just had to act angry, like my reputation was on the line. And you bought it." Jerry's body shuddered, as if demanding more smack or coke.

My fear had laced itself with anger. I almost snarled it out: "All this to support your damn drug habit."

"You hold off right there, girl." The pistol pushed up against my head. I tried to move my head left, but he pushed it farther. He almost wedged me against the window with the barrel. "None of your preaching. I don't want to hear it. You've never been on smack. You don't know how much it needs to be a part of your life."

He pulled the gun away. His voice changed, falling from the tight, almost screeching intensity into a trembling calm. "You know, Romilia, I was getting to like you. I thought, maybe, we could even be friends."

What frightened me about what he said was, I felt the exact same thing. The bastard.

He continued, "But then I knew you suspected something, the moment you wanted to keep my jacket.

I suppose you would have made a trip to ballistics with it and found the gunpowder traces from the forty-five."

I parked the car slowly, but my heart raced, wondering what it would mean the moment I shut off the motor, hearing how he had figured me out.

"Yeah, you're good, Romilia. Real good. You're smart, observant, young... You're even beautiful. You've got your kid and your mom. Everything's going your way. Too bad you're soon going to die from speedballing."

It was the last thing I heard. Except, of course, for the dull slam that echoed through my skull. I barely saw the car's digital clock: 12:13 a.m. Afterwards, all was silent, black, and deep.

CHAPTER THIRTY-SEVEN

The first thing I saw was Sergio. He was smiling at me, asking me to play with him. But his voice was an echo, almost harsh in its sound, its growing absence. Then he left me completely, disappearing from that thin space between forced sleep and the wake to reality, leaving me to stare under the dashboard of the Taurus. I made to rub my head with my hand, but my hand would not obey. Both stayed locked to the handle of the passenger door, right where Jerry had handcuffed me.

"Shit! Shit!" I pulled at the cuffs, stupid as that was. He had obviously laid me down on the seat to keep me from being seen. An invisible baton drummed against the inner lining of my skull from where he had hit me. I scrambled into an awkward seating position and stared up at Vanderbilt Hospital, shrouded in night. Tekún was in the Critical Care Unit, the same place where Gato Negro had been placed. I looked at

the digital clock on my dashboard. It now said 12:17.
Four minutes had passed. He was on his way for
another kill. I knew that, after Tekún, I would be the
last victim. An overdose of speedballing, combining
cocaine and heroin in an intravenous hit. Even with his
frenetic, careless-growing mind, he was still creative.
Even if they caught him, I would be dead. I cursed
again and stared out the window.

I heard the chirp of a car alarm. A doctor walked
toward his BMW just as I had yelled "shit" for the
third time. He must have heard me, for he looked my
way. It was Clancy, the same doctor who had taken care
of Gato Negro. He wore hospital greens, with a thick
coat tossed over his shoulders. His car keys dangled
from a weary hand. He looked over at me. I screamed
at him. Clancy came nearer, saw the situation, and listened to me as I gave him permission to smash the
window and get me the hell out of here.

He found a large stone from the edge of the parking lot and walked around to the back door opposite
me and smashed in the window. I shielded my face
against the seat as he blasted a spiderweb over the
glass. On the third hit he broke through and unlocked
the doors. "What in the world, Detective? What's
going on?"

I explained: a killer just locked me in here before
making his way to murder one of his patients.

He didn't hesitate. He took the stone to the han-
dle, banging away, trying to snap the chain of the cuffs.
It didn't work. The rock bit into the hard plastic, but
did little else. He cursed, "Damnit, damnit, break!"
Then something broke. Not the cuffs, but the handle.
It fell to the floorboard.

I stared at my still-bound hands. But there was no
time. I stumbled out of the car and hit the parking lot

in a sprint. "Do me a favor. Grab my purse and bring it with you." He obeyed.

He ran next to me, making sure I would not fall, not with those cuffs still around me. "What's the quickest way to the Critical Unit?" I asked. Clancy gently grabbed my arm and pulled me to the right.

"Can you run the steps?"

I said I could.

"Follow me." We sprinted.

On the third floor we turned a curve, with the gazes of nurses and other doctors following us. "Listen. Whatever happens, you hang on to that purse," I said. "Don't let it from your sight. If something goes wrong, hand it directly over to Lieutenant Patrick McCabe of homicide."

"What do you mean, if something goes wrong?" I could feel him glancing at me. I couldn't explain as at that moment I saw the door that he had just pointed at. I pushed through it with both my bound hands to see, in the dark, Jerry's sinewy back, his one good arm shaking slightly as he pressed the pillow against the bed. The only other thing I could see was Tekún Umán's olive-colored arms, barely able to lift themselves and struggle against the detective's waist.

There was nothing else to do, so I did it. I jumped on him and flung my hands in front of him, snatching up his neck in the handcuffs' chain.

We both fell back. He let go of the pillow, but it was not to catch himself. He reached down and pulled something from his waistline. His body slammed against mine. "Shit!" I grunted, feeling his full weight crunching my abdomen against the floor. Then I saw the glint of metal that came from below, held tight in his left hand, then shoved back, aiming at my face. I jerked my entire head to the right. But I heard a ripping sound, thick and muffled, right under my left ear. Then I felt the liquid heat pulse through the side of my neck.

I screamed. He reached to his own neck with his right hand, grasped the handcuffs, and pulled the chain off his skin. I dropped away from him. His breath escaped him like a vacuum. Then he stood quickly, his feet trampling against me as he drew his gun.

I could only react by bringing my left hand to my neck, forcing my right hand up as well. I felt the ooze. Then I could smell the odor of fresh blood, as if it were not my own. Three breaths left my lungs, all of them trembling with the thought of a lanced jugular, that I would die here, right now, because of this slice. Yet I could still see Jerry clearly. My vision did not appear to be leaving me.

He looked down at me, the gun pointed straight at my head. From that I could only figure that the knife wound, from his point of view, had not gone deep enough. "You little bitch," he said. It was the snarl of a complete and untied rage.

Behind me stood Clancy. Behind him stood a growing number of hospital personnel. They all looked in. Someone screamed in the hallway. But no one moved, seeing Jerry with the gun aimed at my temple. I yelled back at Clancy, "Get out of here with that purse."

But he didn't move. He glanced over to a woman who also wore greens. He tucked the purse securely into her arms. "Get out of here," he said, "and guard this with your life." She obeyed, leaving the scene.

I had to admit, I liked him for that.

Then Clancy took a step our way. "Don't move, you shit!" growled Jerry. Then he looked at me.

He finally spoke. "What...is in your bag?"

I said nothing. Then he kicked me in the ribs. The crowd behind me sucked in a communal breath.

"The tape recorder, Jerry. The one that you strapped to Miguel." I took another breath, just to get out the words. "Come on, Jerry, give it up. It's over . . ." But for him it was not over. Not until he clicked back the hammer and held the gun up higher and aimed it at his left eye.

Even if the scream had come out of my mouth one-half second before he pulled the trigger, I knew that it would have been utterly useless.

CHAPTER THIRTY-EIGHT

Dr. George Clancy kept admonishing me, saying that I should not be seeing too many visitors. But that didn't stop him from coming into my hospital room every other hour or so. I came to expect him.

"I don't think I'm that bad off, Dr. Clancy," I said the fifth time he came in. "It's really just a flesh wound. It'd be nice to go home."

"Please, call me George. And it's more than a flesh wound, Romilia. He nicked you pretty deep. You were lucky. We all were lucky, I guess," he said, his voice turning humble, embarrassed. He smiled, then grew serious again, professional. "Besides, the whole incident was very traumatic for you. I think it's good for you to rest here for a couple of days."

I couldn't help but think he used his professional authority for personal gains. But I let him. It was nice being waited on hand and foot. And I was tired. Very tired.

Once Mamá came, she never left. She had her sister, my aunt, come up from Atlanta and take care of Sergio at the house. She did allow Sergio to come in once, after I had pleaded, then demanded of her, to let me see my son.

He came in. His eyes kept on me, his face suspended, as if the wrong wind could blow it down. At first he did not come to me, as if afraid, frightened by what he later called "the big Band-Aid" around my neck. I called him over, "*Veníte, mi corazón,*" familiar words for him, ones that beckoned him my way. He stood by the bed. I pushed my fingers through his hair.

"Did you get the bad guys?" he asked, his little voice trickling into my ear.

"Yes, mi *corazón.* I got them."

Then he stared at the bandage. "But they got you, too."

After a short visit, and some coaxed kisses, my aunt led him out of the room, leaving my mother to weep, and me to stare, with tears rolling away from my own sight.

My mother was asleep the time Lieutenant McCabe came in. He had a fresh newspaper rolled up under his arm. He plopped it down on the bed. "Here's some reading material for when you're feeling better. You're the newest Nashville hero."

"Heroine," I said.

"Right. By the way, the mayor called me this morning, after reading the paper. He wanted me to extend to you his hopes that you get better soon, and that he looks forward to seeing you back in service, especially after you've shown yourself to be of such a high

caliber, yada yada yada. He's also very thankful for you
bringing peace to our fair city by clearing up the
death-squad scam that Wilson stirred up."

I laughed, though it hurt my neck some to do that.
"Is this the same guy I barged in on the other day, with
Tekún Umán?"

"Yes, well, the mayor's feeling a little humbled by
the cassette that you got, with Wilson's confession. He
also said he's cutting all ties with Mr. Murillo—or
Tekún Umán—until this is all cleared up."

"Will there be an investigation?"

McCabe sighed. "I'm sure there will be. But Tekún's
lawyers are already making statements this morning on
the radio and television, saying that Wilson's taped confession is not enough to bring their client to court."

"I see. And what about dear Tekún? Is he faring
well?"

Again, McCabe hesitated. Then he just blurted it
out. "He's gone."

"Gone?"

"Yes. Left last night."

"Gone?! Where the hell did he go?"

"Supposedly his personal doctor in Atlanta said
that, due to his peculiar health status, Tekún needed to
be taken directly to his own private-care facilities.
About three hours after Wilson killed himself, a team
of men supposedly came in from Atlanta and checked
Tekún out of the hospital. They had their own emergency health equipment, transportation, everything.
They flew out on a private jet from the airport around
five-thirty this morning. It was destined to land in
Atlanta. But it never showed up there."

Son of a bitch, I thought. No doubt he's somewhere in a ritzy hospital in Guatemala City right now.

McCabe interrupted my quick surge of anger. "Listen. You don't need to be worrying about people like Tekún right now. You've been wounded in action. You've got some health time, plus some of that 'emotional stress' whatever-they-call-it time coming up. Once you check out of here, I don't expect to see you in the office for a couple of weeks."

Maybe four, I corrected him in my mind, adding on my vacation time. But I didn't tell him that.

"Tell me, how did you know so quickly that Jerry had set up to kill Tekún and that boy Miguel? Looks to me like he had set it up to make it appear that Miguel was shooting Tekún."

I sighed, more to catch my breath. "He had. But it was the bullet holes that Tekún had made. They were aimed at Jerry, not Miguel. That made me think about listening to the tape of the shooting sequence. Lucky we had Miguel wired. His recorder caught the whole thing. You can hear it clear as a bell. The bullet sequence is all wrong. Two forty-five shots, then Tekún's shots. Then one parabellum shot after Jerry yelled. That was Jerry's shot, the only parabellum in the room. Jerry had the forty-five in one hand and the parabellum in the other. He first shot Tekún twice with the forty-five, then shot Miguel twice with his parabellum. Then he placed the forty-five in Miguel's dead hand and aimed it at his own arm, wounding himself. This made it look like Miguel had shot Jerry, even leaving gunpowder residue on Miguel's hand. The problem for Jerry was he faked his 'piercing cry' of pain before he had really been shot. Once you hear it on the tape, it sounds almost ludicrous."

"So Jerry carried two guns, and he was shooting with both hands?" asked McCabe.

"He was ambidextrous. I watched him doodle a

great cartoon of Mrs. Hatcher with his left hand. Then I saw him draw his gun on those two illegal Mexicans with his right. He could shoot with either hand."

"So once you suspected your partner," McCabe pondered, "you called the newspaper about the computer..."

"Right. I figured that the whole Kaibil angle was a hoax. Jerry had created that file in Sáenz's computer right when we were all sitting around it. No doubt right when he had 'accidentally' spilled coffee on the table, which distracted Stapleton and me. Jerry also set the computer's calendar back two days, to November first, to make it look like Sáenz had created that computer file before he died. I'm sure he would have tried to correct the date to cover his tracks, but the phone call came about Gato Negro getting beat up. We ran out of the newspaper offices before he could fiddle with the computer any more."

McCabe looked down at my bed, shook his head, and smiled. Then he frowned. I supposed he was thinking about the dead detective, a killer who had worked under McCabe's watch. I wanted to tell him not to think about such thoughts. Before I could say anything, McCabe grabbed my toe underneath the sheet and squeezed it slightly. "Good work, Romilia." With that, he left my mother and me. Mamá still dozed in the chair to my side.

Later that day I stood up to look at the bandage in the mirror. It curved around my neck and held tight to the wound. They had changed it again, so I could not see any stain of blood. They said that there were twenty-four stitches holding it together. My jaw tightened. That hurt. Yet it still tightened, thinking of images of Frankenstein, his head sewn to his neck to keep it in place. I wondered about scarring. I tossed my hair over to the left side of my neck, then tried to imagine how I could cover it completely. "Maybe if I grow my hair out just a little bit longer," I muttered to the mirror. My jaw then started to tremble, as if it heard me planning to hide the scar and take back my appearance. For a quick moment I was glad that the bastard had blown his own head away. Then I knew I was not, for I had seen it, had heard the pistol report, and saw his hand barely jerk as the bullet entered his head and rattled his entire skull for a scant second before making his whole body drop to the ground before me. It would take longer than a couple of weeks to forget that scene. It would take time to try to figure out, or make sense out of the fact that someone I was beginning to trust was in fact a killer. Then, I knew, there would be no figuring out anything. There would only be time in its merciful passing.

A nurse walked in. "You're feeling a little better, Ms. Chacón?" she asked, seeing that I was out of bed. Then she handed me a small package. "Someone delivered this earlier today."

I thanked her and crawled back into my bed. She checked my water pitcher and clipboard, then walked out. Mamá stirred about that time. "What is that?" she asked.

"I don't know. Looks like a card. And a present." I pulled the envelope and the tiny box out of the package. First I read the letter. It had been typed.

Mi amor,

Though I have had to make a sudden departure due to my health, please know that I take you with me. These have certainly been difficult days,

*haven't they? Sometimes it is best to pull back, sur-
vey the world around you, and get a better sense of
the situation you are living in.*

*Yet one thing that I cannot separate myself
from is my memory of you. If it were not for you, I
would not be alive this instant, writing this letter,
thinking about you. It is because of you that I exist.
And now, my existence desires only to think of you.
Yes, I know that some harsh words have been ex-
changed between us recently, but I wish to make
amends, to reconcile, and move on. Much like García Márquez once said, "The heart's memory elim-
inates the bad and magnifies the good, and thanks
to this artifice we manage to endure the burden of
the past." I certainly hope this is the case with us.*

*In the spirit of that same book, I leave you with
this little gift. See it as a true act of commitment,
one which I am willing to wait for. If Florentino
Ariza could wait fifty-one years, nine months, and
four days to tell the woman of his heart that he
loved her, then I too must rise to such challenges of
passion.*

*Forever yours,
Tekún*

Obviously, Tekún had read *Love in the Time of
Cholera.*

My mother appreciated the literary reference.
"Well, now, he truly is a romantic, isn't he?" she said,
beaming at me.

"Mamá, haven't you read the papers? Haven't you
heard what I've told you about him? He's a drug runner, for god's sake! He carved up that boy! And . . . and
Wilson, too."

She just shook her head. I wondered if her tears would come again. "I don't know what to believe anymore..."

I shook my head, then opened the box. It was a ring. The rocks on it almost sung with sparkles.

"*Dios mío,*" my mother exclaimed. "*María y todos los ángeles...*"

I didn't hear her very well. Before she had a chance to tell me what a catch he'd be, I slammed the little box closed, lifted it to the side of my head, and flung it across the room. I'm proud to say it slammed directly into the garbage can.

"*¡Hija!* What are you doing? Have you lost your mind?" She made to retrieve it from the garbage can. Just then a cleaning woman walked in. I had learned her name earlier that day, Betsy Anne. She was a young white divorcé with three kids under the age of seven.

"Mamá, leave it in the garbage can! Do not take it out!"

She heard the forthrightness in my voice, something I rarely used on her. Since it was so rare, she stopped herself.

"But Romi, you can't throw such a ring away, for god's sake. It could be worth a great deal."

"Betsy Anne, you can have it."

"Have what?" she asked, peering into the can.

"That box. It's got a ring in it. Keep it. Sell it. I don't care."

"Why, thanks very much, Ms. Chacón!" she said, fishing the box out of the can.

It was the next day that we learned what Betsy Anne did with the ring. She took it to a jeweler, who estimated its value at four thousand dollars. Betsy Anne called me to make sure it was okay if she kept it. She even told me the price. With no hesitancy I said,

HOME KILLINGS

"Of course. Use it for all it's worth." She did. She sold it to the same jeweler, bought herself some clothes, took her kids out to a nice restaurant, bought them some clothes, then put the rest in the bank.

My mother just shook her head and crossed her arms. She stared up at the television while I closed my eyes. "I don't understand you sometimes."

"I don't expect you to, Mamá."

"I mean, you could have done the same. Kept it. Sold it."

"Yes. But I didn't."

She didn't argue anymore, knowing that I wouldn't move from my ethical spot. Perhaps she agreed with me. She pulled some *tamales* from a bag. I was glad; I had been smelling them for several minutes. "Doña Marina made these just this morning for you. She wants to get over and see you some evening, after she closes up the shop."

"Great," I said. I truly did look forward to the visit.

We sat for a long while, not eating. A tear, silent, ran down my mother's aging cheek. She turned and looked at me. Then she asked, "*Hija*, it's over with, isn't it?"

Then a tear rushed into the corner of my eye as I saw the fear in her face, one that wanted with all its heart to rest, to forget about a beloved country and its bloody history. Yet this had been too hard on my mamá, these recent days in this new city, when the killers of another time and place had supposedly followed us to our new home. I didn't know what I was angrier about: the fact that Wilson had killed, or that he had created a huge façade that had, momentarily, turned this entire city against my own people. Or because Wilson's well-fabricated lie had struck close to home, and had hurled my mother into a painful, unnecessary past. But now everyone knew it had all been a lie. There were no Kaibiles. And that bastard was dead.

"Yes, Mamá. It's over."

We ate the *tamales*. Mamá flipped the television remote that dangled from a cable next to my bed. "This TV doesn't have *Univisión*. How can I keep up with my *telenovelas?*"

Her complaint rang in my ears like a blessing.

ACKNOWLEDGMENTS

My thanks to all the good people at Arte Público Press, for their support and hard work. Special thanks to Nicolás Kanellos for his fine editing (and his allowance of the Salvadoran Spanish throughout the text) and to Marina Tristán for all of her work and most of all her friendship.

I wrote this book while living in an old farmhouse in the deep snows of Iowa. Thus my thanks to the Iowa Writers' Workshop for giving me the great gift of time and Eddie Dunn for the use of the upper room that overlooks his hometown.

Michelle must always be thanked.

MARCOS M. VILLATORO is the author of several books of fiction, poetry, and nonfiction. The *Los Angeles Times Book Review* listed his nationally acclaimed *Home Killings* as one of the Best Books of 2001. It won the Silver Medal from *Foreword Magazine* and First Prize in the Latino Literary Hall of Fame. His second Romilia Chacón novel, *Minos*, was released in fall 2003 to high literary acclaim. His other books include the Pushcart Prize nominee *The Holy Spirit of My Uncle's Cojones* (also an Independent Publishers Book Award finalist), *They Say That I Am Two: Poems*, the novel *A Fire in the Earth*, and the memoir *Walking to La Milpa: Living in Guatemala with Armies, Demons, Abrazos, and Death*.

After years of living in Central America, Marcos attended the Iowa Writers' Workshop. In 1998, he and his family moved to Los Angeles, where Marcos holds the Fletcher Jones Endowed Chair in Writing at Mount St. Mary's College. A regular commentator for National Public Radio's *Day to Day*, Marcos also hosts a book show called *Shelf Life* for Pacifica Radio.

He lives with his wife and four children in Los Angeles, and is now hard at work on the third Romilia Chacón novel, *A Venom Beneath the Skin*. Visit Marcos on the web at www.marcosvillatoro.com.

Dear Reader,

When I first wrote *Home Killings*, I thought this would be a singular novel about a woman named Romilia Chacón. My subconscious had another plan: that little seed, planted on page one, about the murder of Romilia's big sister Catalina, cracked open a whole new story.

In *Minos*, you find out what happened to Catalina. The man who killed her has reemerged after a six-year hibernation. He's killing again, across America. Romilia still has work to do.

Now I see that Romilia will be with me for a while, for personal reasons: she helps me work through some ghosts of my own life. In earlier years I lived in Guatemala, Nicaragua, and my mother's El Salvador. I lost friends to the violence of those years in Central America. Staying with Romilia is a way of looking into the darkness that is murder, and the obsession that is integral to detective work. No doubt Romilia will be in my head for years to come.

[signature]

Read on for an exciting sneak peek at Marcos M. Villatoro's next Romilia Chacón novel,

MINOS,

coming in paperback from Dell in March 2005

December, 2000

I'll never get used to it.

That's when I cried, of course, standing before the mirror. I'd been home from the hospital for three days. I unwrapped the loose dressings from my neck, alone, with no help, pulling the gauze from the cut. There it was in all its glory: twenty-four bindings total. From this angle I could see only six of the twelve outer staples. They pulled the skin of my neck tight over the ten concealed interior stitches, along with the two that pulled together the nick on the external jugular. It was all clean now, little discharge. Ten days of antibiotics had taken care of any infection. A week in the hospital had made me stiff from idleness, my only movement picking at the food they served, sometimes finishing off a tamal that Mamá sneaked into the room.

In the hospital the nurses had done the bandaging. To change them they had combed and tied my hair back, pulling it tight into a pony tail then hooking the tail to the crown of my head. This freed them up to change the dressings. No chance of a loose hair falling and sticking to the cut. The taut hair pulled my scalp and my scalp pulled at the skin of my neck and I felt the pain. Then I knew, but did not say, that this was something I would not get used to: a rip in the cloth of skin that covered my head.

I waited until Mamá left the house, with my son Sergio, before taking off the bandage. I had my eyes closed when she was getting ready to leave. *"Voy donde Marina,"* she had said, meaning Marina's Taquería and Grocery Mart, the first Hispanic-run market in Nashville, over on Nolensville Road. "They say it's going to snow tonight. We better stock up on supplies." Meaning, of course, masa harina, beans, rice, tomatoes, cilantro, cumin, and another CD of *norteño* music, which *doña* Marina had introduced my mother to. "You going to be all right?"

"I'll be fine." I kept my eyes closed. "Could you pick up some bourbon too?"

"¿Qué es bourbon?"

"Whiskey."

"What kind?"

The first name from college years came up. "Wild Turkey. There's a large bird on the label."

"Ay, el chompipe," she smiled. "I think your father liked that one."

He did, as did my sister, Catalina, who used to sneak it as a teenager.

Mamá did not mind that I drank. She probably made little connection to the pain medication that I was on. But I had. Bourbon and codeine. A fine combination.

I wanted to be alone when I changed the dressing, because I didn't want to scare my son. Sergio was three, would turn four in less than a week. He had visited me in the hospital only twice. Both times I could tell he was frightened of me. Not of me, but of the bandage, the unseen scar underneath the gauze. He had said little. Mamá had to coax him to come near me, to place a kiss on my cheek. Then he darted back to his grandmother and held onto her waist.

I was afraid. I had reason to be scared, due to a game of Frisbee Catalina and I played one afternoon, when I was twelve. She was sixteen. I was barefoot at the time. She had launched the Frisbee on a long flight, and I went chasing after it, looking up at the disc, not seeing the high concrete sidewalk with the sharp edge. I kicked it with the full force of the run. The sidewalk's corner cut deep, a string of blood shot toward my shoulder with each limped step I took. Catalina had rushed me to the emergency room, her voice trembling between fear for her little sister and anger over me bleeding on her upholstery, "I just vacuumed the floor mats, *¡Ay la gran púchica!*" Caty had carried me into the emergency room. My head bounced against her shoulder. I could feel her breasts (always larger than mine) pressed against my left arm. I told her she didn't have to carry me, I was fine, though I was getting awfully sleepy.

The doctor patched me up with four stitches. None of that bothered me. It was a childhood adventure.

What disturbed me was the healing afterwards. When my mother took me back to the doctor, and when he unrolled the bandage and pulled off the gauze, Mamá was the first to respond. Her hand went to her mouth, "*Ay jodido*, what happened?"

It looked malformed, as if the healing had gone wrong. Perhaps some awful disease, like gangrene, had set in. But my toe was not green nor black with rot. Rather, it looked like a hard pus had dried over the root of my toe, a solidified jell of bumpy, confused skin, not tan like the rest of my body, nor white like a wound. It was an unsightly tissue, as if in that one half inch area of scar, my skin had turned inside out.

At first the doctor said nothing about it. He instructed me to wiggle my toes. I did. Nothing hurt. He happily declared me healed.

"But, what about that scar?" my mother said.

He shook his head, acknowledging her concern, yet obviously not wanting to make a big deal of it. "That's called a Keloid Scar. Some people are prone to it, though we don't know why. We see it a lot in ethnic people. You're Mexican, right?"

"Salvadoran," Mamá said. She hated it when people couldn't tell the difference.

The doctor didn't catch her rancor. "A Keloid Scar's an abnormal proliferation of tissue over a wound. It's as if your body overcompensates, puts too much scar tissue over the skin to make sure the lesion closes up. It's not very pretty. But it's nothing to worry about." The doctor washed his hands at the sink.

My mother stuttered through some English, then turned to me and asked what she wanted to ask, in Spanish. I translated, "Is it going to look like this forever?"

"Afraid so. Not much you can do about it. If we had had a plastic surgeon on call the day you kicked the sidewalk, we may have been able to do some corrective surgery, maybe tuck the skin a little. But I don't think your insurance would have covered that." He looked at us both, at our obvious worry. "Oh now don't be too bothered by that little Keloid. You're too pretty a young lady to get upset by one scar on your foot that no one will ever see. Why I bet even a pair of sandals would cover it over." He had smiled, then ended with the phrase that now, sixteen years later, sounded like nothing less than a curse, "If you're going to have a Keloid, better that it happens where you'll rarely ever see it."

So as my mother and son shopped for cilantro and sweet breads at *doña* Marina's, I stood at the bedroom mirror, pulled the tape from my neck, and peeled away the gauze. The new me in the mirror cried, seemingly harder than I did.

Caty, at such a moment, would have known exactly what to do. Sometimes I can see her in the mirror, right behind me, pushing my thick hair over the cut, then whispering into my ear, "Now's a fine time to smoke some fine shit."

And that's exactly what we would do. While Sergio ran between the wooden stands of tomatillos and jabanero peppers, and my mother caught up with gossip from *doña* Marina, Caty and I would have rolled a nice fat joint and walked out on the back porch of my little house here in Germantown. We would have looked out on the new Promenade that Nashville had built nearby, north of downtown, an outdoor structure of specialty shops and restaurants that had doubled the value of my property in one year. While getting thoroughly ripped Catalina and I would have talked away from the scar, then slowly back to it, with Caty leading the conversation. Just like she did when I broke up with some creep white guy in high school back in Atlanta, or when some of the girls in our old neighborhood ragged on me about how much I hid behind books. Caty had that way. She would have said something perfect, like "That *pendejo* coward who did it to you is dead. And you're alive. You don't deserve the scar. But you do deserve to live." Something, somehow, perfect. Made perfect by her voice.

But Caty's not smoking grass with me. I don't see her in the mirror. She never entered this house. All because of another killer six, no . . . almost seven years ago. The one they call the Whisperer. The one who got away.

My son Sergio never knew his aunt. He's only seen her in photos that I've hung on the walls. He's only caught a glimpse of her soul in the anger of my eyes. Maybe that's why he never asks about her.

All these men in my life: two serial killers and one drug runner.

The Whisperer is not dead. According to Memphis police reports, he's very alive.

The Jade Pyramid killer committed suicide, which made me Nashville's newest heroine.

Tekún Umán took off.

Though we have no idea where. The Drug Enforcement Administration's Public website is just that: public. General information. Though new to the Internet, I learned quickly that it took some work to find real facts on anything that was worth researching, such as the whereabouts of a now-famous head of a regional drug cartel.

I'm new to computers. A week before I took the bandage off my neck, two men visited me: my boss, Lieutenant Patrick McCabe, and Jacob "Doc" Callahan, the Medical Examiner who worked directly with our Homicide Department. They came bearing an early Christmas gift: a black cloth case that held a very thin, very light laptop computer. Doc unzipped the case, pulled out the laptop, and placed it atop the blankets that covered my legs.

"Is this a joke?" I said.

"Not at all," said Doc. His accent was a bit clipped, as if he were from the upper class neighborhood of West Nashville. "The word is out on how computer illiterate you are, Romilia. Patrick and I decided to take advantage of your condition. We're bound and determined not to leave you in the past millennium. You *will* learn the Internet."

"You bought me a computer."

"Not really," said McCabe. He rubbed the back of his balding head, shoved his other hand in a pocket, like an embarrassed little boy. "The lion's share of the gift comes from Doc."

Doc clarified. "I'm a doctor. Wealthy. I covered the computer. Pat's a cop. He's poor. He got you the first two months of AOL."

Lieutenant McCabe didn't stay long. He was ready to get home. I wondered if he still shied around me because of the Jade Pyramid case, because of how close I had gotten to getting killed under his watch. He also knew me, better than others did in the force. He had my file from Atlanta, which held two incidents that lay like blots of shame on my record. My reputation as a hot-head had followed me to Nashville, but luckily I had a boss who kept that reputation locked in his file cabinet.

It was up to me whether or not others would learn about those previous incidents, the time I slammed a suspect against a wall and gave him a nice, light concussion, and the other fellow whom witnesses had claimed I had pistol-whipped. I still have a different angle on that, but my angle doesn't echo much in McCabe's file cabinet.

Still, McCabe respected me. I had solved the Jade Pyramid serial killings that had haunted Nashville this past autumn. The Mayor of Nashville, Winston Campbell, had congratulated me. So now, while visiting me in my house, McCabe acted a bit sheepish, as if he wanted to become paternal toward me. But he pulled out of that quickly, became my boss again. "Get better. I want to see you back in the office soon." He made to touch my foot under the blanket, but that was too intimate for him. Instead he tapped his index finger against the bed's footboard three times.

Doc stayed. This was no surprise, and in fact pleased me. Though he was old enough to be my father, sometimes I wondered if Doc had a crush on me. He plugged in the computer, hooked it up to my phone. "I'll set up the programs for you," he said.

I slept. When I awoke, Sergio was standing next to Doc. Both of them stared at the screen. Doc allowed Sergio to move the internal mouse with his finger, then taught him the art of clicking, "Now put the arrow right on Buttercup's head, and click. Then it'll give you, see? All the information on her and the other Powderpuff Girls."

"Powerpuff," said Sergio.

"Oh. Right. My granddaughter corrects me on that too."

"They get mad if you call them Powderpuff." Sergio then clicked on Blossom.

I closed my eyes again, listened to them play. Sometimes the laptop chirped, or the voice of one of the cartoon characters giggled and invited Sergio into a game room. After twenty minutes of this, Sergio asked, as if it suddenly had occurred to him, "Why did you get this for my Mamá?"

He whispered, "Oh, because she's my girl."

"*Really?*"

Doc chuckled. I kept my eyes closed.

Sergio was much more enthused about the laptop than I. An hour later Doc had the computer on my lap, and he took me through the same steps of point-and-click. He sat on a chair, leaned over the bed, staring at the screen, showing me how to sign in an e-mail name, how to check my mail (all I had so far were welcome letters from AOL). He wasn't that old. In his late fifties, still handsome, with a strong jaw and very blue eyes and a thick though cropped head of gray hair, once honey-brown. A widower, I had heard from the other detectives. I liked him. Sometimes I wondered if I was, in fact, in need of a father figure. He had a strong, agreeable cologne on, though it could not completely cut the scent of formaldehyde off him.

A father-figure. Or a man. Was I in need of a man? That thought, if spoken, would have thrilled my mother. Sure: I'd love to have a man here, next to me. Doc Callahan? How about that young fellow, Doctor Clancy, who had bandaged me up at Vanderbilt Hospital? How about any guy who could live with a mutilated woman? *Jodido.*

An hour after Doc left, I was still on the computer. I was clumsy at finding websites, but started to get the hang of "surfing." At one point, while looking at a web page on a García Márquez fan club out of Ecuador, the computer spoke up, telling me I had mail. It was from Doc. "I've tried to call, but seems you're still online. I'm glad you're enjoying the computer. Doc." Then his full name appeared below, very formal: Dr. Jacob Callahan, along with his home address. I wrote him back with the "Reply" button, "I'm looking at photos on a *Playgirl* website." I was joking, of course . . . then after sending Doc the note, I moved the arrow to the little white Search Box and typed "Playgirl" in. A slew of website names popped up. It took some clicks, but finally, there I was. So of course right when the young, dark brown fellow with the stomach of Michelangelo's *David* popped up and came into crisp focus, I heard from the side of my bed, "Who's that? He's sure got a big penis." I slammed the laptop shut.

I tried to turn my head, and manage a smile, even with the pain. "Sergio, *mi hijo*. Why aren't you asleep?"

He answered with a shrug of his shoulders. His eyes darted toward the bandage, the one I had yet to pull off. Then he looked at me again.

He smiled, the first smile since I had come home. Perhaps he had seen something relax in me, for which I quietly thanked Doc. His gift had taken my mind off things for a handful of hours. Sergio saw this.

"*¿Querés acostarte vos?*" I asked.

"*Sí,*" he said, and his grin broke open. Then I noticed something about him that I had not paid attention to in days, a detail of his childhood: he twirled his hair with his left index finger. He climbed into bed with me, stretched out underneath the blankets, pushed his toes over my hip. His head lay in the crux of my arm. I had to look at him without turning my neck. "*Te quiero, mijito,*" I said. He reached up to grab my entire head and kiss me, as was his habit. "*Ay, cuidado,* careful there. Don't pull." I forced a smile, not to scare him away. "Just reach up, kiss me on the cheek. There. That's nice." He settled back down and soon was asleep. My mother would carry him to bed soon, but I was in no hurry. Though I was curious: After assuring myself that Sergio slept, I pried open the laptop, touched the "Resume" button. The liquid screen came alive again, right where I had slammed it closed on that lovely man, and . . . Wow. Damned if Sergio wasn't right.

The real Tekún Umán had been a famous Mayan Indian of Guatemala who had died in hand-to-hand combat with the Spanish Conquistador Pedro de Alvarado in the sixteenth century. He was a Central American folk hero. This guy, displayed on the DEA web page, with the name "Rafael Murillo" typed underneath the photo, once told me that la gente had given him the indigenous nickname. All because he took care of poor folks through his store-front façades of nonprofit corporations. The nonprofits not only hid his drug operations, they helped people turn a blind eye from his illegal source of revenue. Tekún had started selling cocaine in Atlanta. That's where he built his first homeless shelters. It was four-star charity. Tekún didn't serve soup, but steak, brown rice, fish, sautéed chicken dishes, and fresh-roasted coffee. His homeless shelters had HBO in every room. On Sunday nights all his rooms were completely filled, with homeless men and women sharing beds and chairs to watch The Sopranos.

The mayor of Atlanta lost a lot of voters when he decided to shut down all of Tekún Umán's nonprofits soon after Tekún left Atlanta and moved to Nashville. It didn't matter how many times he reminded the news media about the connection between the Central American drug cartel and the homeless shelters, how cocaine was keeping these luxurious nonprofits afloat: the papers grilled him, brown and crisp, on the editorial page. Nashville's Mayor Campbell had escaped such embarrassment, as Tekún had only recently arrived in our city when I outed him as a drug lord. Tekún had yet to set up a fully functioning charity program. That's why Mayor Campbell loved me; I had saved him from the news editorials of shame.

I clicked onto Rafael Murillo's face. His photo took over most of my screen. The basic information was listed to one side: his name (and here, in parenthesis, his Mayan nickname, or as the DEA said, "Other Aliases"), age (thirty-seven), race (Hispanic, though I knew that while his father was from Guatemala, his mother was a white woman from Chattanooga. Thus Tekún's connection to the American South). Height: five feet eleven inches. Weight, a slim one hundred sixty-five.

It said nothing of his Armani and Versace suits, his

one hundred dollar cologne, his thousand dollar ear-ring, the aromatic, subtle hand cream from Italy. Those were things I had remembered.

Unlike the Most Wanted mug shots of other fugitives, all grainy and rough, this one showed the handsome look Tekún could strike. The photo had come from *The Cumberland Journal*, a local Nashville paper. He wore a silk tie under one of his Versace double-breasts. He smiled at the camera. His short beard was perfectly groomed.

Drug running, money laundering, dealing mostly in the fledgling yet growing Guatemalan branch of the Latin American cartel. Considered armed and dangerous.

I knew the details behind that last remark. We couldn't charge Tekún for murder; but any court could have charged him for torture. He had a way of making sure his victims never forgot their sins against him. He was a good speller with a knife.

Even though I blew his Nashville drug market, Tekún never came after me. I had saved his life. The Jade Pyramid killer had managed to put two bullet holes into Tekún. Then I had stepped in, got cut, but ended the killings. Tekún survived, then his people flew him out. Now he was hiding out somewhere in Central America.

After he fled, he sent me the letter and the gold ring, proclaiming his undying love for me. *Mi amor*, Tekún had said. No other man had used that line on me. "If it were not for you, I would not be alive this instant, writing this letter. It is because of you that I exist. And now, my exis-tence desires only to think of you." Something I don't be-lieve now. And if Tekún were here right now, standing beside my bed, looking at this scar, I doubt he would either.

Only when my mother is asleep do I flip the computer on and log onto the Internet and type into the white Search Box the words "Serial Killers."

Not Jade Pyramid, of course. But the Whisperer. A name I never say around Mamá.

Obsession becomes easier, more fluid, with the Internet. So many web pages devoted to the careers of Ted Bundy, John Wayne Gacy, Charles Manson. And there are details: Bundy's apartment of dismembered, cooked victims, Gacy's hidden cemetery of little boys, Manson's photo, complete with the swastika cut into his forehead.

There is little information on the Whisperer. Just those same three cases, in Bristol, Atlanta, and now Memphis. Just the names of the victims, small biographies of their lives, the manners in which they were all killed. All murdered with different M.O.s, but the Bureau had decided to lace them together. Obviously something tied the three together, but the specialists at Quantico weren't telling the world everything.

Until recently I had been able to let this go. That was when there were only two cities, Bristol and Atlanta. Then came the news leak while I was still in the hospital, that the murders of three men from Memphis last fall were now considered by the FBI as an act done by the Whisperer. Six years after killing my sister, he resurfaced once again. Six years that had allowed me to believe he was somehow dead and gone.

There are three little boxes with the cities' names. Just a click away and I can read all about them.

"Here is your *Chompipe Loco*." Mamá placed the bottle of Wild Turkey on the dresser drawer, on the other side of the room, away from the bed. She walked to my side, snatched up the bottle of painkillers and tossed them into her purse. "I will be more than happy to fix you a drink. In about twelve hours." She placed a bottle of apple juice where the medicine had sat.

"Mamá, a little drink won't hurt now."

"You think I'm an idiot. Look, *mi hija*, you can change painkillers if you want, from pills to *trago*. But you won't mix them. Tonight, around ten o'clock, I'll fix us both a nice highball."

"But the pain will come back before then."

"So you'll enjoy your drink more. Besides, it's time

you got up and walked around a bit. It will be good for your circulation. I got a call from your physical therapist. She told me to remind you that you can't stay in this bed forever."

Mamá was changing roles, from spoiling caregiver to drill sergeant. She helped lift me from the bed. "The doctor said it's okay for you to sit up. I moved the rocker to the front window for you. You can keep an eye on Sergio and watch television at the same time."

"Where is he?"

"Outside. Playing in the snow."

"He shouldn't be by himself."

"He's fine. He's with little Roy. Come on, up."

She took me to the living room, where a new fire blazed in the hearth. A cup of hot chocolate sat next to the rocking chair. Through the window was my son, tossing a snowball at his friend's head and missing Roy by a good twenty feet.

"Now you just relax here awhile," she said to me. So the care-giving role wasn't completely over. She went to take a shower, which I know would keep her busy for a good thirty minutes. Enough time for me to sneak back into the bedroom and drop a shot of bourbon into the hot chocolate. That first sip was oh so good, rich in chocolate and whiskey. This would be a better day. Perhaps I'd even go outside and try to pop Sergio with a snowball. Little Roy, Sergio's age, would get in the fray. But Roy had a much better aim; his daddy already had him in Pee Wee baseball. Beautiful, to see my son laugh, see his teeth, as he stumbled through the snow with Roy behind him, both boys brown and dark brown against all that white. I was getting soppy. It was the whiskey's fault, making me weep slightly over all that damn joy outside. Even the laptop got happy. I had forgotten to sign off from the Internet. It chirped at me in that white fellow's voice, "You've got mail!" Doc, of course. Probably getting back to me for an update on my porno-surfing. I walked to my bedroom and clicked on the mailbox again. It wasn't Doc's e-mail address, but rather some other name, Cowgirlx14, or something like that, on a different web server. I opened it.

> *Mi amor,*
> *How are you? Convalescing? I hear Wilson left you quite wounded. Nicked in the jugular, and yet you live. Marvelous. No doubt it's that Salvadoran blood of yours. Just too strong, or stubborn, to die that easily.*
> *Tell me, are you the one checking in on that horrible Serial Killer website every fifteen minutes?*
> *There are too many moments in a day, Romi; too many empty opportunities in which I am driven to think of you.*
> *tu*

It was all written in Spanish. Even the accents were there, perfect grammar. And so the lack of an accent on the final word, the signature, was no mistake: he had chosen to use his nickname, or at least the initials of his nickname, Tekún Umán.

Of course, "tu" without an accent also means "yours."

I replied. The only thing I asked was, in English, where that arrogant shit was hiding. "Show yourself, you coward. Come on back to Nashville, so we can finish up business."

An hour later I got a reply, from Cowgirlx14, "Excuse me, but I don't think I know you, and I'd appreciate you not calling me names. And I've never worked in Nashville."

I wouldn't hear from Tekún again for another six weeks, when he sent me the package with the drawings from Atlanta, Bristol, and Memphis.